SEDUCING THE VAMPIRE

Val went rigid as a statue. *What are you doing, Emily?*

She wriggled into a more comfortable position. *Sitting on your lap.*

So I see. But why?

Because I wantd to do this. She reached up and kissed the hollow of his throat. Nuzzled the underside of his jaw. Traced patterns on his skin with her damp tongue. *Because I dreamed of you. Because I am exceedingly curious and I'm tired of you acting so infernally coy.*

He caught her face between his hands. "Not coy, prudent. One of us must be."

"I don't see why."

"Because of this." Val's voice roughened. His emotions swept over her, hungry and dark. Her blood went thick with wanting as he gently loosened her braid and ran his fingers through her hair. "Emily," he murmured.

Val's gaze dropped to her mouth. He clasped her face between his hands and bent his head to take her in a kiss so deep, so carnal, that she forgot to breathe. The feel, the scent, the taste of him burst across her senses . . .

Books by Maggie MacKeever

CUPID'S DART

LOVE MATCH

LOVER'S KNOT

AN EXTRAORDINARY FLIRTATION

WALTZ WITH A VAMPIRE

Published by Zebra Books

Waltz *with a* Vampire

MAGGIE MACKEEVER

ZEBRA BOOKS
KENSINGTON PUBLISHING CORP.
www.kensingtonbooks.com

ZEBRA BOOKS are published by

Kensington Publishing Corp.
850 Third Avenue
New York, NY 10022

All Kensington titles, imprints and distributed lines are available at special quantity discounts for bulk purchases for sales promotion, premiums, fund-raising, educational, or institutional use.

Special book excerpts or customized printings can also be created to fit specific needs. For details, write or phone the office of the Kensington Special Sales Manager: Attn. Special Sales Department, Kensington Publishing Corp., 850 Third Avenue, New York, NY 10022. Phone: 1-800-221-2647.

Zebra and the Z logo Reg. U.S. Pat. & TM Off.

ISBN 0-8217-7826-9

First Printing: September 2005
10 9 8 7 6 5 4 3 2 1

Printed in the United States of America

Who could resist his power?
His tongue had toils and dangers to recount . . .
He knew so well how to use the serpent's art . . .

Excerpt from *The Vampyre,* by John Polidori, published in the April 1819 edition of the *New Monthly Magazine,* popularly believed at first to be the work of Lord Byron.

Chapter One

When an ass climbs a ladder we may find wisdom in a woman.
(Romanian proverb)

It was a dark and dreary night—or, rather, late afternoon—when a small open carriage rattled along the narrow, little-used road that led from Morpeth to the coast of the North Sea. The carriage was shabby, as was its driver, his collar pulled up around his chin to combat the dampness of the day. His passenger was a wee snippet of a lass with masses of frizzy orange hair pulled into a thick braid; a pointed little face with high cheekbones, an awesome number of freckles, and a generous mouth; a sharp little nose which supported a pair of gold-rimmed spectacles; and huge gold-flecked brown eyes. If no one could call her pretty, she had a fey quality. Willie wasn't the first to wonder if her ears were pointed at the tips. He spat over the side of the carriage, and discreetly crossed himself.

The carriage wound through wooded valleys and springy turf fields, past an old stone church and several abandoned cottages, and drew finally to a stop at the base of a desolate cliff. Miss Emily Dinwiddie, newly appointed overseer of the Dinwiddie Society for the Exploration of Matters Abstruse and Supersensible, pushed her wire-rimmed spectacles back up where they belonged and peered at the grim battle-scarred tower that stood harshly silhouetted against the gloomy sky, surrounded on three sides by deep water, the fourth approachable only by a steep slope. "Are you certain this is the right place?"

Of course Willie was certain. Wasna he Morpeth born and bred? Corby Castle this was, or what was left of it, after Robert the Bruce pulled three of the great towers down to almost ground level, and Oliver Cromwell ripped open the gatehouse with a mortar piece. All that remained intact was the three-story keep, which held the Lord's hall and private apartments, not that Willie had seen them himself, nor did he want to, for the place 'twas said to be haunted, and Willie had nae more wish tae be meetin' up wi' gravestane-gentry than wi' the grey folk.

Emily stared at the battle-scarred ruin. It did indeed look haunted. "I'm going inside."

Willie shifted sideways on the seat to gape at her. "G'wa! Haeno' I just been tellin' ye aboot the ghaisties?"

Emily grasped the handle of her umbrella and refrained, barely, from giving him a good poke. "You *will* wait for me?"

Willie scowled at his passenger. Was it no' his luck to be oot in the middle of nae place wi' a fashious female (not to mention ghaisties and gropies and wirriecows) with the gloaming comin' on? "If it's castles ye're after visitin', there's Traquair and Drumlanrig and Sterling. Come away, noo, and I'll take ye someplace better on anither day."

Those other castles didn't house a being old enough to remember fabled Sarmizegetuza, once perched atop a crag in the Orastie Mountains in Romania, or the Dacian god Zelmoxis, or the powerful night goddess Bendis, whose cult involved curious orgiastic rites. Emily produced a gold coin, which she brandished beneath

Willie's nose. The driver's eyes crossed as he took its measure. "Aweel!" he conceded.

"You'll wait." Without giving him further opportunity for protest, Emily clambered down from the carriage, hurried past the dovecote with its many stone nesting-boxes where doves and pigeons had been bred—pigeons being especially tasty cooked in a pastry pie—to provide a source of fresh meat in winter or during time of siege.

A long flight of narrow stone steps wound steeply upward to the castle. Green moss spread over the treads like a perilous soggy carpet. Emily trod gingerly, lest she slip and fall and join the other wraiths wandering the ruins.

The stairs led finally to a small side entrance, although the door was long since gone. Emily walked through the arched opening into the courtyard, beneath the murder hole where castle defenders would once have dropped various unpleasant things—boiling oil, hot sand, sharp rocks—on unwanted guests. More holes gaped in the outer wall near the gateway. Large ragged openings allowed such light as the dreary day provided to filter down from the winching room on the second floor. Courtesy of Cromwell's mortars, no doubt.

Emily peered into a ruined tower, its roof and battlements missing, the west side almost gone. There would have been kitchens here, and vaults. A bake house, a brew house, and chapel. A deep pit where criminals—and those uninvited visitors who had survived the murder hole—would have been thrown and left to rot.

The shadows were lengthening. She could shilly-shally no longer. The tower Emily had seen from down below stood to the left of the gate, three stories high, its domed roof still intact. A strange stillness hung over the place. Not even a bird sang.

No good sign, that. Emily grasped the ancient knocker

and pounded on the door. There was no response but a hollow echo. Feeling slightly foolish, she knocked again, then jumped as the ancient portal swung inward with a groan of unoiled hinges. Half expecting to encounter one of Willie's ghaisties, Emily held her umbrella out before her like a broadsword, and stepped cautiously across the threshold.

The lower floor of the keep was one great empty room, separated from the entry by a wooden screen with a minstrel's gallery above. A raised dais stood at the upper end, and a hooded fireplace was set into the far wall. Broken wooden shutters hung drunkenly at the windows, some of which still held panes of greenish glass behind a forest of cobwebs. The place was damp and drafty and chill. *"Bună!"* snarled a voice from the shadows, startling Emily almost out of her skin.

She spun around, umbrella at the ready. A small shrunken man hobbled forward to plant himself, arms akimbo, smack in her pathway. Bright beady eyes squinted up at her from a face as wrinkled as a raisin. Strands of dark hair were combed carefully across a gleaming pate.

Surely this wizened little man was not he whom she sought! "Count Révay-Czobar?"

"Do I *look* like a count? The name is Isidore." His nose was impressively long for so short a fellow. He gave it a good twitch. "You've come a long way, from the looks of you, and for naught. Strangers aren't welcome here."

Emily looked down her own nose at him. "Poppycock! You will inform your master that he has a visitor, welcome or not. *After* you build up the fire."

Isidore regarded her sourly for a moment, then limped toward the doorway, muttering under his breath.

The hall was cold, dusty, and unwelcoming, bare of furniture save for a couple of carved chests. Stone vaulting supported the floor above. The walls around the dais still bore faint traces of plaster with red lines, representing large masonry blocks, each decorated with a flower. Timeworn tapestries depicted a giant gnawing on the leg of a bear; three archers shooting a duck. A ghastly painting portrayed a dead woman standing in her shroud while worms gnawed her entrails. *Memento mori: remember that you must die.* Emily murmured, " 'Where is now thy glory, Babylon . . .' "

"Better an egg today than a hen tomorrow." Isidore dropped an armful of kindling in the fireplace. A huge silver-gray canine padded through the arched opening of the wheel stairway built into the far stone wall. Emily snatched up her umbrella and fell back a step. The creature's triangular ears were alert, his black-rimmed yellow eyes fixed on her with unnerving intensity.

Emily retreated. The beast advanced. Isidore pulled himself creakily erect. "That isn't the Count either. Drogo, behave yourself."

The animal's fur was shot with silver and gray and black. Its pale, slanted eyes were oddly intelligent, and more than a little menacing. Emily moved prudently behind a dusty carved chest. "Drogo looks like a wolf."

"A wolf knows a wolf as a thief knows a thief." Isidore tossed the last twig onto the fire and hobbled toward the spiral stone stair. Emily wondered if the old man thought she was here to steal the silver. The wolf-dog lay down on the hearth, his pale amber stare still intent on Emily.

Drogo seemed content to remain where he was for the moment. Emily's cloak was damp from the unfriendly weather, and smelled unpleasantly of wet wool. Carefully, one eye on the wolf, she pulled off the pungent garment and draped it over a triangular candle stand missing its candle but embellished with a great deal of dust and rust.

A tendril of springy orange hair fell onto her cheek,

and she impatiently tucked it back behind her ear. Emily's hair was one of the banes of her existence. Thick and curly, it had a distinct will of its own. Try as she might to confine the mass in a tight braid, some invariably escaped. Difficult to look brisk and businesslike and capable when curly tendrils sprang out about one's head in all directions, like Medusa and her snakes.

She edged toward a deep-set window. One pointed ear swiveled in her direction, but other than that Drogo didn't stir. Little enough to see outside, beyond approaching darkness and the wind-tossed waters of the sea.

Darkness. Emily rubbed her arms. According to her studies, creatures of the night couldn't venture into sunlight without burning to a crisp. Not that the sun had shone all this dreary day. Still, Emily assumed that daylight had a similar effect on the ex-animate. Which was why she'd taken care to arrive here before dark and well protected with a necklace bearing a crucifix, the seal of St. Benedict, an evil eye charm from Greece, a tiger's eye, a crescent-shaped charm, and a brass finger ring, salt, and poppy seeds. Lest those precautions prove insufficient, she had also splashed herself liberally with holy water and garlic oil. Emily had studied all the literature, from *Dissertation on the Physical Traits of Bloodsucking Cadavers* to Mr. Polidori's strange, inscrutable Lord Ruthven. Would Count Révay-Czobar be a blood-sucking fiend so foul she couldn't even bear to look at him, let alone ask his help? Would he see her as a tasty tidbit, and thereby force her to defend herself? Would she be able to persuade him to take her seriously when her own papa had not? Emily fingered her crucifix.

Suddenly her skin prickled. The hair on her neck rose. Even her elbows tingled, and in Emily's admittedly limited experience, elbow tingles were almost always a bad thing.

A reflection appeared behind her in the clouded

window glass. Clutching her umbrella, she slowly turned around.

A man stood by the fireplace, rubbing the wolf-dog's ears. He was rumpled, tousled, as if he'd just risen from bed. *Coffin,* Emily reminded herself. Valentin Lupescu was the stuff of which legend was made.

Long, thick auburn hair tumbled loose over his broad shoulders. Golden skin and high cheekbones and a slanted slash of eyebrows hinted of a Tatar somewhere in his ancestry. His jaw was strong, his nose noble, his eyes the blue of fine sapphires, his mouth the most shamelessly sensual Emily had ever seen. Not that she had made a study of sensual mouths, but still. The Count was tall, powerfully built. Easy enough to see that he was splendidly fashioned: his shirt was half-unbuttoned as if he'd just put it on, along with the tight breeches that molded to his powerful thighs. Emily realized she was staring, and where, and quickly returned her gaze to his face.

He arched an eyebrow. "You wished to speak with me, elfling?"

Even his voice was smoky, dark, seductive, with the faintest trace of an accent. Emily collected her scattered wits. "You *are* Count Révay-Czobar?"

The Count inclined his head. "Call me Ravensclaw. It's easier on the tongue."

If here was no graying skin or deathlike pallor, no stink of putrefying flesh—he looked to be no more than five-and-thirty—the Count was definitely preternatural. No mere mortal could be so overwhelming. Emily held her umbrella at the ready, grateful for its nicely sharpened point.

The sensuous lips curved. Ravensclaw's eyes caressed her face, skimmed her forehead, the curve of her cheek; kissed the tip of her nose; lingered on her lips; nuzzled an earlobe.

Emily's knees trembled. Sweat popped out on her brow as a strange melting sensation stole over her, a growing warmth as if his hands were on her body, those long elegant fingers stroking her skin instead of Drogo's thick fur. As if his breath were warm against her ear, whispering of her hunger to be consumed by something greater than herself. Emily wanted to touch him in return, to run her hands over that smooth golden skin beneath his linen shirt, unfasten those snug breeches, and—

Mercy! The Count made her feel things she'd never felt before.

Made her feel them. "Stop that!" Emily said crossly, as she wrenched her gaze away, and reminded herself that she was a sensible, bespectacled spinster, not at all the sort of female this man would have noticed in his prime—and if Ravensclaw was this potent now, what he had been like *before?* Furthermore, she of all people should have known better than to look into his eyes.

He moved again, and was suddenly so close that she might have reached out and touched him. Emily locked her traitorous knees together and thrust out her crucifix.

Ravensclaw plucked the thing out of her hand and studied it. "Excellent workmanship. Solid gold. Byzantine. The sort of thing a Crusader might have worn."

So much for the literature. The Count hadn't cringed or blanched or hissed at sight of the holy relic; he'd touched it with no sizzle of burning flesh. Furthermore, he was standing in what remained of the daylight without any ill effect. Emily found herself fascinated by the length of his eyelashes, which were considerably thicker and darker than her own.

He glanced from the crucifix to her, and sniffed. "*Eau de garlique.* How original. Is this a new fashion of which I'm unaware?"

Emily frowned at him. "Garlic doesn't disturb you?"

"Quite the contrary. I especially like it with chicken, forty cloves and two bay leaves." Ravensclaw released the crucifix. The metal felt warm against her flesh. On the hearth, the silver wolf stirred as the Count reached out with one long graceful finger and pushed Emily's glasses back up to the bridge of her nose.

He was toying with her as if he were a cat and she a witless rodent. Emily stepped back and raised her umbrella to poke her host in the chest. "There's no time for this foolishness. I must ask that you keep your hands— and your thoughts—to yourself, sir!"

The wolf-dog growled. The Count narrowed his eyes as if he might be debating whether to sink his teeth into her throat or hurl her across the room.

Emily took a firmer grip on her umbrella. Not that she wished to skewer Ravensclaw before she had a chance to speak with him, but neither was she eager to make the intimate acquaintance of his fangs. At least not yet. Although she *did* have a certain curiosity—

And then, without the slightest hint of fangs, he smiled, a roguish captivating grin that said you're-the-most-delicious-thing-I've-seen-in-a-long-time-and-I'm-going-to-gobble-you-up-slowly-and-savor-every-nibble as clearly as if he'd spoken aloud.

Emily blinked. Ravensclaw was surely the most irresistibly, wickedly beautiful being ever put on God's green earth. In whatever century that had been.

She could hardly look at him without drooling.

It was clear from his amused expression that he knew it.

Oh, bloody hell.

Chapter Two

Bees that have honey in their mouths have stings in their tails.
(Romanian proverb)

Emily brandished her umbrella. "We're wasting time. I know what you are, Count Révay-Czobar."

"Ravensclaw," the Count reminded her, then said: "Isidore?" The old man quickly appeared, as if he had been eavesdropping just out of sight. "Have tea brought to the Lord's Chamber."

"Tea. The Lord's Chamber." Isidore twitched his nose.

The last thing Emily had anticipated was taking tea with an aberration. "There's no time for this!"

"There's always time to observe the proprieties," the Count said primly, his eyes alight with mischief. "And there's all the time in the world for us to become acquainted. Your driver has departed without you."

Emily turned to the window, noticed that it had grown quite dark. Ravensclaw said soothingly, "No doubt he was afraid of the ghaisties. The natives are a superstitious lot. Wheesht, lassie, didna Kiuttlin' Kate lepit off the castle wall into the loch after cuddlin' with one lad too many and findin' herself biggend? Doesna Gawkit Gordy haunt the stables, or what were once the stables, where he was murthered by a manservant under circumstances best not thought aboot?"

The Count's Scots accent was cannily accurate. Emily suspected he was laughing at her. "You jest."

"Not at all. We also have a woman in white who is most often seen on the stair, and the ghost of a dog."

Emily couldn't stop herself from glancing at the wolf. The animal rose from the hearth and moved toward her. She backed away. The Count murmured, "I assure you Drogo is no ghost. Touch him and see for yourself."

Emily had no intention of doing anything so fatwitted. Not that coming here had been especially wise. She thought of Mr. Polidori's Lord Ruthven, the fearless world-traveling aristocrat who lured innocent women to their death so that he might feed on their blood. Ravensclaw didn't *look* like a fiend from hell. And even though she'd roused him from his slumber, he'd been nothing but polite.

"Tea awaits. Permit me to escort you to the Lord's Chamber." The Count offered his arm. Emily eyed it dubiously. "After all, you wish to speak with me, do you not? And it seems you are to be my guest tonight."

His guest, or his supper? But if Emily lacked courage she wouldn't have come here in the first place. She didn't take his arm, however. The Count looked amused by her refusal and gestured for her to precede him up the winding stone staircase.

The Lord's Chamber was a lofty, domed six-sided room with false ribs, once brightly painted with red and black chevrons, springing from corbelled colonettes. Set into the walls were a fireplace and an arched cupboard and four windows, three comparatively wide with stone benches, the last a narrow slit with a stone sink in the sill. Behind a carved screen, a doorway led off to a smaller room.

The chamber was furnished with opulence enough to suit the most hedonistic Romanian boyar. Heavy oak furniture embellished with intricately carved animals and flowers; a cabinet with checkerboard parquetry, another inlaid with what looked like precious stones; a writing table of silver-inlaid ebony; and bookcases everywhere. Fine multicolored rugs lay on the stone floor. Tapestries depicted historical and mystical scenes, a medieval garden complete with lush foliage, animals, and even insects. Illumination was provided by oil lamps suspended in metal rings.

A tea tray rested on an inlaid chest. "If you will do the honors?" said the Count. With a sense of unreality, Emily went about the familiar, soothing ritual. Ravensclaw preferred his tea with a chunk of crystallized ginger. Emily took hers with milk. From somewhere, Isidore had produced raisin scones served warm with clotted cream.

Ravensclaw settled back with his teacup, as proper as if he sat in any London drawing room. Not that Emily knew many—if any—gentlemen who drank tea. And not that she was particularly familiar with London drawing rooms. She had been more hungry than she realized, and the scones were very good. Emily observed the Count keenly, alert for signs of blood lust, a reddening or glowing of the eye, an elongation of his teeth.

"You have me at a disadvantage." Ravensclaw raised his gaze from the pulse point at the base of her throat. "Perhaps you might permit me to know your name."

This entire meeting was nothing like Emily had imagined it. In an attempt to take control of the situation, and herself, she briskly set down her teacup. "I know, Count Révay-Czobar, that you are familiar with the Dinwiddie Society."

His eyes narrowed just a little bit. "I am."

"I am Emily Dinwiddie."

He studied her. "Daughter of Professor Bartholomew

Dinwiddie, creator of several strange inventions, most notable a portable engine, in the way of a tobacco-tongs, by means of which a man may climb over a wall. Known to his many detractors as Professor Dimwit, a sobriquet resulting from his invention of a sundial for a gravestone that placed particular emphasis on the anniversary of the deceased's dates of birth and death. Or perhaps it was his amphibious horse-drawn vehicle. You are a considerable distance from London, Miss Dinwiddie. I assume you traveled here alone."

Fortunately her papa's detractors hadn't learned of the little ladder that enabled spiders to climb out of a hipbath. The automaton that could play a flute. The mechanical quacking duck which appeared to digest and excrete its food. Emily picked up the teapot. "You surprise me, Count."

Ravensclaw gestured at the considerable reading material in the chamber, which at a glance ranged from early studies of anatomy, treatises on fungi and pharmacology, to Sir Walter Raleigh's *The Discovery of the Large, Rich and beautiful Empire of Guiana, with a relation of the Great, Golden City of Manoa (which the Spaniards call El Dorado)*, Albertus Magnus's *The Alchemist*, and, unless Emily's eyes deceived her, *The Egyptian Book of the Dead.* "I'm a victim of insomnia. Reading scholarly treatises helps me to fall asleep. Did you know that the ancient Egyptians were in the habit of annually burning alive an unfortunate individual whose only crime was to have hair the color of yours? You look disturbed, Miss Dinwiddie. Have I said something to upset you?"

Emily poured more tea into her cup. "I *meant* I was surprised that you should think I might arrive here with a retinue." Not that one was "alone" when traveling on the common stage, even though one might heartily wish to be. Emily had been more than happy to part company with her traveling companions in Morpeth, a matron with several offspring, a parson, and several unhappy chickens in a cage. "Perhaps you're unaware that my father died recently in an accident in his laboratory. At least everyone else insists it was an accident. Myself, I am unsure. In any event, I am now overseer of the Dinwiddie Society."

The Count raised an eyebrow. "You?"

Emily scowled. "Don't you *dare* point out that I'm a female."

He smiled. "I seldom state the obvious, Miss Dinwiddie. Moreover, you misjudge me. I was merely thinking that you're very young for such responsibility."

"I am four-and-twenty. That's not so very young. Nor am I entirely ignorant, Count Révay-Czobar. In addition to my extensive formal education, I worked with my papa, and consequently know about vampires and ghouls and shape-changers." Emily glanced pointedly at Drogo, snoozing on the hearth. "And werewolves."

Ravensclaw picked up a cucumber sandwich and looked politely interested. "How nice for you."

For all her experiences with the Society—or the experiences she had read about in her role as her papa's amanuensis, no one having been willing to let her *do* anything because she was a mere female—Emily had never met a supersensible being in the flesh. If "flesh" was the proper term. Emily watched in amazement as the Count gave every evidence of enjoying his repast. A plump, black long-haired feline oozed through the doorway. Upon sight of Emily, it hissed.

"Machka," said the Count, when Emily glanced questioningly at him. "Romany for cat." The creature jumped into his lap and purred.

According to the literature, animals didn't like the preterhuman, yet here Ravensclaw sat like any ordinary man, with a cat on his lap and a dog sprawled on his hearth. Not that there was anything ordinary about Count Révay-Czobar, or the dog that could well be a lycanthrope, or the cat that was probably his familiar. Emily touched her necklace with its assorted charms. "Let us return to the purpose of my visit. I've come here to ask your help."

Ravensclaw stroked the cat. "Whatever gives you the impression that I'm a man who rescues damsels in distress?"

Emily hadn't the impression that he was a man at all. "How many times must I tell you that I *know* what you are! Shall I remind you of Mercea the Wise, Vlad Tepes, Michael the Brave? You have lived in palaces and huts alike, foraged for food in the mountainous regions of Wallachia, Moldavia, and Transylvania; have seen Greeks fight Romans, Romanians fight Hungarians and Tatars, Turks fight Russians and Austrians. Having apparently come to the not unreasonable conclusion that it is human nature not only to covet one's neighbor's land and goods but also to attempt to destroy each other in the process, you decided numerous decades past that you preferred to observe the human tragicomedy from a less volatile vantage point than Romania."

Ravensclaw didn't react as Emily might have expected to her recitation. Calmly he said, "You're well informed about my ancestors."

"I'm well informed about *you!*" Emily flung herself out of the chair and began to pace. "Let me reassure you, sir. The Society has a live-and-let-live-except-in-isolated-instances philosophy. We believe that evil is in the eye of the beholder, and morality is a point of view."

"Fascinating," murmured the Count.

Emily eyed the fireplace, over which hung a thirteenth-century sword, a sharpened rod of triangular cross-section drawn to an acute point at one end and hilted at the other; and wished she might whack her host over his aggravating head. How much was safe to tell him? Dared she take a chance and trust Ravensclaw?

He hadn't offered her harm yet. Nor, from what she knew of the Count, was he likely to do so unless she threatened him or his. "My papa spoke highly of you, sir. And so I'll tell you now that the Society has, or had, in our possession a double-bladed athame with a cabochon ruby and a Celtic pentagram set into its hilt."

Ravensclaw's blue gaze sharpened. "The d'Auvergne athame. It vanished centuries ago."

"Was stolen, I'm afraid. In 1544, to be precise, by Isobella Dinwiddie, and thereafter kept locked in the Society's vault."

Ravensclaw said nothing. Emily drew a deep breath. "It gets worse. A number of other things are also missing. You must help me get them back."

His expression was unreadable. "Must I?"

Provoking creature. Emily strove for patience. "Since the athame was originally stolen from you, you surely know its powers."

Ravensclaw had ceased petting the cat, and Machka jumped down off his lap. "Stolen from my ancestor, you mean."

Emily threw up her hands in exasperation. "I suppose you'll also try to tell me it's your ancestor whose name is on the Dinwiddie list, which was stolen as well! The Society has known about the Breaslă for some time, Count Révay-Czobar. Do stop wasting time! We must go to Edinburgh. I'm convinced the missing items may be found there."

The Count stretched his long legs out before him. "You are too impatient, Miss Dinwiddie. Tell me about your father's accident."

Impatient, was she? Ravensclaw had no idea. Emily's first supersensible creature was causing her to wish to box his ears.

"Papa had become interested in electropathy. He was attempting to create a pair of galvanic spectacles, applying electric current to the optic nerve by means of a small zinc and copper plate to the nosepiece." Emily pushed her own spectacles back up where they belonged. "Something went amiss. A considerable amount of current was instead applied to himself."

"How unfortunate. My condolences."

"Thank you. As you might imagine, things were at sixes and sevens for a time. There are those in the Society who thought Papa should be more aggressive than he was. That the Society had become little more than a mere repository of arcane lore. It was some time before I discovered that the athame had gone missing." Emily reached into a pocket and pulled out an odd silver charm of the sort that might have dangled from a gentleman's watch fob. Provided said gentleman had esoteric interests. "This was left behind."

The Count glanced at it. "The *vrajă* is familiar to you?"

Emily noted that Ravensclaw had called the charm by its correct name. And that he wisely hadn't touched the thing. "I believe this *vrajă* to have been in the possession of a man named Michael Ross. He is—*was*—a particular friend of mine." She paused, embarrassed by the sharpness of her tone.

The Count was studying the charm. "It's not an unusual piece. Could the *vrajă* have been left behind at some other time?"

"I would have found it previously, were that the case, since I'm the only one Papa trusted to tidy up his laboratory. And Michael had it when I spoke with him earlier that day. Can we please go now?"

"Humor me, Miss Dinwiddie. What do you expect to find in Edinburgh?"

"I shall find Michael, of course."

"And then?"

Emily blew out an irritated breath. "I don't know. Ask him to return what was stolen. Steal the dratted things from him. Or maybe you can make him give them back."

Ravensclaw reached for the teapot. "Perhaps a little more subtlety might not come amiss. Particularly if you suspect this young man of having something to do with your father's death."

Emily didn't want to discuss her suspicions. "Naturally you would prefer to travel under cover of darkness." Alas, the Count didn't look like he had any intention of moving from his chair. She added, "Unless you can sprout wings and fly like a bat?"

His brow quirked again at her sarcasm. "You intrigue me, Miss Dinwiddie. If I was what you think me, shouldn't you be afraid?"

She *was* afraid, but not about to tell him so. "You admit it, then?"

"I admit nothing." The Count stood. "You'll spend the night."

Pass the night at haunted Corby Castle? Emily opened her mouth to protest. Ravensclaw raised his eyes to hers and instead she contemplated the pleasures of the flesh, imagined the brush of those knowing lips against her throat, wondered if he would like the taste of her skin.

He rose from his chair, the cat draped over one shoulder. Emily stepped back, a hand raised to fend him off. Her fingers brushed his bare wrist.

A dizzy sense of mysterious dense forests, high rocky mountains, lush green upland pastures, a harsh climate and heavy rainfall. A two-roomed cottage of solid well-hewn logs, roofed with laths. Wood floor covered with home-

made woolen rugs. Similar rugs arranged neatly on the bed.

A woman with chestnut hair, wearing a sleeveless jacket of fine white lambskin, richly embroidered in many colors and decorated with little straps of dark leather, pierced metal rings, and loops of lace. Around her waist an ornamental belt of different-colored wool interwoven with golden threads, a skirt woven in strips of light and dark red wool, with silver thread shining in between. Her heavy wool stockings were striped white and red and black.

She backed away from him. "Trădător! Nelegiuit!" cried Ana, and made the sign against the evil eye.

Ravensclaw looked startled. Emily jerked her hand away.

Chapter Three

An ape's an ape, a varlet's a varlet, though they be clad in
silk and scarlet.
(Romanian proverb)

Thunder rumbled through the heavens. Raindrops
rattled against the window glass. Emily slept fitfully.

The dense wild forest was all around her, the small
cottage a long distance away. Moonlight cast eerie silver
shadows. She threaded her way through tall spruce trees
to a mountaintop meadow where aromatic grasses and
flowers grew.

He was waiting there for her. "I hunger. Let me taste
you." He spread his dark cloak on the meadow floor.

She was powerless to resist him. "I know what you
are."

He reached out his hand to her. "I also know what
you are, iubită."

Closer she moved to him, closer, though she had no
awareness of moving at all. "You do?"

Cool fingers slid through her hair to caress the nape
of her neck. "It's a matter of scent."

His eyes weren't blue now but black and bottomless.
Breathlessly, she said, "Scent?"

"You smell enticingly of garlic." He lowered his lips to

*her throat. Pleasure hummed through her veins. His
teeth found her pulse, nipped and licked. A strange melting sensation, a growing warmth—*

His eyes burned crimson as the flames of hell.
His teeth had turned to fangs.
He was nibbling at her neck.
And she didn't give a damn.

The warm molten feeling of the dream evolved into
the metallic taste of blood in her mouth and a heavy
weight on her chest. A quick investigation, and Emily
discovered she had bitten her own lip. Perhaps an incubus had invaded her dreams, that special sort of
demon who stole upon sleeping women at night and
made them long for things unimaginable in the practical light of day. Which would explain the hunger still
burning in her, if not the fact that, though the night
was over, something still squished her breasts.

Cautiously Emily opened one eye. No incubus perched
atop her, but Machka. The cat's whiskers twitched. They
were almost nose to nose. Emily held very still. After a
moment's slit-eyed contemplation, Machka butted her
head against Emily's chin, and began to knead her neck.

Gingerly, Emily patted the creature. She hoped her
necklace of talismans would prove effective against whatever Machka was, although they weren't protecting her
against the sharp claws that pricked her throat.

The stone chamber was small and sparsely furnished,
the bed a simple cot. A single deep-set window offered a
pleasant view and a clear field of fire for anyone de-
fending the castle walls.

A tap on the arched door, and it swung open. A
maidservant bustled into the room. "Good morning,
miss. I've brought you some chocolate. Ah, the naughty
pisică!" She shooed a hissing Machka off the bed.

Maidservant? Emily reconsidered. The woman more

resembled a tavern wench, brown-haired and buxom, with a fine color in her cheeks and plump pouting lips. Emily pulled her sheet up to her chin and shifted herself into a sitting position. "What's your name?"

"Zizi, miss." Zizi put down the tray, which contained not only a pot of chocolate but also a plate of biscuits.

This was not the servant who'd brought Emily to her bedchamber the evening before. "How many of there are you?" she asked.

"Just three, miss. And old Isidore."

Emily lifted her chocolate cup. "How long have you been with the Count?"

Zizi scooped up Machka, who was inching toward the biscuits. "As long as I can recall."

Glamour, Emily decided. Although Zizi, as opposed to being pale and wan as befit an undead's victim, was awesomely robust. Nor were there any fang marks on the startling amount of creamy neck and bosom that were on display. "Indeed?"

"Sometimes it seems that way." Zizi shrugged. "Ravensclaw treats his people well. None of us would want to be elsewhere."

They wouldn't, would they, if Ravensclaw had bespelled them? It was only sensible of the Count to have servants do his bidding in the daylight when he couldn't be abroad. He would blind them with his powers to the monstrous creature he really was.

Oh, drat! No incubus had sent her dream, but Ravensclaw. Emily couldn't have resisted him no matter how hard she tried, and now he would know that she hadn't tried at all. Zizi added, "Himself says that as soon as you're ready, we'll leave for Edinburgh."

Emily paused with her chocolate cup halfway to her mouth and stared at the bright sunlight streaming through the window. "Himself?" Perhaps she'd misunderstood.

Zizi looked at Emily as if she were addled. "Ravensclaw. Isn't that why you came here, miss? Because you wished the master to go with you to Edinburgh?" Machka hissed and lashed out with sharp claws. Zizi cursed and dropped the cat. Machka jumped up on the bed, raised one back leg, and began to lick herself. "*Căţea!*" muttered Zizi. "Will you need help getting dressed, then?"

"Thank you, no." Zizi closed the door behind her. Emily took off her nightgown and folded it neatly. Though Willie had proved himself a coward, at least he'd left her valise behind at the bottom of the steps. She donned another serviceable and somewhat wrinkled dark gown, and went in search of her host. Machka jumped down from the bed to trail at her heels.

Emily found Ravensclaw in the Lord's Chamber. Drogo was dozing at his feet. The Count raised his eyes from the slender volume in his hand. "I was just reading a formula for the manufacture and use of a magic carpet. A virgin is required, as well as poppies and autumn gentian."

Emily glanced at the grimoire. "Indeed? *I* have read that one may vanish a nosferatu by stuffing his left sock with graveyard dirt and cemetery rocks, then tossing it into water flowing away from the area one wishes to protect. And also that the demised may be controlled by the use of spiritwood and rum."

Again, that bewitching smile. "One needs to be naked during that particular ritual, I believe."

Emily resisted the temptation to think of Ravensclaw naked. "Alternately one might make a stake of ash, hawthorn, or maple and pound it into the corpse, put garlic in its mouth, and pound a nail in its head. Remove the heart and cut it in two. Incinerate the decapitated body and throw the ashes to the wind." Any of which, she admitted, would be a great pity in the present case. "You have a reflection. I saw it in the window yesterday."

"Why would I not have a reflection?" Ravensclaw closed his book. "I assure you, elfling, that I'm quite corporeal."

He was entirely too corporeal for her peace of mind. Emily was embarrassed to feel herself blush. Her papa would consider this befuddlement as further proof that the feminine mind was prey to overstimulation. The Count said, "Miss Dinwiddie? Are you all right?"

He knew quite well that she wasn't. Emily retorted, "I understand that we're to go to Edinburgh."

Drogo opened one yellow eye. Ravensclaw scratched the wolf's ears. "Am I mistaken? I thought that was what you wished." The Count was dressed for traveling in glossy boots and fawn breeches that clung to his muscular thighs, snowy linen, and a superbly cut brown coat.

"I've always wished to travel without the annoying restrictions placed on females. I almost arrived here disguised in masculine attire, thinking that I would be less, um, palatable." And maybe the Count had bespelled *her*, that she spoke so freely to him. Emily bit her lower lip.

"My dear," Ravensclaw said gently. "What nonsense."

"Oh." Emily pondered this startling revelation. "I didn't realize your sort were . . . um . . ."

"Amphierotic? Oh yes. Umbivalent, actually. I know this only because of my vast reading, of course." Drogo parted his great jaws and yawned.

Umbivalent? Suspiciously, Emily said, "Are you mocking me?"

Ravensclaw's eyes twinkled. "No, elfling, I'm enjoying you. It's a very different thing."

Enjoying her, was he? Emily was absurdly pleased. Gruffly, she said, "So we're to go to Edinburgh. How do you intend to transport your, ah, resting place?"

The Count stood. Emily couldn't help but notice the graceful way he moved. Or the somewhat annoyed expression on his face. "Has anyone ever told you, Miss Dinwiddie, that you're a very exasperating young woman? Come with me." He led her to the room adjoining the Lord's Chamber and stepped aside to allow her entry. "*This* is where I sleep."

Tapestries hung on these walls also. Rugs worked in Turkey wool were scattered on the floor. A huge cupboard stood against one stone wall. Drawn up to the fireplace were carved chairs made comfortable with crimson pillows. Dominating the chamber was a huge canopied bed standing on a dais, its headboard and posts elaborately carved with figures in bas-relief. Emily was assailed by naughty images involving the fur coverlet and smooth sheets. Cheeks aflame, she bent to peer beneath the bed.

There was nary a speck of dust in sight. Or dirt. But the literature stated that the insensate must return to the earth for a certain period of time each day. "I thought revenants couldn't go far from their native soil."

"I don't know about revenants, but *I* can go anywhere I please."

His voice was above and behind her. Emily realized he must be gazing on her upthrust rump. Hastily, she righted herself. "And can you cross running water, sir?" she snapped.

His voice was warm. "I swim. I also bathe. Would you care to join me, Miss Dinwiddie?"

As if a splendidly masculine being like Ravensclaw would care to share his bath with someone like herself. His naked bath. Emily's cheeks flamed hotter yet. Unwilling to face her tormentor, she stared at a carved bedpost, and discovered to her shock that the bas-relief figures were erotically entwined.

She squinted. The lovers were sitting face to face, heels locked around each other's waists. What a strange position! Was such a thing physically possible?

"Miss Dinwiddie?" Ravensclaw sounded even more as if he wished to laugh out loud. "You're anxious to leave for Edinburgh, I believe?"

She was anxious to remove herself from Ravensclaw's bedchamber, and this wicked bed. Before she entirely lost her senses and dragged him down with her onto it to explore what was possible and what was not. "Yes! Fine!" Emily stalked out of the room with as much dignity as she could summon. Which, she suspected from the Count's merry expression, hadn't fooled him a whit. Although she might have been mistaken. He had donned small, dark round-lensed spectacles to protect his eyes.

Outside, a traveling coach waited, its dark wood embellished with a coat of arms. Emily watched as Ravensclaw walked out into the sunlight. Despite his assurances, she half expected him to burst into flame and crumble into dust.

He held out his hand, his expression unreadable behind his dark spectacles. Emily ignored this offer of assistance and climbed into the coach.

The interior of the carriage was lined with crimson upholstery and boasted numerous amenities, including locking shutters, a compass, silver-plated furnishings, and three lamps. Drogo and Machka were to travel with Emily and the Count, Drogo taking up a great deal of the floor, and Machka sprawled on Emily's reluctant lap. Isidore climbed onto the high box seat. Emily hoped the old man had the strength to control the spirited team. Zizi and her companions followed in a less conspicuous vehicle. Emily wondered where all this equipment had been kept, and what other amenities were hidden in the castle ruins.

The carriage moved forward, beneath the rusted portcullis with its wicked-looking spikes, across an ancient drawbridge that looked as though it couldn't bear a mouse's weight. Emily threaded her fingers through Machka's soft fur and was rewarded by the prick of claws against her thigh.

She had never before realized the intimacy of a closed carriage. But then, Emily had never before ridden in a closed carriage with Ravensclaw. Privately, she admitted to being a little afraid. As well as astonishingly attracted to him, which she assured herself wasn't surprising, since the dead-alive were said to be of a seductive nature, and in this instance at least the literature was correct.

The attraction she didn't mind, not really, curious as it was. Emily was a creature not of the senses but of the intellect. What choice had she, with her freckles and spectacles and frizzy mass of orange hair? But she very much minded being afraid. Emily's intrepid ancestress Isobella wouldn't have been frightened of Ravensclaw. From all accounts Isobella Dinwiddie had been frightened of nothing, which perhaps was why she'd met an untimely death. The d'Auvergne athame wasn't the only thing Isobella had stolen during her adventurous career. Emily yearned to be more like Isobella. Not that she wished to drink poison or dally with other women's husbands. But she definitely wanted more adventure in her life.

Well, she was having an adventure, wasn't she? And she might as well take advantage of the opportunity to ask the Count some of the questions that intrigued her. "Is it true that your kind can change shapes at will? Make yourselves invisible? Can you really fly?"

He stretched out his long legs until one muscular calf rested against her skirts. "You remind me of a terrier with a rat, Miss Dinwiddie. The dog sinks its teeth into its prey and refuses to let go until the rodent's neck is broken."

"Are you comparing yourself to a rat?"

"No, little one. Nor am I comparing you to a cur.

However, much as I hate to disappoint you, I'm not what you think me. Although I *have* perused much literature on the subject during my bouts of insomnia. I especially enjoyed *On the Masticating Dead in their Tomb* (1728), and the notion that having a virgin boy ride naked bareback on a virgin stallion will point the way to an inanimate's resting place. And before you ask me, since I've read so extensively and am therefore something of an expert, I consider it most unlikely that any being can crawl headfirst down a castle wall, or turn himself into a wisp of fog."

Could she be so mistaken in him? Emily narrowed her eyes. "Why are you accompanying me to Edinburgh if you refuse to take me seriously, Count Révay-Czobar?"

Ravensclaw reached over and plucked Machka from her lap. "Because you're a very reckless young woman, Miss Dinwiddie. And I am of a more chivalrous nature than I had realized."

Chapter Four

An arrow shot upright falls on the shooter's head.
(Romanian proverb)

Edinburgh was a perilous city built upon an extinct volcano, the medieval Old Town's dark tenements piled up like a great haphazard pile of rocks glowering down upon the New Town's neoclassical terraces and squares. The two areas were separated by a deep, broad bridge-spanned ravine planted with trees and shrubbery, once a lake where countless accused witches met their deaths, most of them being exonerated of all charges in the process, for only the innocent drowned. Ancient Edinburgh Castle towered above everything.

In the heyday of the Old Town, several prominent Elizabethans had chosen to live in the then less congested area of the Canongate, commuting to and from Edinburgh Castle by sedan chair along the Royal Mile. Count Révay-Czobar chose to live there now, in a tall, narrow townhouse that rose five stories and terminated in two pointed gables of unequal size. Curving forestairs jutted out onto the pavement westward of an arcaded ground-floor frontage consisting of two round-headed arches stained from centuries of billowing black smoke, fog, and rain. A lentil stone bore the date 1622 and the words FEARE THE LORD AND DEPART FROM EVILL. The interior of the townhouse was highly decorated, including tiled chimneypieces and fine tempera work.

The master bedroom was richly decorated also, its beam and board ceilings brightly painted with flowers and fruit. A deep arcaded frieze adorned the stone wall above the fireplace and the curved wall that marked the turnpike stair, surmounted the tall, deep-set shuttered windows. Upholstered armchairs were scattered around the chamber. A coffer with a dolphin motif inlaid with holly and bog oak sat against one wall, near it a great carved bed. Ravensclaw lay there amid gryphons and unicorns, his hands folded on his chest, as still as the mythical beasts. Or perhaps not precisely as still. One eyebrow twitched.

Abruptly, the Count wakened. If it could be called that. This was hardly sleep as he remembered sleep. Not that he thought much about the past, any more than he dwelled upon his own history. Valentin Lupescu experienced no regret at being what the Dinwiddie Society would consider an aberration of nature. In fact, all things considered, Val thought himself damned fortunate.

Fortunate, if alone in his bed at the moment. He opened one eye. Looking even more dour than usual, Isidore hovered just inside the door. Val said, "Where are Zizi? Lilian? Bela?"

Isidore twitched his nose. "They didn't think it would be proper to be in your bedchamber with a young lady in the house."

Propriety. What an odd concept. Especially in connection with Zizi, Bela, and Lilian.

Miss Dinwiddie was complicating Val's existence. He didn't mind. She was such a serious, stubborn little creature that she appealed to his well-developed sense of the absurd. Although he found most people amusing, if not especially original, Emily promised to provide more potential entertainment than Val had enjoyed in a decade.

And more problems. It had been obvious that, with or without him, she would travel to Edinburgh, a curious lamb blundering into a lair of hungry wolves. Although "lamb" was hardly a proper term for a young woman bent on a bit of blackmail. Val would at some point have to destroy that blasted list.

In the interim, he would help Emily retrieve her missing items. If he took few things seriously, including himself, Val took the d'Auvergne athame very seriously indeed. And he thought it very unlikely that Professor Dinwiddie's death by electrocution had been a mere mishap.

Isidore had been waiting patiently. Now he cleared his throat. Val threw back the covers. "*What?*" he said.

"I decided the chimneys needed sweeping. However, it seems that Miss Dinwiddie has strong feelings about chimneysweeps. This particular chimneysweep was caught trying to steal a silver candlestick. By Drogo." Isidore almost smiled. "Scared the *puşti* out of a good year's growth."

Val reached for his clothes. "What did you do with our young thief?"

"He that may not do as he would, must do as he may." Before Val could either comment or cuff him, the old man shuffled out the door.

Val pulled on his breeches. Though he was personally acquainted with the Dinwiddie Society, an old and long established family foundation whose true purpose wasn't publicized, he had *not* known that the Society was in possession of the d'Auvergne athame. Now he wondered what else he didn't know.

He also wondered how far Miss Dinwiddie would go in her attempts to protect herself from his perceived menace. Hopefully she wouldn't drape herself about with bleached bones, or eat grave dirt. He was smiling as he buttoned his shirt.

Contrary to custom, Val didn't let out each story of his townhouse like a separate flat, the ground floor occupied by a tradesman and his workshop, the lower floors provenance of aristocrats and prosperous merchants who wished to get away from the dirt and stench of the street and yet to avoid the steep and often noisome climb up the common turnpike stair. The highest floors were home to servants or poorer workmen who reaped some benefit in that they, at least, could see some degree of sunlight. The bottom floor of Val's house was indeed occupied by a small cloth merchant's booth, but the MacCamishes were in his employ, and made sure that in his absence the rest of the dwelling was kept secure and in good repair. Val's kitchen and dining room were on the first floor, the drawing room on the second, his bedroom and adjacent study on the third, guest and servants' rooms above.

Val descended the narrow stair. His drawing room was a cozy chamber, with walls paneled green, faded rugs on the wood floor, and a simple chimneypiece. Chairs, sofas, and stools were covered with leather and studded with nails, or fashioned from imported hardwood delicately inlaid with pearl and rendered comfortable with quilted upholstery. Books littered almost every available surface, interspersed with maps of the world, a calculating board, and a perpetual almanac in a frame.

Val paused unnoticed in the doorway. His houseguest stood in an errant patch of sunlight that glinted off her spectacles and turned her fiery hair every shade from copper to gold. Her fair skin was almost translucent, at least that part of it not covered with freckles. She was clutching a raggedy little urchin by the elbow and delivering a lecture on the penalties for theft, which ranged from branding to transportation to simply being hanged.

"Contermashious sassenach," muttered the sweep. Miss Dinwiddie gave him a good shake. Machka rubbed against her ankles. Emily looked even more annoyed. Drogo sprawled in the doorway.

Val walked into the room. "Isidore informs me that we have a guest." The chimneysweep was no bigger than a minute, and covered head to toe with soot.

Emily dragged the boy behind her and prepared to do battle. "Can you imagine what it's *like* to be a chimney-sweep? These old buildings are built of wood and the chimneys have to be swept continuously to ensure coal dust doesn't build up and lead to house fires. Children, being small, are naturally best suited to this task. Did you know that a child can be employed as young as four years old as a sweep? *If* he lives past his twelfth birthday, which is unlikely, a sweep's average life expectancy being six months, his body is already deformed by the constant pushing of his limbs against the chimneys' brick walls. Most need crutches to walk by the time they reach adulthood and are unfit for any other kinds of jobs. My papa was so appalled by the widespread cruelty to such children that he invented a system of elongated hinged poles and a pulley apparatus to be used in our home." She paused for breath. Her captive muttered something uncomplimentary to do with bumbaleeries and bletherskates.

"Poles and pulleys. What an excellent notion. You must tell me all about it, Miss Dinwiddie. In the meantime, your young friend has a somewhat noxious aroma about him." Unlike Emily, who smelled enticingly like pasta tossed with sautéed garlic and olive oil. "Isidore. Take this noisome whelp away." The servant hobbled forward.

"I'm nae bastartin' whelp!" protested the sweep. "Me name's Jamie."

"*Neisprăvit!*" muttered Isidore, in the strangled tones of someone attempting not to breathe through his nose.

"No!" said Emily in the same moment, and clutched the boy's filthy jacket all the harder. "You shan't have him for your—er!"

For his breakfast, perhaps? Val was annoyed that Miss Dinwiddie thought he meant to harm the little wretch. "Isidore will find the lad's master and buy him off. Zizi, Bela, and Lilian will give the brat a bath. They'll enjoy it, but he won't. Still, he'd much rather have a bath than have Drogo eat him, I think." The wolf blinked one golden eye. "Crivvers!" ejaculated Jamie, and suggested that the gent awa' and bile his heid.

Much as Val disliked imposing his will on others, sometimes there was simply no choice. *Go with Isidore. Now. Behave yourself.* Jamie looked confused. Isidore grasped the lad's ear and led him from the room.

Drogo padded after them. Machka twined around Emily's ankles, for all the world as if she liked their guest. What Machka really liked was to be an annoyance. Val picked up the cat and set her on his shoulder. Machka licked his ear.

Emily righted her spectacles. "I've decided that I want Jamie as my page."

Val decided that Miss Dinwiddie was unfamiliar with the adage concerning fools and angels and the placement of their feet. "Be truthful. What you want is that I shan't have that miserable morsel as a snack. You may set your mind at rest. Not that I expect you'll believe the word of a conscienceless monster such as you clearly believe me to be."

Emily squinted at him. "You're angry with me."

Yes, and wasn't that interesting? Anger wasn't an emotion with which Val bothered much. "First you invade my castle and demand I bring you to Edinburgh. Now you introduce a filthy little thief into my household and insist on having him as your servant, although I doubt he knows what a page boy is and will probably rob you blind. And no, I don't mean you should turn him back out into the streets. Mrs. MacCamish could handle a regiment of Hussars. She'll brook no nonsense from a cheeky little scamp."

Emily was startled. "Mrs. MacCamish?"

"My cook. I have an exceedingly well-developed palate, Miss Dinwiddie. You shan't starve during your visit here. And as to that—" Val contemplated her drab gown. "I made some inquiries last night, after you went to sleep. Your Mr. Ross is a familiar figure in Edinburgh society. I think—no, I'm certain—we must find you some different clothes. And a chaperone."

Emily returned his regard through narrowed eyes, and with a betraying color in her cheeks. "A chaperone?"

How suspicious she was, and rightly so, because Val was enjoying the notion of how she might look clad in nothing but her own freckled skin. "A young lady like yourself can't reside in a gentleman's establishment without female supervision. Your reputation would be ruined."

"Hang my reputation!" retorted Emily. "Anyway, who would know?"

"Everyone. You'll be the cynosure of all eyes when we appear at"—Val rifled through a stack of invitations, and extracted one—"Lady Cullane's musicale."

Emily plopped into a chair and stared at him. "You can't mean what I think you mean. I'm not going to any wretched musicale."

"Ah." Val was sympathetic. "You don't know how to go on."

"Of course I do!" Emily retorted. "I was trained in all the ladylike arts before my mama died. Afterwards, however, I devoted myself to my papa and his studies. I have little interest in frivolity."

Val flicked the invitation with an elegant finger. "Then Lady Cullane it is. One must make sacrifices, Miss Dinwiddie. I guarantee your Michael will be there."

"He's not my Michael. You are the most exasperating man." She heard herself, and paused.

Val didn't even try to resist temptation. "You called me a man. Does that mean that you've decided I'm not a grotesquerie?"

Emily looked at him over the rim of her spectacles. "Whatever you are, you're exasperating. And what am I to tell Michael when I see him, pray? As far as he knows, I'm still in London. And I *am* still in mourning for my papa."

"So you won't dance. You've come to Edinburgh to find solace for your grief. In the bosom of your family."

"I don't have a family."

Val stroked Machka. "You do now."

Chapter Five

Plant the crab-tree wherever you will, it will never bear pippins.
(Romanian proverb)

Cleaned up, young Jamie was revealed to be a gap-toothed freckled lad—"fernitickles," he called them, noting that Emily had her own goodly share—maybe ten years of age, with a sandy-colored "coo lick" springing up from the crown of his head. Jamie confessed to having never had such good food, or clean clothes, or so warm a place to sleep as the wall bed near the kitchen hearth. He assured Emily he had no thought of running away, for Isidore had warned him that if he was to scarper, that great wolf would track him down and gobble him alive. If Isidore was crabbit (grumpy), Mrs. Mac-Camish was couthie (kind); and Zizi, Bela, and Lilian were—Och. Words failed him. Or words he could use in front of a young lady like herself. Isidore had given Jamie strict instructions on how to behave.

Isidore hobbed into the kitchen and wished he might give similar instruction to Miss Dinwiddie, if not grill her over the fire on the brandiron, because he had been searching for her everywhere. "The master is waiting for you, Miss Dinwiddie," he said sternly. "Along with Mme. Fanchon and Lady Alberta Tait."

Emily felt rebellious. "If he's waiting for them also, then a few moments more will hardly count."

Isidore's nose twitched. "No, miss, *they're* all waiting. For you. In the drawing room."

Emily wrinkled her own nose. Ravensclaw had only to voice a wish to have it granted. It was most annoying in him.

Tail straight up in the air like some sort of furry directional device, Machka led the way across the flagstone floor and up the narrow stair. So far Emily had managed—barely—to avoid either kicking or tripping over the annoying feline.

She hesitated in the doorway of the drawing room. Ravensclaw and his guests were seated around a mahogany table, enjoying a fine selection of delicacies, coffee, and tea. The younger of them was eyeing Drogo with trepidation. "Forgive me for asking, Count Révay-Czobar, but is that a *wolf*?"

"It's a common error, Mme. Fanchon. Drogo is a rare Carpathian *copoi,* or sleuthhound."

"Cabbage twice cooked is death," muttered Isidore, and gave Emily a none-too-gentle shove.

Three pair of eyes turned toward the doorway as Emily stumbled across the threshold. Four including Drogo, who additionally swiveled an ear in Emily's direction before he returned his attention to the guests.

Ravensclaw performed introductions. Lady Alberta Tait was a woman of considerable age, all wrinkles and powder and rouged sharp angles, her short curls blacker than ever intended by nature. Mme. Fanchon was fair-haired and plump, impeccably dressed and coiffed. In front of Lady Alberta sat a plate bearing remnants of smoked salmon omelet with watercress cream. Mme. Fanchon had confined herself to a cup of tea. Ravensclaw appeared to have enjoyed a bowl of thick and wholesome porridge, which Emily thought queer in him indeed.

Ravensclaw set down his teacup. "We're in grave need of your assistance, Mme. Fanchon. Miss Dinwiddie requires a new wardrobe." Mme. studied Emily, then murmured fervent agreement. Emily felt like kicking them both.

"Her coloring!" tsk'd Lady Alberta, after swallowing a last mouthful of omelet. "That hair. There's entirely too much of it. She reminds me of a hedgehog. No offense, my dear! And it's so *bright* a shade."

"*Desordonnée!*" agreed Mme. Fanchon. "*Vulgaire!*"

And you're no more French than I'm a water kelpie! Emily pushed back a ringlet that had come loose from its long braid. "Leave the hair alone. I like it," said Ravensclaw, just as she was on the verge of turning on her heel and walking out of the room.

"As you wish, of course." Lady Alberta applied herself now to herrings with oatmeal. "Perhaps the spectacles—remove them, Miss Dinwiddie, and let us have a look at you."

Instead Emily folded her arms across her chest. "I can't see without my spectacles."

Lady Alberta waved her fork. "You don't need to see, my dear, merely to be seen. Perhaps there's a substantial dowry, Val?"

Val, was it? The informal nickname suited Ravensclaw. Since she could hardly hover in the doorway indefinitely, Emily perched on the edge of an upholstered chair. Machka jumped up and rearranged Emily's lap to suit herself. Lady Alberta reached for a treacle scone.

Ravensclaw nudged the serving plate closer. "Miss Dinwiddie's financial situation is irrelevant. We're not trying to find her a husband, merely make her presentable."

Emily stiffened at the suggestion she wasn't "presentable." Machka kneaded and purred. "Not that I don't consider Miss Dinwiddie to already be perfection," Val added. "However, it's not my attention she wishes to attract."

Perfection. How absurd. And as for attracting his attention . . . *When pigs may fly!* Mme. Fanchon was staring at Ravensclaw, obviously fascinated with his high cheekbones and golden skin. Not to mention broad shoulders and muscular thighs, showcased today by a well-cut blue coat and doeskin breeches. He turned his head and a long lock of auburn hair fell forward on his cheek. Emily thought the *modiste* would drop her teacup. Her own hand twitched to reach forward and tuck that errant strand of hair behind his well-shaped ear. Emily stroked the cat instead.

Lady Alberta dabbed at her lips with a napkin. "Fortunately, I thrive on challenge! Forgive me, Miss Dinwiddie, but have you eaten garlic recently? A definite odor of it accompanied you into the room. Young ladies shouldn't smell of garlic. Lavender, perhaps. Rosewater. Patchouli."

Lady Alberta was fortunate that Emily only smelled of garlic. The Japanese believed a raw fish would keep a decedent from the room. "I have a fondness for garlic myself," murmured the Count. "You look a trifle peaked, Miss Dinwiddie. Didn't you rest well last night?"

She'd rested, well enough. *I hunger. Let me taste you.* The feeling of cool fingers against the nape of her neck, of teeth or, rather, fangs . . . "Quite the contrary, Count Révay-Czobar! I slept like the dead."

"Not pink, with her coloring," ventured Mme. Fanchon, who was less enamored of a challenge than Lady Alberta. "She's a little old for girlish hues. You'll forgive my plain speaking, *mademoiselle,* for it is the truth."

Emily succumbed to temptation, and met Val's gaze. Never had she seen eyes that blue. He said, "Green would suit her. Or azure. However, since she's still in mourning, we must restrain ourselves."

Emily pushed away a thought of the various ways in which Ravensclaw might restrain her. "Perhaps you should drape me in brown to match my freckles! This is absurd."

"Your freckles are hardly brown." His voice was a caress. "Amber, perhaps. Sun-kissed gold."

Emily felt her cheeks redden. She didn't recall ever blushing in her life before she met Ravensclaw and now she couldn't seem to stop. Perhaps he *had* bespelled her. She touched her necklace of charms. Machka raised a lazy paw to bat at the brass finger ring.

"What an unusual necklace!" remarked Lady Alberta. "It will have to go."

"No," retorted Emily, as she held Machka immobile on her lap. The cat hissed.

Lady Alberta looked astonished. *"No?"*

"The necklace is of great sentimental value to Miss Dinwiddie," interrupted Ravensclaw. "It remains, along with the hair."

Lady Alberta eyed the assorted talismans. "Perhaps," she said dubiously, "we might set a new style."

Emily didn't want to set a new style. All she wanted was to retrieve the list and the stolen items and return to her home. She stole another glance at Ravensclaw. Well, maybe that's not all she wanted. Which was exceedingly foolish in her.

"To set off Miss Dinwiddie's, er, striking looks," ventured Mme. Fanchon, "I would suggest a *robe en caleçons,* perhaps."

The Count had a few suggestions of his own. Morning dresses, evening dresses, walking dresses; petticoats and stockings, shawls and scarves, half boots and satin slippers, an entire rainbow of gloves . . . Emily sat back and let the conversation swirl around her. What did Ravensclaw think she would do with all these clothes? Chair a meeting of the Dinwiddie Society wearing satin slippers and lavender gloves?

She could hardly let him pay for her clothing. Though Emily was far from a pauper, her head spun at the thought of the expense. As well as at the thought of how many women Ravensclaw might have dressed—or undressed— in his long career. When the conversation moved on to a discussion of stays—jean or buckram, long or short, whether the bosom should be pushed up or compressed to achieve an agreeable and graceful shape—Emily could happily have sunk right through the floor.

Mme. Fanchon rose briskly, filled with energy (if not enthusiasm) by visions of the small fortune to be made on this commission. Ravensclaw escorted her from the room. When he returned, Emily pushed a reluctant Machka off her lap and brushed ineffectually at the considerable amount of cat hair left behind on her skirt. "You will wish to speak with Lady Alberta privately. I have some business of my own—"

"No." Ravensclaw caught her wrist in his strong fingers. "You'll wait until I am free to accompany you. It would be unsuitable, Miss Dinwiddie, for you to venture into the streets of Edinburgh alone."

Dangerous, he meant. But nothing could be more dangerous to Emily than Ravensclaw himself. No sensation of cool forests overcame her now, but tingles that began at the nape of her neck and tickled their way down to the tips of her toes. As if he'd brushed his fingertips against her bare skin. Or his wicked mouth. Those lips that could tease and tempt and tantalize could with her blessing nibble their way from her earlobes to her throat and from there downward to—

Botheration! There had been no warning in the literature that being in the presence of a gone-but-not-departed made one start thinking like a pumpkin-head. While she stood here swooning over Ravensclaw, Michael was up to heaven knew what mischief with the athame. Perhaps Michael's *vrajă* might have protected Emily from Ravensclaw. Why had she left it behind in her room?

Val's eyes twinkled, as if he knew very well why she'd left the dratted thing behind. "Most unsuitable!" said Lady Alberta, who had been talking all this time. "Especially here in the Old Town. You could easily get lost in these narrow alleys and wynds. Or worse! Most of the Edinburgh of early times still exists beneath the city streets. Cold, damp dirt and stone-lined corridors. Underground chambers with rats and sewage seeping in from above. Not to mention the criminal fraternity. And then there are the ghosts. There must be hundreds of ghosts in the Royal Mile alone." She tilted her head to one side and studied Emily. "Dinwiddie. I don't believe I've heard of any Dinwiddies. Are you well-connected, my dear?"

Emily could only be grateful Lady Alberta hadn't heard of the Dinwiddies. Val murmured, "Well enough. I am an old friend of Miss Dinwiddie's family."

Very old, thought Emily. There was mention of a Count Révay-Czobar in the Dinwiddie Chronicles as far back as the thirteenth century, in the unending battles between Wallachia and the Turks.

"Ah well, then!" said Lady Alberta. "Of course I'm happy to oblige you, Val, though it's patently absurd to think that under your protection Miss Dinwiddie might come to any harm."

"Absurd, indeed," agreed Val. "And now I'll leave you ladies to become better acquainted."

Emily didn't want to become better acquainted with Lady Alberta. She didn't want Ravensclaw to leave off turning her insides to pudding by tracing lazy circles with his thumb on the inside of her wrist.

He smiled. She blinked. Lord, she *was* a featherhead. Emily snatched her hand away from his.

She could hardly chastise Ravensclaw in front of Lady Alberta. Emily turned her back on him instead. And was still aware of the very moment he was no longer in the room.

Drogo had gone with him, and Machka. Lady Alberta stared pointedly at the empty scone plate. "I believe Val said your home is in London, Miss Dinwiddie? I hear poor Prinny has got so fat he's afraid to mount a horse."

In point of fact, the headquarters of the Society were some distance outside London; but the fewer people who knew Emily's true purpose in Edinburgh the better for them all. "London. Yes."

"And you have, of course, had a Season, waltzed at Almack's, been presented to the Queen? Forgive my impertinence, but one needs to know what one is working with."

"Yes to all your questions." Alas, Emily believed in her heart of hearts that her disastrous London debut had hastened her poor mama's death. "I'm also familiar with the British Museum and the Horticultural Society. I assure you, Lady Alberta, that I know how to behave."

"So you say." Lady Alberta propped her elbows on the table and with one finger trapped an errant crumb. "Frankly, Miss Dinwiddie, I really don't care."

Emily took a closer look at her newly acquired chaperone. "You don't?"

"I don't. I'd prefer that you refrain from embarrassing me, but beyond that—" Lady Alberta shrugged. "Val is paying me handsomely to lend my assistance to your endeavors, whatever they may be. As well as putting a roof over my head."

Emily entertained and quickly dismissed the notion that Lady Alberta was one of the insensible. Nor was the older woman likely to possess so excellent a constitution that she could eat everything in sight and still remain painfully slim. Her simple gown was so many years out of fashion that even Emily noticed, and Emily was hardly *au courant* with such things. Ravensclaw was doing a kindness in offering employment to a gentlewoman fallen on hard times.

Ravensclaw was full of surprises. "If you don't mind me asking, how well do you know Count Révay-Czobar?"

Lady Alberta flicked a finger against her empty plate. "How well does anyone know Ravensclaw? He's a true man of mystery. And *such* a splendid specimen. We females all run mad for him. But you know how that is."

Emily was gaining a good notion. "If you don't mind, Lady Alberta, I believe I shall ring for more tea."

"As you wish." Lady Alberta beamed. "Whatever your purposes in coming here, Miss Dinwiddie, I mean to see that you enjoy your stay. Edinburgh is a very progressive city, for all we're considerably smaller than London. We have the University, the acknowledged world leader in medical instruction, and the *Edinburgh Review;* John Dalton and his atomic chemistry, Robert Fulton, John McAdam, George Stephenson with his steam locomotive that draws a passenger car on wheels. Edinburgh leads the world in medicine and law, architecture and philosophy. Not for nothing are we called the Athens of the North."

Civil engineers and doctors and bodysnatchers, mused Emily. *But we don't talk about that!* "I like to read aloud of an evening," added Lady Alberta. "Are you familiar with Keats' *Endymion,* Thomas Love Peacock's *Nightmare Abbey,* Mary Shelley's *Frankenstein?* A man destroyed by the monster he created. There's a lesson in it, don't you think?"

Dissertation on the Physical Traits of Bloodsucking Cadavers. Historical and Philosophical Divertation on the Gnawing Dead. "A lesson, indeed, Lady Alberta. Are you familiar with Mr. Polidori's *The Vampyre?*"

Chapter Six

Fair is not fair, but that which pleases.
(Romanian proverb)

The hour was far advanced, the street nearly deserted. Fog had settled on the city, muffling sight and sound. Not that Val's senses were affected. However, he lived as best he could like an ordinary man, not from any inane desire to be mortal, but because otherwise things rapidly became deadly dull. Val disliked nothing more than boredom. And so he took steps to make sure he was entertained. Such as keeping about him an ancient manservant who spouted proverbs at him, maidservants who were no better than they should be, and now Miss Emily Dinwiddie.

His quest for entertainment took Val this night along the High Street. He walked along an arched passageway between two tall structures, emerged in a closed courtyard with old tenements towering all around. Light glimmered from the windows of one building. Val approached the door. A knock, a nod, and he was granted entrance. No door in Edinburgh was closed to Ravensclaw, not opera hour or oyster bar, New Town mansion or Old Town gaming hell, although later some might wonder why he'd come, and what he had done there.

A suite of rooms on the first floor was given over to various games of chance. On one side of the front room stood a buffet covered with food, liquor, and wine. In the middle of that same chamber was the *rouge et noir* table. On each side sat a *croupier* with a green shade over his eyes and a rake in his hand.

Val's entrance didn't go unnoticed. A voluptuous blond woman quickly made her way to his side. "Ravensclaw. To what do we owe the honor of your presence? I doubt you've come for the play."

He raised her gloved hand to his lips. "Perhaps I simply wished for the pleasure of your company, Kate."

She laughed, without offense. "No you didn't. I'm not at all in your style. You're here, as usual, to ask questions. To say truth, I'm glad for the diversion. Fetch me a glass of wine, and I'll tell you whatever you want to know."

Val beckoned a waiter. Kate had aged since he'd seen her last. The sporting life didn't suit her well. Still, it was the life she'd chosen, having abandoned a husband and babe to take up with a Captain Sharp, and so it was the life she was stuck with, and there was no use in crying over spilt milk.

She didn't realize that Val knew her thoughts, of course, any more than she realized she welcomed his presence in this place because he neither wanted something from her, nor set himself up as judge. Kate was perhaps all of eighteen, and already weary of nights spent strolling around these crowded rooms in a gown cut so low it showed rather more than the tops of her plump breasts.

The waiter returned with Kate's wine. Val handed her the glass and said, "Michael Ross."

She studied him over the rim of her wine glass. "Interesting that you should mention him. Mr. Ross has picked up his crumbs finely of late, though not that long ago the gull-gropers had got their talons so deep in him no one thought he'd ever contrive to get clear. There's considerable speculation about how the gentleman made such a come-about after having been so purse-pinched."

"And the conclusion is?"

Kate lifted her plump shoulders. "Rumor is he's found himself an heiress. If it's true, he'll empty her pocketbook quick enough, poor thing."

Val disliked this revelation, though it was no more than he'd suspected. "Mr. Ross is a gambler, then."

Kate laughed, without mirth. "Some become addicted to opium, some to cards. He's in the other room, if you'd like a look at him." Plump hips swaying so provocatively that some of the punters looked up briefly from their cards, she led the way.

Michael Ross had contrived to tow himself out of the River Tick. Val wondered if he had accomplished that by selling stolen items, among them the d'Auvergne athame. And if so, who had purchased it. The young fool would be back in the hands of the cent-per-centers soon enough if he insisted on wasting the ready in establishments where the elbow shakers played with loaded dice.

Interesting, what Kate had said about an heiress. Miss Dinwiddie didn't given the appearance of a young lady who was plump in the pocket, not that she would care about such stuff. "There he is," murmured Kate. "The sprig of fashion in the claret-colored coat."

Val followed her gaze. Michael Ross was quite the fashionable young buck. In addition to his claret-colored double-breasted coat, he wore tightly fitting inexpressibles, gleaming Wellington boots, a cravat tied in the Gordian knot. Dark hair tumbled over his pale forehead. Sideburns extended down toward his chin. Val was surprised at the practical-minded Miss Dinwiddie's preference for so callow a specimen.

Not that Emily had told him she had a preference. She hadn't needed to. And not that she'd be grateful for his assistance. Val could almost hear her demanding he be less busy about her affairs. Perhaps he'd tell her what he'd done tonight just for the pleasure of a scolding. Miss Dinwiddie wasn't one to mince her words.

Michael Ross glanced up and caught Val's gaze. In the brief instant before he lowered his gaze, Val realized the young man was cup-shot. He was also badly overextended. It took no supersensible abilities to read the panic in his eyes.

Addicted to the bottle as well as to cards? Emily had chosen poorly indeed. Val resigned himself to playing Good Samaritan. He thanked Kate for her information and prepared to employ his luck at basset. *"A bon chat, bon rat,"* she murmured. To a good cat, a good rat. Not inappropriate to think of rats in view of the character of this establishment, and the nature of the play.

It was said that basset had been invented by a noble Venetian, who was punished with exile for his creativity. The game had been prohibited in France by Louis XIV after countless people of distinction were ruined and the princes of the blood themselves stood in danger of being undone.

Basset was a sort of lottery. The banker, or *talliere*, had the sole disposal of the first and last cards, and a much greater prospect of winning than those who merely played. However, the game was of so bewitching a nature, because of the several multiplications and advantages that it seemed to offer to an unwary player, that it was vastly popular despite the fact that the odds were altogether in favor of the bank.

The punters sat around a table, the *talliere* in their midst with the bank of gold before him. Each player had a book of thirteen cards and lay down the number that he pleased, with stakes. The *talliere* took the pack in his hands and turned up the bottom card or *fasse*, and paid half the value of the stakes laid down by the punters upon any card of that sort.

So it went. "King wins, ten loses." "Ace wins, five loses." "Knave wins, seven loses." Val paid little attention as the game progressed. He was more interested in Michael Ross.

That young gentleman was not destined to win tonight. Or so the *talliere* had decided, for it was in his power to let a player have as many winnings as he found convenient, and no more. However, it was one of Val's many small amusements to influence such things. He considered it in the nature of the cat giving the rat a sporting chance. As a result, when several fairly remarkable strokes of fortune brought Mr. Ross's stake to *soissante-et-le-va*, thereby breaking the bank, the dealer was even more shocked than Mr. Ross himself.

Michael sank back in his chair. The high points of his crisp shirt collar had wilted like lettuce during the excitement of the play. He was relieved, exhausted, and not entirely well.

Val rose from the table, his time sufficiently well spent. He was a couple hundred pounds richer himself, it being virtually impossible for him to sit down to play and lose, even when he didn't direct his will toward the cards; and he had gained some insight into Michael Ross. The young man was a dilettante, perhaps even a wastrel, and something weighed heavily on his mind. What, Val could not quite determine, perhaps because Mr. Ross was quite drunk.

Was Emily an heiress? From what Val knew of the eccentric Professor Dinwiddie, she might well be. Emily was an only child, her mother having been dead for several years. She had already said she had no other family. She had also said she was now overseer of the Society.

An heiress, without a family to protect her. The fortune hunters would swarm at her heels. Or they would if they knew about her situation, which didn't seem likely, in view of Miss Dinwiddie's firmly expressed dislike of Society. Which left the field clear for Michael Ross.

It wouldn't do. Emily deserved better than an inept gamester. Val had already decided to introduce the unpredictable Miss Dinwiddie to what passed for the *ton* in Edinburgh, an enterprise which promised to be vastly entertaining. She would hate every moment, and thereby amuse him even more. And since she was under his protection, no one would dare snub her, no matter how outspoken she might be.

Perhaps he might amuse himself further by finding her a husband. Not that Val imagined for a moment that Emily wanted one, which made the challenge greater. Considering Emily's unsubmissive nature, it would be little short of a miracle if he succeeded.

He found Kate by the buffet table, and pressed his winnings into her hand. "An expression of my gratitude," Val said, and then wished he'd kept the money, because of the bitter expression that flashed across her face.

Val liked women. All women. Light-skirt or lady, virgin or soiled dove. And he had gifts that ordinary men lacked. Therefore, he drew Kate's hand through his arm and said, "Stay with me for a while."

Chapter Seven

Talk of the devil and he is bound to appear.
(Romanian proverb)

Emily stared at herself in the looking-glass. Silvery grey merino crepe over black sarsenet, trimmed with lace and artificial roses around the hem—Ravensclaw must have paid Mme. Fanchon a fortune to have the gown sewn up so quickly. It was the most beautiful garment Emily had ever owned.

She hated it. Almost as much as she hated what Zizi was doing with that hair brush. "You're hurting me!" Emily snapped.

" 'Tis all for the sake of beauty, miss." Unrepentant, Zizi gave the brush another brisk tug. "Being as you'll be with the master, it's only right you're at your best." She stepped back to regard her handiwork. "Fine as fivepence, if I do say so myself."

Emily conceded that she'd never appeared to better advantage. She didn't look the least bit like herself. Zizi's clever fingers had arranged her rebellious hair in an antique Roman style, the long braid wound up back and around, a few curls allowed to casually fall free. Emily was afraid to move her head for fear the whole thing would come tumbling down. Zizi had not achieved this transformation without assistance. Also crowded into Emily's bedroom were Lady Alberta and Ravensclaw's two other maidservants, Bela and Lilian, both of whom bore a marked resemblance to Zizi in the bosom department. One was dark, the other fair.

Lady Alberta was in especially high spirits, perhaps because she also had a lovely new evening gown, yellow with a draped tunic, and a turban headdress. "Edinburgh society is similar to that of London, only smaller. We have theaters and assemblies and musical evenings, gentlemen's clubs that rival Watier's or White's." Bela applied lavender water with a liberal hand while Lilian pinched some color into Emily's pale cheeks.

At last they were done poking at her. Lady Alberta arranged a crepe scarf around Emily's shoulders and handed her a pair of black kid gloves. Emily snatched up her reticule. She might have been persuaded to leave off her necklace, but her various protections would still accompany her, shoved into her reticule alongside a little mirror and a charming vinaigrette fashioned from bloodstone, its aromatic contents meant to "correct the bad Quality of the Air." These items were intended not so much to protect her against Ravensclaw, who didn't seem to mean her any harm—for which she couldn't decide whether to be grateful or disappointed—but one never knew what other manner of supersensible creatures one might encounter out in the world. Emily settled her spectacles more firmly on the bridge of her nose.

Ravensclaw waited at the foot of the staircase. He wore full evening dress: tight-fitting pantaloons and dark blue coat; white linen shirt and waistcoat; starched cravat with discreet sapphire stickpin in its folds; highly polished shoes. His long auburn hair was tied at the nape of his neck with a velvet cord. He was both sophisticated and savage at the same time, and so devastatingly breathtaking that Emily almost swallowed her own tongue.

Ravensclaw stepped forward and raised her hand to his lips. " 'Fair as is the rose in May.' You are lovely, little one."

Pleasurable prickles tingled along her skin. Thank heavens she was wearing gloves. Although she half wished she weren't. "Roses don't have freckles," retorted Emily.

They descended the outside staircase. A carriage waited in the narrow street. With Ravensclaw's assistance, Lady Alberta climbed inside.

He turned back to Emily, bent to smell her hair. "Lavender. Very nice. Although I rather miss the garlic." His breath was warm on her cheek.

Breath? Did the insensate breathe? Emily murmured, "I thought you wanted me to be 'presentable.' "

Val touched the crucifix that still hung round Emily's neck. That particular talisman she had refused to tuck away out of sight. "Did that rankle? I apologize. You are more than presentable." She shivered, and he frowned. "Don't be frightened. You're safe with me."

Emily barely refrained from snorting. *Like a hen is safe from the fox.* "If I'm frightened, it's not of you. How can I make you understand how urgent it is that we find Michael and retrieve the athame?"

"I understand that nothing is served by cramming our fences. Your Michael is not so all-powerful as you may think."

"I don't think Michael is powerful at all. The athame is another matter. If only we knew that he has it."

Ravensclaw's fingers lingered lightly on her throat. "We'll find out soon enough."

His lightest touch sent her senses humming. *Concentrate, you ninny!* "Um. How will we do that?"

"He'll tell us. Have you not read of the persuasive abilities of my kind?"

"Then you admit—"

"You are so very serious. I couldn't help teasing you a little bit."

Val was smiling as he helped her into the carriage. Emily was not. She settled beside Lady Alberta, who immediately began talking about the popular Professor Leslie's lectures on light and heat, during which he amazed the audience by turning a cup of water into ice in seven minutes, after which, like a good practical Scot, he sold an apparatus devised for this domestic end at twenty guineas each. Ravensclaw took the opposite seat and stretched out his long legs.

Lady Alberta was also knowledgeable about Dugal Stewart's lectures on philosophy. Mr. Stewart rejected metaphysics as a vain attempt to fathom the nature of the mind and in its place proposed inductive psychology, the patient and precise observation of mental processes without pretending to explain the mind itself. Emily mused that her own mental processes weren't working as effectively as once they had. She glanced out the window as the carriage jolted and swayed.

Edinburgh's Old Town was a wilderness of narrow streets and wynds and lofty irregular tenement houses known as "lands," some as many as eight stories high, built higgledy-piggledy like a child's city of playing cards, the rooftops an ocean of chimneys arranged at dizzying heights under an external pall of fog and smoke, many twisted and angled instead of straight up and down. Between the lands, which formed a continuous wall from one end of a street to the other, lay narrow passages called closes, which ran down the sides of the ridge on which the city was built and gave access to the properties behind, frequently small open areas with tall buildings peering down.

Picturesque shops extended along the street they traveled, their exteriors painted with pictures of the merchants' wares. Each story from top to bottom was chequered with different forms and bright glaring colors—red, yellow and blue on black—until the whole resembled the stall of a fair. Fog wreathed the streetlamps, gave a queer half-life to a black quartern loaf perched directly over a black full-trimmed professor's periwig, caused a Cheshire cheese and a rich firkin of butter to dance above advertisements for stages, child-bed linen, and petticoats. Easy enough to believe this place was haunted, especially when Lady Alberta began talking about Johnny One-Arm and Cat Nick; the Mercat Cross, site of countless public tortures and hangings; Lady Glamis, burned alive on the Castle Hill. Ravensclaw was curiously silent. Emily wondered how much of Lady Alberta's ghoulish history he had witnessed firsthand.

The narrow, twisting streets of the Old Town gave way to the wider—and hopefully less haunted—neoclassical avenues of the New. Lady Alberta explained that Charlotte Square was the only part of the city to be designed, by Robert Adams, as a single unified scheme, with houses integrated into an entire block appearing to be an urban palace with a grand central edifice and less imposing wings, each side three stories high, plus attics and basement.

The carriage drew up before a residence in one of the less imposing wings, which boasted great wide pilasters above Venetian windows with balusters at first-floor level, and delicate decorations that included sphinxes at the roof line. Liveried footmen in white stockings and powdered wigs waited outside an arched doorway. Emily took a deep breath, and prepared herself to see and be seen.

The hall lobby was painted green, its ceiling and cornice a warm white, its floor glazed tile. The room was furnished with a wooden-seated hall chair for waiting servants, a lobby table for calling cards, hat and greatcoat stands. A tall clock stood at the foot of the stair. Lamps in wrought-iron brackets lit the stairway to the drawing room.

Lady Cullane's townhouse was crowded with the *crème de la crème* of Edinburgh society, all of them professing themselves eager to hear such musical treats as "A Highland Battle" on the violin, and variations on "Bonnie Jean of Aberdeen"; "The Pic-Nic" on fiddle, "Black Jock," and "The Sow's Tail." Within moments Emily realized that this was just like every other musical evening she'd ever attended—save for the Scottish music—which had been as few as possible. The drawing room was furnished with the same classically inspired furniture and crystal chandeliers, exquisite paintings and marble fireplace, pier glasses and perfume burners and porcelain vases; adorned with the same pale-gowned young ladies whispering behind gloved hands and fans and simpering each time a gentleman younger than their papa came within spitting distance, fluttering their eyelashes and looking so innocent butter wouldn't melt in their mouths. The same matchmaking mamas with their gimlet eyes sizing up their daughter's competition, and calculating their matrimonial prospects. Only the windows were different, set deep in curtain boxes with draw-up festoon drapes.

"You're frowning," said Val, at her elbow. "Remember why we're here." Emily relaxed her forehead before Lady Alberta could remind her that proper young women didn't scowl.

They made their way further into the crowded chamber. The two women might as well have been invisible, but Val immediately drew every eye. *Glamour,* thought Emily again. Although perhaps it also had a little bit to do with muscular thighs and broad shoulders, high cheekbones and golden skin. Cynical blue eyes. Long auburn locks. Tempting wicked lips. If she had been skeptical of magic—her papa hadn't believed in shielding children from knowledge of the supersensible, and Emily clearly remembered her mama having hysterics at finding her playing with a shrunken head—she would have become a convert on first sight of Ravensclaw.

A young woman's rendition of "The Hen's March o'er the Midden" on the harp sounded, alas, more like a limp. Emily was distracted by another round of introductions. Between the two of them, Ravensclaw and Lady Alberta surely knew everyone present in this place tonight. And then the crowd parted, rather like Moses and the Red Sea, and Emily found herself staring at the most beautiful woman she had ever seen. "Devil take it," murmured Val, under his breath.

The woman was tall, and voluptuous, and moved with the graceful assurance of one who knows she is universally admired. Her features were perfection, her skin the palest porcelain, her hair so dark it drank up all the candlelight. She wore a gown of crimson-colored gauze, the bodice cut low with vandyked trimming and corded edging, the sleeves shot with Spanish slashing, the scalloped skirt trimmed in twisted ribbon rolls. Her lips were also crimson, her eyes thick-lashed and raven black. In her dark hair gleamed a strand of pearls.

At the vision's side stood a tall man as handsome as she was beautiful, dressed entirely in somber colors, his eyes the color of violets, his hair a startling silver-grey almost as long as Ravensclaw's, but allowed to fall loose over his shoulders. Add lace at his throat and wrists, and jewels on his hands, and he would have perfectly portrayed the dissolute aristocrat of an earlier time. Following behind them was a second man with chestnut hair and ice-green eyes and a harsh chiseled face marred by a scar slashed across one cheek.

Perhaps it was shallow to judge on physical appearance alone, but sometimes one couldn't help oneself.

The silver-haired man caught Emily's gaze, and smiled. His was not a seductive smile like Ravensclaw's, but instead a little cruel, which was perhaps fortunate, since Ravensclaw's smile turned a person into a giddy goose.

The woman's gaze flicked dismissively over Emily. "Ah, Val, you are so surprised to see Lisbet that you forget to introduce your little friend."

The muscles of Val's arm tightened under Emily's fingers. "Lisbet, may I present Miss Emily Dinwiddie. Emily, before you is Elisabeta Boroi. And this gentleman is Cezar Korzha. You both know Lady Alberta Tait, of course." He nodded to the third man, who remained in the background. "Andrei Torok."

"Mea amant," murmured Lisbet. "So civilized."

"Of course!" said Lady Alberta. "Although I have not seen either of you for some time. You were traveling, I believe, Mr. Korzha, in some exotic clime. India, was it? Or the Orient?"

"Merely Budapest." Cezar bowed. Then he turned his startling eyes on Emily. "Miss Dinwiddie. Val is full of surprises. Where has he been hiding you?"

Emily roused from wondering what Val was like when he wasn't being civilized. With his hair falling down around his shoulders as he knelt on his satin sheets. With candlelight gleaming on his golden skin.

All his golden skin. Emily's throat felt dry. "Hardly hiding," she managed. "Count Révay-Czobar is an old friend of my family."

"Yes, indeed!" Lady Alberta displayed an enviable talent for prevarication. "Both Ravensclaw and I have known Emily since she was a babe. And such a precious child she was!"

"I'm sure," murmured Lisbet. "All those freckles. All that hair."

The dratted woman didn't have a single mark to mar her perfect skin. Or a hair out of place. Or a bosom that required a miracle of engineering to give it any prominence. "In some cultures," retorted Emily, "freckles are regarded highly. The more freckles, the more beautiful a woman is thought to be."

"And in others, freckles are thought to be an indication of a contentious nature," remarked Val. Emily shot him a sharp glance.

Cezar looked as if he wished to laugh. Lisbet's dark eyes narrowed speculatively. "And now, if you'll excuse us," Ravensclaw murmured. "Miss Dinwiddie is expecting to meet someone." A frown flickered across Lisbet's perfect brow before she graciously inclined her head.

"Val," said Cezar, as they turned away. "I must speak privately with you." Val hesitated, and then nodded. "Never fear, Miss Dinwiddie. We shall return your 'old friend' to you safe and sound." Lisbet's crimson lips curved mockingly. Andrei's watchful eyes scanned the room.

Emily adjusted her spectacles. Innocent she might be—to her growing regret—but not naïve. Of course Ravensclaw would have a mistress. Several of them, probably.

Not that Emily was jealous. Why should she be? This queer feeling in her stomach was simply because she was trussed up like a pullet for the cooking pot. As soon as this matter of the d'Auvergne athame was satisfactorily resolved, she would return to the business of the Society, and Val would return to the business of being a supersensual—did ever a label fit so well?—and their paths wouldn't again cross. Her adventure would be at an end.

Ravensclaw tucked a finger under her chin and turned her face up to his. *Lisbet Boroi is of no consequence. You will not be disturbed by anything she may do or say.*

I will not—Emily was stunned to realize he could invade her most private thoughts. And then anger took its place. *I will be disturbed by whomever I wish whenever I please! Don't tell me what to do.*

Val's fingers tightened. *Do that again. If you can.*

"Ravensclaw!" murmured Lady Alberta. "Remember where you are!"

Emily stared up at him. "I don't know if I can or not. I was just so angry that you—" An approaching figure caught her eye, and she pulled away. "I just saw Michael."

Chapter Eight

A cat in gloves catches no mice.
(Romanian proverb)

Damn and double damn! Emily realized Ravensclaw could read her thoughts. Hopefully, not all of them, or he would know of the strong attraction that she felt for him. And of her equally strong desire to see Lisbet Boroi trip and fall on her oh-so-perfect face.

No time to wonder about that now. The music changed to a lively tune played on hammered dulcimer with bombarde accompaniment as Michael Ross made his way across the crowded room. Michael was no less handsome than Emily remembered him, pale and poetically brooding in the fashion made popular by the unfortunate Lord Byron, with a lock of dark hair draped artfully upon his brow, a soulful expression in his charcoal grey eyes. He was cropped and curled and clad in trousers that fitted without a wrinkle, a fashionable tailcoat with French riding sleeves and cuffs, and shoe buckles of polished cut steel. At least, unlike some of the gentlemen present, he hadn't decked himself out in a kilt. Emily was briefly distracted by the thought of Val in that costume.

Michael looked forbidding. It was hardly the expression one might expect from a gentleman unexpectedly glimpsing the object of his affections. Not that Emily believed herself to be the object of his affections. At least, not anymore. But neither did he need to grimace like he'd seen a specter risen from the dead. Ravensclaw drew Lady Alberta discreetly toward the refreshment table as Michael reached her side.

"Hell mend it, Emily! What are you doing here? Has there been some new development?" he asked.

Definitely not loverlike. Why should she be surprised? "Any manner, I should think. Prinny has begun building the new Royal Apartments, though his Pavilion at Brighton is not yet completed. Portable gas cylinders have been introduced in London, at thirty atmospheres. The *Raith* from Leek was wrecked . . . Or perhaps you were inquiring about something else?"

He frowned. "What the devil's wrong with you? I was referring to the circumstance that you're here instead of being closeted with your grief like any normal young woman should be."

Had he always been so irritating? "I'm not aware that there's anything 'wrong' with me. Despite whatever corkbrained notions you may cherish about normalcy!"

Michael ran his hand through his hair, disarranging his carefully styled curls. "Forgive me. I'm making a mull of this. I didn't expect to find you in Edinburgh, Emily."

Not surprising if he hadn't. The last time Emily had seen Michael he was pledging his eternal devotion to her, after which he disappeared without a word. Which had bothered her immensely at the time. Interesting to discover now that she didn't care a fig. "It's nice to see you, too, Michael. Of course you didn't mean to leave London without telling me. Your letter must have gone astray."

A muscle clenched in his cheek. "Forgive me. I can explain."

And a pretty pack of lies it would be, she'd warrant. "You owe me no explanations. It's not as if we're betrothed." Even if she *had* accepted his proposal in a grief-stricken moment, Emily had refused him several times before, partly because she mistrusted his motives, and partly because professions of devotion were so novel an experience for her that she had wished to hear them again.

Michael looked at her as if she were a loony. "Of course we're betrothed. I was suddenly called away on business. Surely you understand."

Emily smoothed her black kid gloves. "I too am in Edinburgh on business. Since the Dinwiddie Society is now my responsibility."

Came a brief silence while Mr. Ross attempted to curb his temper. "I think that you must be the most muleheaded female I've ever known. You can't seriously think you're capable of overseeing the Dinwiddie Society. What's more, you're still in mourning. You shouldn't even be here."

"Need I remind you that the Society can only be overseen by a Dinwiddie?" Emily wished she hadn't been persuaded to leave her umbrella behind. It would have been immensely satisfying to jab her suitor with its sharp tip. "And I don't need lessons in propriety from you, sir."

"Good God, Emily, don't go off on one of your queer starts now." Michael caught her hand in his. "Be reasonable. You must marry me. It's what your father intended. I shall take your name."

"You may take your fine self to the nether regions. I think *I* should know what my father intended better than you do. Are you trying to break my fingers?"

"Sorry." Michael relaxed his grip. "Shortly before his sad accident, the Professor and I discussed the matter of our union. Yours and mine, that is. I'd meant to allow you sufficient time to recover from your grief, but since you've recuperated sufficiently to come to Edinburgh—" He winced as a bagpipe assault left the audience's ears bruised. "Something about you is different tonight."

Different. How flattering. Although it was probably unfair to expect pretty words from a gentleman wholly enamored with his own reflection in the looking-glass. Surely Emily's papa wouldn't, despite his habitual distraction, have wished her to wed such a starched-up popinjay.

How she missed him. Were the Professor himself to see his daughter in such finery, he would most likely marvel at the miracle of engineering that was her corset, because the thing almost made it seem like she had a bosom. The thought made her smile.

"So do you look different, Michael. I hadn't expected to find you such a gentleman of fashion." Emily's smile faded as she realized what she'd just said. "That is, I didn't *expect* to find you here, of course. How would I know you were in Edinburgh?"

The bagpipes had—thankfully—been succeeded by the bell-like sound of a Scottish *clarsach*. Michael moved closer, lowered his voice. "I live here, don't I? As you knew. You needn't pretend, Emily, I understand. The anguish of separation was too much for you to bear. Of course I'm delighted to see you. You just took me by surprise."

Emily was appalled. Michael thought she had pursued him to Edinburgh in hope of resuming their romance, which was most unlikely for a number of reasons, not least among them the circumstance that he reeked of Rowland's Macassar Oil. "You misunderstand. I have family here." She tried to tug away her hand.

Michael clasped it all the firmer. "What family?" he asked.

Excellent question. Peering up into his handsome face, Emily wondered if Michael's smug assumptions held some truth. Had she followed him to Edinburgh because of the stolen items—or because her pride had been stung by his desertion? Now that she was standing here talking to the man, she couldn't convince herself of his involvement in the thefts.

He was waiting for her answer. Emily collected her scattered wits. She had just told Michael she had family here. "Since you are so familiar with Edinburgh society, perhaps you're also acquainted with Lady Alberta Tait."

Michael glanced at that worthy, who was hovering near the punch bowl. "Everybody knows of Lady Alberta. What has she to do with you?"

"Lady Alberta is my aunt."

"Your father never mentioned Lady Alberta." In his astonishment, Michael relaxed his grip. Emily snatched her hand away from his.

"Why should he have? This may surprise you, but Papa didn't tell you everything. Anyway, they were estranged. Lady Alberta, um, doesn't approve of the supersensible." Before Michael could question her further, Emily opened her reticule, and pulled out the *vrajă*. "I believe this is yours. I gave it to you myself, as I recall."

He started, and scowled, but made no move to touch the charm. "Where did you find that?"

"In Papa's laboratory." Emily dangled the *vrajă* in front of Michael's face. "It has me in a puzzle, since Papa didn't permit anyone to enter his laboratory other than myself."

Michael wrenched his gaze away from the charm. "Perhaps it belonged to the Professor. It isn't mine."

"Oh? I notice you're not wearing yours."

Michael's hand moved to his waistcoat. "It didn't seem appropriate for an occasion such as this."

Since Emily had never seen Michael on an occasion

such as this, she couldn't quibble with his statement, although she would have liked to, very much. "You're sure, then, that this *vrajă* doesn't belong to you."

"Certain," retorted Michael, though his fingers twitched as if he wished to snatch the thing out of her hand.

"Then I'll keep it." Emily dropped the charm back into her reticule.

Michael's eyes moved from her reticule back to her face. Emily thought he would question her further, but instead he said, "I'm anxious to call on you. What is Lady Alberta's address?"

He was anxious to convince her she was fit only to marry him. Perhaps he was not altogether wrong. If only Emily hadn't waited so long to delve into Society business—hadn't shirked her responsibilities while she floundered in grief—but she had and now there was no way of telling how long the athame had been gone. Emily didn't want to alert Michael of her suspicions in case she was mistaken in him.

Be conciliatory, she told herself. *Act as though you're pleased to see him.* "My aunt and I are both residing with Lord Révay-Czobar."

Michael's mouth dropped open. "Ravensclaw? Impossible!"

Emily almost smirked at his thunderstruck expression. "Why is that?"

Michael sputtered and turned almost as red as Libset's gown. "You can't stay there a moment longer! Good God, Emily! You must know what he is."

What was it about her that made everyone think—mistakenly!—that they could **tell** her what to do? Emily abandoned any attempt at being conciliatory. "And just what *is* he, pray?"

Michael lowered his voice and leaned closer. "A rakehell and a libertine, at the very least. I have it on good authority that Ravensclaw is the devil's spawn."

Said authority being the pilfered Dinwiddie list? "Poppycock! Ravensclaw is no such thing. I see Lady Alberta beckoning to me." With obvious reluctance, Michael let her go.

At last the interminable evening ended, after a series of ballads sung in a sweet soprano voice, which—having progressed from *Loch Lomond* ("and me and my true love will yet meet again") through *The Three Ravens* ("she was dead herself ere evensong time") to *Mary Hamilton* ("the land I was tae travel in, or the death I was tae dee")— left a great many of the revelers in a somewhat somber frame of mind.

Ravensclaw's carriage waited at the door. Lady Alberta was again the first inside.

Val lifted Emily into the carriage as if she weighed no more than a feather. "I'll speak with you later, little one."

"Later? But I must tell you what Michael said." Or didn't say, but that was beside the point.

Ravensclaw looked regretful. "I'm sorry. I must go."

Go where? Silly question. Emily glanced at Lady Alberta and lowered her voice. "You don't understand. I think Michael suspects what you are."

Val stepped back and closed the door. "If Mr. Ross's knowledge is on a par with yours, I don't think I'll tremble in my boots just yet."

Emily sank back on the carriage seat. Had Ravensclaw just admitted what she thought he had? And if he *had* admitted it, then how dare he abandon her with a thousand questions buzzing about in her brain?

"It may be unchristian of me to say so, but Lisbet Boroi is *not* a nice woman!" remarked Lady Alberta. "And I have my doubts about Cezar Korzha! Not that I mean to say that Korzha is a woman, because any fool can see he's not, which isn't always the case. At any rate, it's a great pity they didn't stay in that godforsaken place."

Counts who were Other, dogs that were werewolves—

that sort of thing Emily could accept. But men who were women? Her companion must have imbibed more than was prudent of the champagne punch.

"Lady Alberta, how well do you really know Ravens-.claw?" There was no answer. The older woman's head had fallen forward on her chest. She was sound asleep.

Emily stared through the window at the darkness, thinking of the events of the evening, and of Michael, and Val. Once she had admired Michael. Now he held no more appeal for her than an old boot. And probably wouldn't, even if she didn't still suspect he had something to do with the items stolen from the Society.

It was all because of Ravensclaw. Who, after such dreams as she'd had, could be content with an ordinary man? Or even an extraordinary one? Which Michael demonstrably was not.

Ravensclaw, who was probably even now with Lisbet Boroi, nuzzling and nibbling and sinking his teeth into her neck. *Fangs!* Yes, and why had she been able to speak silently to him? Emily wound her fingers in the chain of her reticule.

Chapter Nine

Do not all you can; spend not all you have;
believe not all you hear; and tell not all you know.
(Romanian proverb)

Darkness was fading with the approach of dawn. The air was damp and chill. As well as noxious, since the sanitary arrangements in Edinburgh's Old Town were considerably inferior to the New. Edinburgh was perhaps less dangerous than London, but still unsafe after dark, due partly to the numerous parties of young men who spent their evenings in the taverns, and the occasional outbreaks of mob violence. Not to mention resurrectionists. Supersensible creatures. Lady Alberta's ghosts. Val wondered how Miss Dinwiddie felt about ghaisties. She would no doubt tell him in good time.

Wisely, none attempted to interfere with him, not man nor beast nor specter; and at length Ravensclaw climbed the exterior wooden stair to his front door. His servants, long accustomed to his nocturnal habits, were snugly abed. Val made his way up the inner stairway to his own chamber, where he found Drogo stretched out on the hearth, and Machka and Miss Dinwiddie stretched out on his bed. One of them was snoring. He doubted it was the cat.

Drogo rolled over on his back. Val paused to scratch

the wolf's belly, then walked closer to the bed. Machka opened one incurious eye and yawned. As he had expected, the snoring didn't cease. Emily's spectacles lay abandoned atop a book opened to Gottfred Bürger's *Lenore*, the tale of a maiden who rode off with a ghostly lover only to have him crumble to dust under the rays of the sun. One bare foot peeped out from beneath the practical cotton wrapper that she wore over a voluminous night gown. A fragile little foot, with painful-looking blisters. Val took it in his hand. Emily's new slippers hadn't fit her any better than the role she'd played in Lady Cullane's elegant drawing room. Miss Dinwiddie would be much more at home with her Society's musty tomes and fantastical tales.

She turned her head on his pillow. Tendrils of hair escaped from their braid to caress her face. Val rubbed her sole with his thumb.

. . . She lay on the woolen rug before the fireplace. He lowered his lips to her throat. Pleasure hummed through her veins. His teeth found her pulse, nipped and licked. A strange melting sensation, a growing warmth . . .

The young woman was preoccupied with throats. Val thought he would advance her understanding a little bit.

. . . His lips slid across her silken skin to the soft flesh of one breast. He teased her rosy nipple with his tongue until it pebbled, begging him for more. His mouth closed around her. She shuddered and moaned . . .

Her scent surrounded him. A surprisingly erotic scent that tickled his nose. And elsewhere. Not garlic now, or lavender, but just Emily. *Emily. Wake up.*

She stared nearsightedly at him. *You said you weren't what I thought you were. You lied.*

Val traced the arch of her foot. *What did you expect? I am vampir.*

She considered this, and the hand that clasped her. *Are you lying now?*

No. Are you frightened, little one?

Maybe. A little bit. Emily watched fascinated as he traced a pattern on her ankle with his thumb. *What are you doing to my foot?*

Caressing it. Do you mind?

Oh. Emily blinked at him. Her ankle twitched. On the hearth, Drogo stirred. Machka reached out a sharp-tipped paw.

Emily snatched back her foot and tucked it beneath her. "What are you doing here?"

Val shrugged off his jacket. "I sleep here, remember? Perhaps I should ask you the same thing. This is hardly so large a house that someone might get lost."

Emily fumbled for her spectacles. "I wanted to talk to you. Earlier, you brushed me aside."

She was irked. He didn't explain. Where Val had gone, and what he'd done there, might try even Miss Dinwiddie's tolerance. "This chat of ours couldn't wait until tomorrow?"

Emily glanced at the window and the brightening sky outside. "It *is* tomorrow. Don't think to put me off again. Especially now that you have—finally!—admitted what you are." She wrapped her arms around her knees. "Why *did* you tell me the truth?"

Not entirely for his amusement, though that was part of it. "Has anyone ever told you, Miss Dinwiddie, that you are as tenacious as a cocklebur?"

"Papa, when he didn't want me to know things. As if ignorance could ever be preferable to knowledge." Emily tilted her head and studied him. "How did you become *vampir*? I think it must be more than having lived a wicked life. Not that I mean to infer you lived a wicked life. Although looking as you do, I don't imagine that you died a virgin. I think the literature may also have been mistaken on that point. Did dogs jump over your corpse? Were you born the seventh son of a seventh son?"

"None of the above." Most females who made their way into his bed didn't treat him as a scientific curiosity. Val casually removed his waistcoat and cravat. Unbuttoned his shirt. Pulled the velvet cord out of his hair. "Shall I continue?"

"Yes. I mean, no!" Emily barely caught her spectacles before they tumbled off her nose.

Val scooted Machka out of the way and stretched out beside her. "Then talk we shall if that is what you wish."

Emily cast a sideways glance at the strong leg that pinned down her skirt. "Excellent!" she croaked. "I know there is more than one traditional way to become a vampire. Perhaps you were set upon unawares and drained to the point of death."

Val smoothed his own elegant fingers over Machka's fur. "I'm sorry to disappoint you. It was nothing like that. I became what I am by choice."

Emily's eyes widened in astonishment. "Why would anyone become a vampire by choice? I mean, I'm sure it's very nice to be a vampire, aside from what you must drink! And as for that, can you feed from other of the undead, or from animals, or must you confine yourself to human blood? How often do you need to hunt? Do your eyes turn red?"

Val hoped Miss Dinwiddie's inquiring mind wouldn't be the death of her. Or him. "I thought that you wished to talk to me about your Mr. Ross."

She wrinkled her nose. "I'm being unforgivably *pushing*, aren't I? It's just that you are my first supersensible creature and there are so many things I must know. Such as where you prefer to bite someone. On the wrist? Sole of the foot? Throat?"

"On the chest between the breasts. And then there is a luscious vein here—" Val pointed. "In the groin."

She shook her head. "You're teasing me again. Perhaps you think I can't keep a secret. I promise you I can. Is it true that the nonliving have remarkable regenerative powers? Hugely heightened senses? The ability to cloud people's minds?"

He was going to have to cloud her mind, eventually. "Pray concentrate your thoughts. You wished to warn me about your Mr. Ross."

"*Not* my Mr. Ross." Emily toyed with the edges of her robe. "He informed me tonight that you are the devil's spawn. Which makes me think he must have seen the Dinwiddie list. He was different at home. Michael, I mean. We met him at a lecture on the dyeing processes in Leydon and Stockholm papyri. He used to attend demonstrations at the Society, and stay to talk with Papa."

Val settled himself more comfortably and decided he was definitely going to have to interfere with Mr. Ross's carefully contrived plans. "You appear to know him well."

"Not as well as I thought I did." Emily considered she was exhibiting remarkable self-possession for a young woman who had never before found herself sharing a bed with a half-clad gentleman who, thanks to his unbuttoned shirt, was exposing a considerable amount of bare furred chest. "Now, thanks to your insistence that I appear at Lady Cullen's dratted musicale, Michael thinks I followed him to Edinburgh."

Machka was also interested in Val's chest. He pushed the sharp-clawed cat aside. "It was your intention, wasn't it, that we should flush out your fox? And why should

he think you followed him? Unless you told him of your
suspicions, and that you found his *vrajă*. Did you return
it, by the way?"

"Of course I won't! And of course I didn't." Emily
cleared her throat. "Before my papa's death, Michael
was, ah, courting me."

Val was amused by her expression. "Miss Dinwiddie,
you are a *femme fatale*."

Emily drew herself up with immense dignity. "Don't
poke fun at me."

"I'm not poking fun at you." Val studied her. "Why
do you think that you are not desirable?"

"I know precisely what I am. Which is not pretty or
charming or amenable. However, I do have a sizeable
dowry. And now that Papa is gone, I am a considerable
heiress to boot." Emily puffed up her cheeks and blew
out an exasperated breath. "Oh, why don't you just
reach out and *find* the athame?"

"Because I can't."

"Oh. I assumed your preternatural senses . . . Isn't
that unusual?"

"It is. Whatever the degree of his involvement in this
business, I think we must assume your Mr. Ross is up to
nothing good. Yes, I know he isn't yours! But I'm afraid
you must act for a little while as though he is." It took
no preternatural senses to hear the sound of grinding
teeth. Val reached out and caught her hand.

Emily studied his fingers. "You're going to do that
thing again. Where you know my thoughts." *I also
wished to speak with you about that. I dislike it. I think you
must have bespelled me, and I wish you would stop.*

Miss Dinwiddie grew more and more intriguing. Any
other maiden would have run shrieking from the room—
or tried to—as opposed to calmly sitting on Val's bed
with her hand in his. *I haven't bespelled you, little one. I
won't do this again. Unless you wish me to.*

Images flooded his mind. Of the circumstances under which she might wish such a thing. Which had to do with nibbles and kisses. And nips. Then there was nothing, as if she'd slammed shut a door. Val released her and leaned back. "You've told me what your suitor wants. What do *you* want, Emily?"

Emily flushed, not surprisingly, considering the recent tenor of her thoughts. "What I *don't* want is to marry Michael and give him control of the Society and my pocketbook. For that matter, I don't want to marry anyone, although I suppose I eventually must, because the law doesn't consider females fit to manage their own affairs. Oh, stop watching me as if I were some entertaining oddity and pay attention to what I'm telling you! You aren't taking this business seriously enough."

Understandable, perhaps. Val had already been hanged, shot, and staked, none of which was particularly pleasant, but he had lived (so to speak) to tell the tale. "You're serious enough for us both, elfling. Don't you ever laugh?"

She scowled. He smiled. "If Mr. Ross has the athame, it wasn't with him last night."

Emily's expressive eyebrows climbed her forehead. "How do you know that?"

Val raised an eyebrow of his own. She frowned at him and snapped, "I can't imagine why your servants are so devoted to you. You must have swayed their minds."

"That would be unsporting of me."

"And you never take advantage?"

"Sometimes I do. Indulge my curiosity, Miss Dinwiddie. Most well-bred young women would settle for marriage at any price."

Emily drew up her legs and wrapped her arms around her knees. "I don't know that I'm particularly well-bred, although Mama certainly tried. My parents had a marriage of convenience. Her dowry and his convenience, that is! Oh, they rubbed on well enough together, except when his experiment with a reverse magnetosphere went awry, and we had rabbits in the drawing room, and Mama fainted into the teapot. Since I know I'm not the sort of female a gentleman would wish to marry, except for my fortune, I've decided I shall try and make my own way in the world."

Perish the thought! Val said, "Indeed?"

"I've learned a great deal about many subjects, but what use is simply knowing things? However, that's about to change. *Has* changed: here I am with you."

"Which is very bold of you," said Val.

Emily sighed. "I suppose I am ill-mannered. I don't mean to be. Please try and understand: there are so many things I wish to do and see. While I'm here in Scotland, I hope to visit one of the Scottish mermaids who uses their beauty to lure sailors to them, not that I would try to capture one even if she *would* grant me a wish. I would especially like to meet a kelpie, though I'd prefer it looked like a handsome man with seaweed in its hair rather than a black horse-bull beast with two horns. And I certainly shouldn't let it lead me to a watery grave."

More likely she would lead the kelpie to one. Val eyed the charms Emily had replaced around her neck, which were of no more practical use than the line of salt and scattering of seeds she habitually placed outside her bedroom door with the absurd notion that the undead had a compulsion to count everything in their path.

On the other hand, he wouldn't be at all surprised to discover she'd hidden an axe beneath the pillows. "You speak of legends. What happens when you discover that these creatures don't exist?"

"What happens when I discover that they do? Like

you. The point is, I'll have found out for myself. As I mean to find out what has happened to the athame. And why."

Val glanced at the window. Sunrise was too near. "We'll find your answers, and we'll retrieve your athame. Now you must return to your room."

"Since when do your kind care about the proprieties?"

"I don't. Lady Alberta does. The household will soon begin to stir." And it was doubtful that even the inquiring Miss Dinwiddie would care to see him turn into a corpse before her eyes.

She slid off the bed, dragged her feet across the carpet like a sulky child being made to go bed, hesitated in the doorway. "No!" said Val. "I will *not* tell you what it's like to bite someone. Although Drogo might be persuaded to show you." The wolf rose and bared his teeth. Emily hastily backed out onto the stair.

Chapter Ten

If an ass goes a-traveling, he'll not come home a horse.
(Romanian proverb)

Emily's foot still tingled where Val had stroked it. She hoped he didn't know how close he'd come to seducing her without trying. For Ravensclaw to seduce females must be as natural for him as drawing breath.

Not that he drew breath.

She really must try to remember that.

What *had* she been thinking? Ravensclaw had found her in his bed. It must have been the champagne punch.

Not that he had seemed surprised. Probably Ravensclaw was accustomed to finding females in his bed. It was that golden skin. Those amused blue eyes. Those sinful lips.

That glorious muscular chest with its furring of auburn hair. Emily reminded herself that the *strigoii* of Romania had two hearts. That red-haired men who rose from the dead had the power to transform themselves into frogs. She snickered. Perhaps in his true form Ravensclaw was ugly as a toad.

That snicker drew the attention of the other occupants of the drawing room. Lady Alberta looked up from the *Gazette*. Zizi, Bela, and Lilian paused in their efforts to instruct Jamie in the proper handling of a tea tray, it being customary for the first pot to be prepared in the kitchen and carried to the lady of the house. These being early efforts, Jamie carried a book—*A Greene Forest, or a Naturall Historie,* divided into three sections, Animal, Vegetable and Mineral, an encyclopaedic digest prepared by John Maplet in 1567—on the tray instead. Thus far he'd only spilled it thrice. Machka lent her efforts by winding around his feet. Drogo sprawled in his usual spot on the hearth and watched the proceedings with lupine disbelief. Lady Alberta said, "Is something amusing, dear?"

Indeed. The notion that Ravensclaw might seduce her. Emily smiled.

Jamie did a nice turn with the tray. "Och, she's in a wee dwam."

"I'm no such thing," protested Emily. "Whatever it is."

"A dwam is a daydream." Lady Alberta abandoned her *Gazette* to reach for an oatcake. "And I think you were."

Perhaps she was. Emily couldn't decide whether she should be pleased with her initiative at bearding the dragon in his lair, or appalled at herself. Bearding dragons was one thing, falling asleep in their beds something else entirely. She watched Jamie attempt to maneuver the empty tray, and felt a pang of guilt. She had brought him into this strange household, and then abandoned him to the tender mercies of its occupants. At least one of whom was a nightwalker.

A nightwalker who despite his fondness for tea and oatmeal must surely dine on something more substantial. "Jamie, has Count Révay-Czobar"—how best to phrase it?—"er—"

Jamie stared blankly at her. As did Lady Alberta, Bela,

Zizi, and Lilian. Emily cleared her throat. "Has he perhaps offered you advances that seemed, um, unusual?"

"G'wa!" Jamie hadn't survived ten years in the streets of Edinburgh by being slow on the uptake. "Are ye thinkin' that himsel' is a mop-molly?"

Now it was Emily who looked blank. "A mop-molly?"

"A deviant, my dear," Lady Alberta said comfortably. "A gentleman who prefers relations with a member of the same sex. Or with an animal. Which should be somewhat difficult, I'd think." Drogo growled. "But to each his own!"

Umbivalent, actually. Emily hadn't believed him at the time. Perhaps instead of learning about matters supersensible, she should have devoted herself to the study of anatomy.

Jamie snorted. "Himsel's nae jessie."

"One ass scrubs another." Isidore carried a huge bunch of roses into the room and plopped them on a table. He looked sternly at Emily. "And someone should have her mouth washed out with soap."

Someone wished she'd never opened said mouth. "I didn't mean—oh, never mind!"

"She's in a fankle," observed Jamie. "Dinna fash yersel', Miss Emily. How wid ye ken such things, bein' unkenand lak ye are?" Zizi, Bela, and Lilian giggled behind their hands. Isidore rolled his eyes heavenward.

Emily was exasperated. "I'm not!" she snapped. All attention turned on her. Lady Alberta dropped the oatcake she'd had halfway to her mouth and even Drogo looked up. "Why is everyone gawking at me?"

"Young Jamie said that you were unknowing. You said that you weren't." Lady Alberta glanced regretfully at the fallen oatcake. "We were talking about gentlemen and their preferences. You understand our astonishment."

Bright-eyed Zizi offered, "You just said you weren't a virgin, miss."

"What's a virgin?" murmured Bela. Lilian giggled again.

Emily ignored them, and Jamie's gap-toothed grin. "I *meant* I'm not in a fankle, whatever that is. At least I think I'm not. Where did the roses come from, Isidore?"

"You have a visitor." The old man peered at the calling card he held between forefinger and thumb. "Mr. Ross. Shall I send him up?"

"You'll *bring* him up and announce him properly!" Lady Alberta fixed Isidore with a stern glance. "Pretend for just a moment that this is a properly run household. You hussies stop gawking and do something with this mess. And"—she snatched the book off Jamie's tray— "we shall need more tea!" Zizi hurried to the kitchen. Bela and Lilian quickly tidied up the chamber. The carpet was already in pristine condition, Drogo—being almost as fond of oatcakes as was Lady Alberta—having licked up all her crumbs.

"Jamie, wait." Emily followed the boy to the stair. "When Mr. Ross leaves, I want you to follow him. Don't let him see you. Then come back and tell me where he went."

Jamie regarded her with censure. "I hae ma doots ye'll be unkenand long, miss, if ye keep on lak this."

Did the entire household know she'd fallen asleep in Ravensclaw's bed? Emily said, with commendable patience, "Mr. Ross may have something of mine. I want it back."

Jamie brightened. "Shall I mak' the dive? Pick his pockets, miss?"

Emily was tempted. However, there was no assurance that Jamie was any better at picking pockets than filching candlesticks. "No. Just tell me where he goes." She returned to the drawing room. Lady Alberta picked up the *New Monthly Magazine* and resumed where she'd left off when she was distracted by the arrival of the *Gazette*. " '... the tale of the living vampire, who had passed years amidst his friends, and dearest ties, forced every year, by feeding upon the life of a lovely female to prolong his existence for the ensuing months ...' "

Isidore appeared in the doorway and dramatically announced: "Mr. Michael Ross!" Michael stepped into the room, a vision of sartorial splendor in a violet-colored coat, cream-colored breeches, and gleaming leather boots. In one hand he carried a tall beaver hat and leather gloves. These items he tried to give to Isidore. The old man flapped his hands and backed away.

Lady Alberta continued reading. " '... the dead grey eye, which, fixing upon the object's face, did not seem to penetrate, and at one glance to pierce through to the inward workings of the heart ...' " Michael gazed nervously about, took in every detail of his surroundings from the plaster ceiling to the perpetual almanac in its frame. Emily was not unhappy to see him ill at ease.

Botheration! She had forgotten to warn Lady Alberta that they had suddenly become kin. "Michael, I don't know if you have met my aunt, Lady Alberta Tait. Aunt, uh, Bertie, may I present Mr. Michael Ross."

"Who brought these lovely roses." "Aunt Bertie" shot Emily a wry glance. "How nice."

"Lady Alberta." Michael's uneasy gaze fell upon Drogo. "That's a wolf!"

"Nonsense. Drogo is a rare Carpathian sleuthhound." Emily gestured toward Machka, who appeared fascinated by the tassels on Michael's highly polished boots. "And that is a cat."

Michael hastily moved his foot away. Machka followed, a hunter stalking prey. "I dislike cats," he said. "Shoo. Go away."

Emily was getting a headache. She snatched up the

cat and plopped it on her lap. Machka hissed. Emily swatted her. "Stop that or I'll pull your tail. Do sit down, Michael."

Lady Alberta looked up from her magazine. "Are you familiar with Mr. Polidori's *The Vampyre,* Mr. Ross? '. . . his dead eyes sparkled with more fire than that of the cat whilst dallying with the half-dead mouse . . .' "

"An interesting account." Michael deposited his hat and gloves on a small table atop a copy of *Egyptian Secrets, White and Black Art for Man and Beast.*

Lady Alberta was distracted by the arrival of Zizi with the tea tray. "Ah, black buns! I am especially fond of black buns." She popped one into her mouth. Drogo was also fond of black buns—a rich fruitcake made with raisins, currants, chopped almonds, brown sugar, and finely chopped peel, flavored with cinnamon and sugar. He edged closer to her chair.

Emily thought a change of subject might not come amiss. "Michael, did the Professor ever show you a cere-monial knife? With a cabochon ruby and a Celtic pen-tagram set into its hilt?"

Michael shook his head. "I'm certain he didn't. Is it important?"

"Important? No. I only wondered because the knife went missing about the time the *vrajă* appeared."

"As you can see, I still have mine." The charm was prominently displayed on his watch fob.

Emily had already noticed the *vrajă,* as well as the sprig of hawthorn stuck in Michael's lapel. Hawthorn was useful in repelling the nonliving, according to the literature, which had thus far been proved wrong more often than right.

Michael tapped his fingers on his knee. He was fid-geting about as if he expected Ravensclaw to pop out of the teapot and bite him in the neck. Emily leaned closer and whispered: "The devil's spawn is out cavorting with his fellow fiends from hell. You've nothing to fear."

"That shows all *you* know!" snapped Michael, then took in a deep breath. "Forgive me. I had hoped to speak privately with you."

To be private with Michael was the last thing Emily wanted. "Don't mind Aunt Bertie, she's deaf as a post. The roses are lovely, Michael. What is it you want to talk about?"

Michael looked doubtfully at Lady Alberta, who made no reaction to this slander, and drew his chair closer to Emily. Machka leaped onto the table, where she settled down near Michael's hat. "I wish to apologize for my behavior yestere'en. I realize that I was perhaps a trifle high-handed, but you must know that I have your best interests at heart. I've made arrangements for your return home. I'll join you there when I can."

He really did flatter himself that she would let him lead her around by the nose. "Take a damper, Michael. I'm perfectly comfortable where I am."

"So I see." His voice dripped disapproval. "Which I can only think another excellent indication that you aren't in your right mind. Someone must look after you, Emily, and you must see that I'm the properest person for the task. We shall be married right away."

What Emily could foresee was the disbandment of the Society in that event. Michael was far more interested in lining his pockets than in any arcane lore. "No, we shan't. And don't tell me again that you don't think me capable of bearing responsibility."

"I wasn't speaking of responsibility." He leaned closer. "But offspring."

Emily blinked. "Offspring?"

"You know, children. To carry on the Dinwiddie name. It was the Professor's dearest wish."

Emily tried to imagine Michael touching her the way Ravensclaw had touched her in her dreams—and hadn't what he'd done to her bosom been interesting? Emily had not previously been aware that bosoms could be the source of such sensations. She was curious to find out what else she didn't know.

But not from Michael. And if Michael told her once more what her papa had wanted, she would box his ears. Emily raised her voice. "Aunt Bertie! Did my papa ever tell you that his fondest wish was for me to bear offspring?"

Lady Alberta marked her place with her fingertip. "Why no, dear, I don't believe he did. Although perhaps he *wouldn't*, because he knew that I was unable to do so myself. Such a tragedy, I thought at the time. Although I have since changed my mind. Children are so unpredictable. You never know how they'll turn out. Why, I have a friend—"

"Why would he tell her anything?" muttered Michael. "You said they were estranged."

Perhaps Emily would box Lady Alberta's ears instead. "They *were* estranged. Sometimes. And sometimes they weren't. Oh, let's have done with this! I know you made off with the knife, Michael. You have no idea how dangerous it is."

Michael wore an expression of astonishment. "Are you accusing me of theft? You wound me, Emily. How can you think such a thing?"

"You don't want to know what I think of you in this particular moment!" Emily snapped. "The knife is missing. I must have it back."

"You shouldn't have lost it in the first place. Don't you see, Emily, this is precisely why you need me?" Michael cast a glance at Lady Alberta, who was seemingly oblivious, and dropped to his knees. "Marry me, dammit, Emily. I'll help you get back your blasted knife."

Emily pushed up her spectacles. "You look very silly kneeling there. Do get up off the floor."

He flushed and rose to brush off his breeches. Lady Alberta read aloud: " ' . . . the dreadful shrieks of a woman mingled with the stifled, exultant mockery of a laugh . . .' "

"Very well! But I've no time to go a-wooing, so don't expect me to dangle after you like a lovesick swain!" Michael snatched up his hat and gloves and stalked out of the room. His voice drifted back from the stairwell. "My hat! That damned cat clawed my hat!" Then there came the slamming of a door.

Emily looked at Machka. "Good kitty," she said.

Lady Alberta reached for another black bun. "It's none of my affair, nor do I wish it to be, but I feel compelled to point out that one catches more fleas with honey than vinegar."

Emily rubbed her temples. "I think it's supposed to be flies. And I don't wish to catch Michael."

"I didn't think you did, my dear. But I think you want *him* to think you do. At least for a little while. It might be interesting to pretend that you wish to marry him and see what happens. You can always cry off. No, don't confide in me! I truly do not wish to know."

Chapter Eleven

Who keeps company with the wolf will learn to howl.
(Romanian proverb)

Edinburgh's Royal Exchange boasted a fine piazza, home to a custom-house and thirty-five shops, some with living-rooms above; ten other dwelling places; two printing shops, and three coffee houses. The Exchange had been built on the steeply sloping site of several old closes, with the result that though around the quadrangle which faced the High Street it was only four storeys high, its north wall rose like a great grey cliff to the height of twelve.

Down around the cellars of the Royal Exchange could be found the cobbled way of Mary King's Close, flanked by remnants of ancient houses and shops. A tavern. A sawmaker's establishment. A stockroom, its ceiling still hung with gruesome hooks. Leading off Mary King's Close were a warren of interconnecting rooms where entire families once lived.

The close was silent now, abandoned in the belief that it was haunted by residents who'd died of the plague. Bold explorers who ventured here returned speedily to the streets above with garbled tales of unearthly screams and mysterious noises, a ghostly black figure with jaws agape and burning eyes, a woman covered in blood uttering deep groans and moans, tall men with cloven feet dressed in dark blue cloaks.

Abandoned though the close might be, it was not entirely deserted. The secret meeting place of the Breaslă was here, deep beneath the cobbled streets of the Royal Mile.

Candles burned in ancient sconces set into the walls of a filthy cobwebbed room, which boasted the additional amenity (in case an explorer grew too curious) of manacles hanging from the ceiling and a skeleton built upright into one of the stone walls. In the middle of the chamber was a table of the sort used by anatomists, though the chamber was mercifully free of fragments of limbs, intestines dangling about like discarded party streamers, grinning heads and gaping skulls.

The table was not empty. On it lay a corpse. An especially unattractive corpse, battered and drained of blood. The head had been lopped off just below the chin, leaving a rough stump. The dense, cloying smell of decomposing humanity filled the chamber, reminiscent of rotting fruit and meat.

The body was naked, and female. Young, despite her deflated breasts. From the lower classes, judging from the condition of her hands and feet. "A pretty present," murmured Val.

Cezar gestured and Andrei flung a blanket over the grim sight. "I found it on the doorstep. Rather a pointed statement, don't you think?"

"You believe one of us responsible?" Only in case of extreme emergency did a member of the Edinburgh Fraternitae kill. This looked less like an emergency than outright savagery.

"I don't know what to think. The beheading suggests

a vampire slayer." Andrei remained standing by the table while Cezar moved away. "However, there remains the matter of the missing blood."

Val studied his companion. Cezar was clad in black. He made a dramatic picture, his silver hair loose around his shoulders, his astonishing violet eyes. Their kind were civilized on the surface only, and frequently fought among themselves, and jostled constantly for position in the hierarchy of the clan.

Cezar was dominant at the moment, and had been for some time. It was due entirely to Cezar that the Edinburgh Fraternitae was among the less violent of the Breaslă. *Use sense when indulging your nature; don't flaunt what you are in public places; never indulge or get careless; appreciate the gift of life; never let the Darkness enslave your will.*

Perhaps the athame would make it possible for someone to wrest control from Cezar. It hadn't before occurred to Val that the problem posed by the stolen artifact might be as immediate as this. He owed Cezar his allegiance, and would do so even were Cezar not his Stăpân. They had roamed the forests of their youth together in search of food and shelter, untried and naïve enough to believe that malicious fairies dwelt in the reeds of marshy streams, and werewolves haunted the narrow mountain valleys, and witches flew over upland pastures on moonlight nights.

Cezar adjusted his coat cuff. "It was unlucky to come across a strange dog first thing in the morning. If someone passed a priest, or an elderly woman with an empty pail, he dare not speak to either of them or he'd have bad luck that day. What are you keeping from me, Val?"

Val glanced at Andrei. All three of them had fought alongside Constantin Brâncoveanu, and seen him beheaded at Mogosoaia. Had been present at the Walachian Vespers, when Michael the Brave summoned his creditors to his palace and had them massacred. Would never forget St. Bartholomew's Day 1459, when Vlad ordered thirty thousand of the merchants and *boyars* of Brasov impaled. Andrei remained expressionless.

La dracu! He hated politics. Cezar was closer to him than a brother. Therefore, much as Val disliked it, Cezar must be told. "The d'Auvergne athame has resurfaced. I suspect it may have something to do with your uninvited guest."

"That accursed athame." Cezar gaze grew cold. "I thought it was lost."

Val propped one foot on the old chest. "So did I. However, I admit to having been a trifle distracted. Now it turns out the Dinwiddies have had the thing all this time."

Cezar studied the blanket-covered corpse. "Your Emily intrigues me."

Val had expected that she might, which was why he hadn't mentioned the athame before. Cezar was unpredictable. "My Emily, as you have it, knows about us. Not us, specifically, or at least not you, but that our kind exists."

Cezar's violet eyes narrowed. "She knows what you are? How, Val?"

"I told her." Val took perverse pleasure in seeing Cezar rendered speechless. "Lisbet had upset her, you see."

Cezar looked as though perhaps he saw too much. Before he could comment, Val added, "Emily then informed me that she would be upset by whomever she pleased whenever she pleased and I was not to tell her what to do." He smiled at Cezar's expression. "Miss Dinwiddie is an original."

Cezar's lips curved. "Val—"

"Emily is very curious as to how I became what I am. She doesn't think it's because I led a wicked life. Although she wouldn't wish to infer that I *did* lead a wicked life. Nor does she imagine that I died a virgin. I particularly liked the suggestion that a dog jumped over my corpse."

Cezar by this time was laughing. Even Andrei's grim face wore a faint smile. "What did you tell her?"

"That I became what I am by choice."

"And then I hope you're going to tell me that you re-arranged her memories. After she gasped and shrieked. Or perhaps sank into a faint."

"*Then* she asked if I could drink from other vampires, or from animals, or if I must confine myself to human blood. How often I had to hunt. Where I preferred to bite someone." Val grinned. "And if my eyes turned red. After which she apologized for being so *pushing*, but explained that I was her first supersensible creature and there were many things she wished to know."

Cezar's laughter faded. "Has it occurred to you that you may be mistaken in Miss Dinwiddie?"

"Constantly. In what way do you mean?"

"Professor Dinwiddie not only invented an amphibious horse-drawn vehicle and an automaton that could play a flute, he duplicated the Everlasting Light of Trithemius, and had remarkable success in extracting metals from fruit. Lead from bladderwrack, as I recall. And mercury from Irish moss. I wouldn't underestimate his daughter. She may be playing a deep game."

As might Cezar himself. Val wouldn't make the mistake of underestimating his Stăpân. "Miss Dinwiddie is more interested in natural wonders than in alchemy. She hopes to meet a water kelpie while she's here in Edinburgh." Val dropped his foot to the floor and resumed his pacing. "In addition to the d'Auvergne athame, there are other items missing also."

Cezar's gaze was thoughtful. "Miss Dinwiddie confided in you freely, knowing what you are."

"Miss Dinwiddie is a very practical young woman. She wants my help."

Cezar continued to watch him. "Miss Dinwiddie claimed you are an old friend of the family. Does she know how truly she spoke?"

"No. And I don't intend to tell her."

Cezar's eyes never left his face. "What are you doing, Val?"

"Protecting our interests." Val contemplated the skeletal wall decoration. "There *is* a possibility that she may be influencing my mind."

"How would she do that? You are *vampir*. You're supposed to be influencing hers."

Val snorted. "I don't think Miss Dinwiddie is easily influenced by anyone. She can close her mind to me. If we're touching, unless I block her, she can read my memories. I should be able to hear her thoughts. She should *not* be able to hear mine."

"You want her." Andrei's voice was hoarse, his throat damaged by the same weapon that had slashed his face.

Val considered the comment. Did he want Emily? Probably. If to call him jaded was perhaps injustice, he had had a long time to appreciate females, and consequently had become something of an epicure. Although he could not recall that freckled virgins had ever before been on his menu.

"Miss Dinwiddie amuses me. I respected her father. I feel a responsibility for the athame." This was more explanation than he would have offered to any other, but Andrei was Cezar's *Locotenent* and closer to him even than Val; a onetime fellow member of the Order of the Dragon, a group of soldiers who had protected the lands of Eastern Europe from the Turks.

Andrei looked skeptical, Cezar even more so. "Your studies have not yet borne fruit?"

"So near and yet so far." Val turned back to the shrouded body. "What will you do with that?"

Cezar, too, glanced at the table. "You mean, with her. She was the keeper of a cabbage-stall in the High Street who from all accounts possessed an unusually long set of canine teeth. Perhaps I shall invest in one of those patented spring-closure coffins outfitted with cast-iron corpse straps to keep the body snatchers from stealing her. Can you imagine the uproar if the anatomists got hold of such a corpse? And I think I must do it now, before our miscreant grows even more bold. One more thing, Val."

"What?"

"If Miss Dinwiddie has the d'Auvergne athame in her possession, she can do more than push you from her mind. Watch your back, *camarad*."

Chapter Twelve

A woman, a dog, and a walnut tree,
the more you beat them the better they be.
(Romanian proverb)

As structures in the Old Town had climbed higher and higher, their foundations had sunk deeper into the soft sandstone. The steep slopes on either side of High Street had enabled builders to dig sideways into the ridge, allowing underground levels to be built at depths not possible elsewhere. The foundations of the tenements resembled rabbit warrens, levels of cellars built one above the other, cold and damp. Beneath the steep winding streets sprawled a maze of tunnels and underground chambers teeming with beggars and criminals and other outcasts of society. Water for cooking and washing was carried by hand down the winding tunnels, the same tunnels into which the residents threw their household waste.

Having sufficiently appalled his companion with this grim recitation, Jamie then pointed out an ancient cemetery with high walls and railings and watchtowers. Some graves had additional safeguards in the form of individual railings and walls. The Edinburgh resurrectionists were the city's primary public enemy, for the Scots preferred their dear departed to arrive in heaven

in an unkenand condition, as opposed to missing one
or several body parts. Grieving families went so far as to
pour vitriol and quicklime into the coffins of their loved
ones to render the corpses unfit. Which rather begged
the question, mused Emily, of arriving in heaven in one
piece. Before she could voice this opinion, Jamie
launched into the tale of Black Annis, a hideous witch-
like creature with blue skin and a single piercing eye,
most often found perched atop a pile of bones outside
a Highlands cave, who captured humans and ate them,
and if humans weren't available dined on sheep and
deer. Miss Dinwiddie responded by saying that she was
all the more determined, then, to visit the Highlands,
and if Jamie didn't stop shilly-shallying she would box
his ears.

He shilly-shallied all the harder. Jamie was more than
a little familiar with the Old Town, having been left as a
babe on the doorstep of an orphanage there. However,
he didn't think it proper he was guiding Miss Emily
through those narrow streets. Not that anything about
Ravensclaw's household was proper. Jamie had been
down enough chimneys to know that. Still, Miss Emily
was a fine wee lass, even if she was a bit camstairy and
had caused him to have to take a bath. He smoothed
the sleeve of his fine new set of clothes, fine practical
clothes, not knee breeches and coat like footmen nor-
mally wore. Jamie had been learning all manner of new
things, such as how to set a table, though Isidore wouldn't
allow him near the silver or let him pour wine. And if
he wasn't especially excited about cleaning the hearth,
at least he wasn't expected to carry out the slops. He
wished Miss Emily would buy something so that he
might carry it for her, like a proper footman. "It's no'
right," he repeated. "A young lady like yersel' shoulna
be daverin' aboot the Old Town alone."

Emily regarded him with exasperation. "So you have

said, several times already! Must I point out that I'm hardly alone? You are with me, and Drogo is with both of us. Not that I consider this a blessing, but he refused to be left behind. Furthermore, we aren't wandering. You're going to show me where Michael went."

Jamie kicked at a piece of broken cobblestone. "Nae need t' be abstrakulous. I should hae gi'n him a cuddy lug."

"No, you shouldn't." Emily caught the boy's shoulder and gave him a shake. "Listen to me, Jamie. Mr. Ross isn't the gentleman he seems. He has stolen something from me. In truth, various somethings. And I mean to get them back." For that matter, the pilfered items weren't even hers but belonged to the Society, and would in turn pass to her descendants, although Emily thought her papa might have been a little optimistic on that point, since she had pretty much decided she didn't want to marry Michael and there were no other suitors lining up at her door.

Michael insisted they were betrothed. Probably he justified his theft as only taking what would eventually be his.

Well, they weren't betrothed if Emily had anything to say about it, which she did and would.

Jamie pulled away from her. "And I wadna wonder if ye're no' also a wee bit daft! Ye shouldna be here, miss. Come awa' noo. 'Afore Isidore finds out where I brought ye and gie me a skelpit dowp!"

"I'll give you one if you don't stop scolding! For the last time, show me exactly where Mr. Ross went."

The air was damp with a grey mist, the "haar" Jamie called it, that was blowing in from the Firth of Forth. Emily's hair had already sprung every which way about her face until she must surely look a quiz.

Along the High Street they traveled, toward the Royal Exchange. Emily was tempted to stop and warm herself in the coffee shop, listen to gossip and peruse the latest newspapers to learn what folly Prinny's Tory ministers had most recently committed, and discover who of interest had lately gotten married, disgraced themselves, or died. Jamie led her down a flight of dark, narrow stairs, worn and sloping from centuries of traffic, into another steep and winding street. They rounded a corner into a narrow close, where crowstepped gables and chimneystacks perched at crooked angles against the sky.

Jamie pointed. "There." Daft was not the half of it. Miss Emily was a regular dare-the-deil.

Even Drogo thought so. The wolf growled, he snarled, he slavered; he crawled on his belly; the fur on his back stood straight up in the air.

Emily hesitated in front of the dark archway. It hardly looked welcoming. But neither had Corby Castle, and she'd marched right up to the front door. Not that Emily wished to march up to Michael's door, merely to search his lodgings. Resolutely, she moved forward.

"I dinna think," protested Jamie, "that ye should go down there." Drogo seemed to be in agreement: the wolf blocked her path.

"Stop it, the both of you!" Emily plopped her hands on her hips. "I have decided I must take a more active hand in the proceedings. Oh, get out of my way!" This latter was addressed to Drogo, who didn't budge an inch. She squinted at Jamie. "Why are you staring at me as if I'd grown horns?"

Jamie blanched. "Behind ye, miss!"

Emily spun around. Three hulking brutes loitered at the mouth of the close. Now that she had spied them, they abandoned all pretense of idleness, and advanced. Rather, two advanced. The third jerked like a puppet when he walked, his pale face twitching spastically. In one hand he clutched a sack.

She might have run, but Drogo was in her way. The

wolf couldn't seem to decide whether to fight or flee. Emily adjusted her spectacles, raised her umbrella and prepared to defend herself.

No one could fault her courage. She stomped on the instep of one assailant, whacked another in the shin, would have gotten a good grasp on the hair of the third had not the twitching man thrown a sack over her head. Jamie, being of shorter stature, went directly for the crotch and was flung into a refuse pile. Drogo took to his heels.

'Twas a right bourach. Jamie flailed about in the slippery, stinking rubbish. Emily kicked and flung her arms about, cursing all the while. "Bloody, blooming, blasted—"

Her captor punched the sack, hard. The blow knocked the breath out of her, and Emily went limp. She would have a sore belly tomorrow. If she saw tomorrow. Perhaps these were resurrection men in search of a fresh body to steal and sell. Extremely fresh, considering that she was still very much alive.

Why they would want her Emily couldn't imagine, little bit of nothing that she was. While wondering how to save herself, she eavesdropped. Her abductors were a contentious lot. The word "feartie" was mentioned, and more clearly, "sweerbreeks."

Oxter and Mowdiewarp were the more vocal. Emily was interested to learn that these were not resurrection men, but ruffians for hire; and it was just as well their employer didn't want the lass dead instead of tossed over Twitcher's shoulder like a sack of potatoes, because none of them had the stomach for such work.

Jamie stirred. He couldna just sit there lak a doolally, greetin' over the puir mawkit condition of his nice new clothes, now slechered in nasty substances he didna want to know the nature of. He must gather his wits about him so that he might follow when the bajins took Miss Emily away.

In the end, they took her nowhere. Drogo reappeared at the far end of the close. With him was Ravensclaw, who moved with startling speed to smash one man against the wall of a building and fling another onto a rooftop. The third escaped a similar fate only because he was carrying Emily. His brains being in his ballocks, Twitcher took one look at the newcomer and promptly dropped her in the dirt. Ravensclaw caught him by the throat. The man's eyes bulged, and not merely because he was dangling in midair: Twitcher was goggling at a vampire's fangs.

Twitcher kicked and gurgled and struggled for breath. Slowly, Ravensclaw lowered him to the ground. "None of this happened. You spent the past two hours getting drunk as David's sow in that tavern on the corner. You and your companions. If you go near this young woman again, I will tear out your liver and wrap your intestines around your neck. Do you understand?"

Twitcher shuddered. "Aye." Ravensclaw released him and he jittered out of sight.

"Och!" Jamie emerged from the pile of rubble. "Some grand teeth ye hae! I thought ye wid bite that bajin's heid in twa. Be Miss Emily a'richt?"

Miss Emily was still sprawled on the cobblestones. Ravensclaw bent to lift her in his arms. "Heed me, Jamie. You saw no teeth. You were never here. Go on home."

Jamie opened his mouth to argue, then a blank expression stole across his face. Without another word, he turned and walked away.

Emily's eyes opened. "Yes, he did. Teeth. Saw them. So did I." Now Ravensclaw would try and erase her memory as well. He wouldn't want her to remember what she'd seen.

However, she had no intention of forgetting. When Ravensclaw set her on her feet, Emily reached up and touched a curious finger to one fang. Winced as she cut her finger on the sharp tooth. Said, "Oh, my."

Ravensclaw stepped back from her. Turned away. Turned back and caught her hand and licked the blood from her cut finger. Emily took in a sharp breath. Drogo growled.

Abruptly, Ravensclaw released her. "Go now. While you can." Emily took a last look at his grim expression and obeyed.

Chapter Thirteen

He that would eat the fruit must first climb the tree.
(Romanian proverb)

Emily set down her book, an ancient grimoire which contained such fascinating information as a shape-shifting spell that involved sticking twelve knives in the ground at intervals and somersaulting over each one; and the use of wolfbane seeds to achieve invisibility. She leaned back her head and contemplated the plaster ceiling. It felt like every muscle in her body ached.

Machka leaped into her lap. "It seemed like such a good idea at the time," said Emily, as she stroked the cat's soft fur.

Machka sank her claws into Emily's thigh. Drogo, in his customary spot on the hearth, rolled one expressive eye. Emily didn't even want to think what would have become of her if the wolf—or rare Carpathian sleuth-hound—hadn't fetched Ravensclaw.

Ravensclaw. She marveled at the memory of his tongue wet and hot against her fingertip. Emily's under-standing of the ways of maids and men—or maids and the nonmortal—was increasing at a marvelous rate. First his touch, then the dreams, and now . . . She regarded her wounded finger with awe. If a little finger-lick could be so sensual, what must it be like to feel a vampire's teeth? To experience a full-fledged fanging, so to speak?

Instead she had run away. The terrible stark beauty of Ravensclaw's face had overwhelmed her. In that moment, she had seen the predator.

Now here Emily sat, waiting for him to come home. The drawing room was pleasant in the daylight, a chamber meant not for entertaining guests but for everyday use, with its maps and almanac and counting board, and the books piled everywhere. The only discordant note was Michael's roses, great luxuriant crimson blooms that hadn't yet begun to fade. Jamie and his clothing were being divested of their noxious stench by Zizi, Bela, and Lilian (a skelpit dowp having turned out to be punishment delivered to the backside), and Lady Alberta was shopping in Princes Street for a corset that promised to give her figure the graceful curves of youth.

Emily had ceased her stroking. Machka bit her hand.

Val walked into the room. "Isidore said—" He saw the roses then, turned pale and clutched his throat, and pointed. "Aaargh!"

"Isidore! *Isidore!*" Emily stood up so abruptly that Machka sailed through the air to land atop Nostradamus's *Centuries,* snatched up the roses and ran into the stairwell. Isidore hobbled toward her. She thrust the vase at him. "Isidore, Ravensclaw is ill!"

Isidore took the vase. "The master is allergic, miss."

Over the rim of her spectacles, Emily regarded the old man. "Yet you brought the roses into the drawing room."

"They were a gift. For you." Isidore's nose twitched. "From your young man."

"He is *not*—" Emily stopped herself and drew in a breath. "What can we do for Ravensclaw?"

"There's nothing *to* do. He'll be right as rain." Isidore nodded to the roses. "As soon as I take these away."

"Then why don't you do that?" Before she bashed him over the head with them. "*Now,* Isidore!"

"The butcher looked for the knife and it was in his mouth." Having managed to get in the last word, the old man hobbled down the stair.

Emily hurried back into the drawing room, flung open the windows, waved her hands to shoo the scent of flowers from the room. Ravensclaw was not so pale now. "Roses?" she said. "Not garlic or crucifixes or holy water, but *roses?*"

Val nodded, and loosened his cravat. "Roses are the devil," he said, his voice strained. "Surely in all your reading you've come across the superstition that a branch of the wild rose placed upon a corpse keeps a *vampir* trapped inside its grave."

Emily shrugged. "I've also read that blood baths cure leprosy, and that the crowing of a rooster will scare away the undead. I presume this means you don't strew rose petals about for your lady friends to lie upon?"

He raised a brow. "What would you know about strewing rose pedals, elfling?"

"Only what I've read. Perhaps you could substitute some other flower. Daisies. Lilies." *Forget-me-nots.* "I wish to thank you for saving me today. It was most impressive, the way you clouded Jamie's mind. He thinks he accompanied me on an errand and had an unfortunate encounter with a rubbish cart." Drat it, she was babbling. Emily took a deep breath. "You frightened me, Ravensclaw. Those wretched roses. I thought I was going to see you crumble to dust before my eyes."

He picked up Machka. The cat settled on his shoulder. "Would that distress you, little one?"

"Of course it would. I've grown, um, used to you."

Ravensclaw frowned. "Emily, we have to talk."

She had been talking. Rather too much. "About what?"

Val stroked the cat. "About what you're feeling. No, I haven't eavesdropped on your thoughts. It's what everyone feels after they've encountered one of us."

How serious he looked. How remote. In Emily's experience, when gentlemen became serious and remote, they were about to be annoying. She could also be annoying. "One of you? Oh, you mean the walking dead."

Val overlooked her sarcasm. "Naturally you liked it when I took your blood. Everyone enjoys it when one of us takes his—or her—blood." He paused. "Well, almost everyone."

"I'm glad you qualified your statement." Emily took off her spectacles and gave the lenses a brisk polish. "I don't imagine it's particularly enjoyable having one's throat torn out."

"Emily—"

She crossed her arms beneath her bosom. What there was of it. "Fiddle! I know all of this. If you didn't make people think they were enjoying it, no one would ever let you feed. But I don't think you were *making* me feel what I did. Because to *make* me feel it, you would have had to overwhelm my senses, and I would have known." She paused. Honesty compelled her to add, "Not that it wasn't overwhelming, because it was. But it was my own overwhelming, not yours. Anyway, it's not as though you bit me. It was only a little lick."

He still wore that closed expression. Emily stamped her foot. "Don't just stand there brooding at me! I have a thousand questions, and I won't be put off. For instance, is this your true form?"

"I only have one form. As for my abilities . . . I can do only what a man can." A twinkle lit his eye. "But better, of course."

Emily didn't care to dwell on what things Ravensclaw might do better. At least not in this particular moment.

"A pity; I should have liked to see you turn yourself into a man-sized bat. Is it true that blood-drinking is an adjunct of the amorous congress?"

Val ran a lazy finger over Machka's purring head. "I assure you that I'm capable of amorous congress, Emily."

She didn't doubt it for a moment. "Do you and Drogo, ah?"

"Ah?"

"You *did* say you were umbivalent."

"I have said any number of absurd things to you. Since you seem to bring out the worst in me, no doubt I will say more." Ravensclaw walked toward the doorway. "Isidore! I know you're lurking somewhere. Bring tea."

Thank goodness! For a moment, Emily had thought he meant to leave the room.

She folded her hands primly in her lap. "You said you became what you are by choice, but *how?* Have you ever made someone? Brought them across? Turned them? Whatever you call it?"

He studied her. "No."

"Why not?"

"It's not so easily done as you seem to think." Ravensclaw plucked Machka from his shoulder. Sulkily the cat curled up in front of Drogo. The wolf licked her head.

Lilian arrived, puffing, with the tea tray. "There's no black buns left. Lady Alberta ate them all."

Emily waited impatiently until the maidservant left the room. Her hands shook slightly as she prepared Ravensclaw's tea. "If you were to drink from me, I wouldn't become like you are?"

Ravensclaw took the cup from her. Gently, he said, "No. But the more I drank from you, the more you would become attuned to the Darkness. You don't want to become attuned to the Darkness, Emily."

What she wanted to become attuned to was him.

Emily touched the charms she wore around her neck. "No!" he said. "Don't even think it. I refuse."

Emily could see it now. Her very own addition to the Dinwiddie Chronicles: *The Curious Episode of the Vampire Who Wouldn't Take Advantage.* "From whom do you feed?"

Ravensclaw rose from his chair. "I am a creature of sanguine nature. You must never forget that. As for who provides me with sustenance, that's a very personal question, don't you think?"

Personal? Emily glared at him. "So is what you do in my dreams!"

He moved to a table, unlocked a drawer, and extracted a small carved chest. "Allow me to offer you somewhat more protection than those charms of yours."

Curious, Emily ran her hands over the wood. The chest was very old, covered with unfamiliar symbols. "Open it," Val said.

Inside, on black velvet, lay a necklace wrought of intertwined gold. Emily touched a reverent finger to the pendant, a large blood-red ruby set against a Celtic pentragram. On the reverse was etched in tiny letters verse fifteen of Psalm xxxvii: "Their swords shall enter into their own hearts, and their bows shall be broken."

"Marie d'Auvergne's amulet," she murmured. "Created to match her athame. I thought the thing was only legend."

"It should also at the very least protect you from witchcraft and sorcery and those who wish you harm. Consider this an inferior replacement for what was stolen."

"Hardly inferior, at least in appearance. It's beautiful. You think I'm in danger, then?"

"You were in danger earlier today. That was no random encounter. Turn around."

Emily obeyed. "Those men were following me?"

"They'd been following you for some time." Val fastened the pendant around her neck. "Who have you annoyed lately, elfling?"

Beside Michael, who wanted her to bear his offspring? Who'd said he had no time for proper wooing and perhaps had decided to have her snatched up instead?

What an absurd notion. Emily swung around. "I've changed my mind. I want you to touch me again. With your thoughts."

Val's eyes went dark as midnight. "I'm trying very hard *not* to touch you, Emily."

"But I want you to."

"How am I to convince you that what you want is dangerous?"

She huffed in exasperation. "I'm a Dinwiddie, remember? Dinwiddies thrive on danger. Adventure. Exploring the unknown."

"You will remember that I warned you?"

"Ravensclaw. Shut up."

Val laughed and raised his hand, ran one finger lightly over her skin, along the line of her jaw, coming at last to rest on the pulse beating wildly at the base of her throat. *Let me in, little one.* Emily took a deep breath and deliberately let down her guard.

Mind touched mind, a thousand times more erotic than skin brushing skin, for that contact was from outside, and this was from within. Emily felt Val's power, his hunger. His darkness. His desire for her. Her legs grew weak, her mouth went dry. He caught her arms and drew her close.

Pleasure stole over her, and warmth. A sensual exhilaration. Emily was floating, flying, far above the ground. Soaring toward the heavens, on the wings of some hot unearthly bliss. Or perhaps very earthly. Fire licked along her veins—

Emily.

Mm?

The d'Auvergne athame, Emily. Is it in your possession now? Do you know where it is?

The d'Auvergne athame? In this moment of intense intimacy, all he could do was ask about the d'Auvergne athame? Emily plummeted back down to earth. *If I had that blasted athame, I'd be safely at home instead of wasting my time with bloody obstinate stupid manipulative vampires!*

She felt his regret. *I'm sorry. I had to ask. We cannot lie to one another when we are touching like this.* He withdrew from her mind and dropped a chaste kiss on her forehead.

He could not lie to her? Emily grabbed his wrist and concentrated very hard . . .

. . . Wind howled outside the cottage. A fire burned in the hearth, gleamed on the fair skin of the woman who sprawled on a rug before the fireplace. Ana's lambskin jacket lay discarded on the floor beside her, along with her gold-threaded belt, her red woven skirt. She wore only her embroidered blouse, and her striped stockings, and her long brown hair.

As if sensing an intruder, she looked up. "Valentin . . ."

Ravensclaw broke away. "What are you that you can do this to me?"

Emily felt somewhat unsettled herself. "I don't know. I mean, I know what I am, which is a somewhat frumpish female with a perhaps overly inquiring mind, but I don't know why that happened. It must have more to do with you than me. Since I suspect those are your memories." She paused but he didn't argue. "Who was Ana?"

Val moved toward the window, his back to her. "My wife."

Ravensclaw was hundreds of years old. Of course he'd had a wife. Probably he'd had several wives. Only a goose would be jealous.

Emily was a goose. "What happened to her?"

His voice was expressionless. "I presume she died."

Emily wasn't deceived for a moment. Ravensclaw wasn't as detached as he wished her to believe. She moved to stand beside him at the window, and touched his sleeve. "There's no mention of an Ana in the Dinwiddie Chronicles."

He shrugged her off. "Ana was before. Emily, I know this goes against your nature, but for your own safety you must allow yourself to be guided by me."

First he kissed her on the forehead—the forehead!— and now he acted as if she were an ignorant schoolgirl. Icily, Emily said, "I suppose you think my powers of intellect less acute than yours. Because you are a male."

Val winced. "Perhaps I might have phrased that better. You are not acquainted with the Darkness, for which you may be grateful. I am."

"The Dark Ages, you mean? But we are no longer living in the Dark Ages, Ravensclaw. Females today do all sort of interesting and dangerous things."

"Such as?"

Emily chewed her lip, distracted by thought of all the interesting and dangerous things she'd like to do with Ravensclaw himself. "No one will let me do anything," she muttered.

"I will," said Val. "We're going to the theater. Tonight."

Chapter Fourteen

It is idle to swallow the cow and choke on the tail.
(Romanian proverb)

Emily disliked the theater. Specifically, she disliked seeing Val murmur low to the lovely Lisbet Boroi, while Michael nattered in her own ear. There was nothing to complain of in the Theater Royal, which was said to compare favorably with any outside London, for it was managed by W. H. Murray and his sister Harriet Siddons, related by marriage to the great Sarah Siddons and John Kemble himself; and this evening's offering included the popular *Rob Roy MacGregor; or Auld Lang Syne* in addition to *The Falls of Clyde*, a mélange of tragedy and comedy, action and pathos, dialogue and music all jumbled together in one grand mishmash. Lady Alberta was in fine fettle, discussing Sir Walter Scott with a number of her friends: the poet was suffering a case of gallstones so severe that many people in Edinburgh thought him to be on his deathbed. Lady Alberta did have a more youthful shape this evening, though that was perhaps due less to her new corset than the number of black buns and oatcakes she had lately consumed. Her gown of purple-blue taffeta suited her, as did the turban she wore on her dyed hair. Emily felt rather fine herself in a gown of dark shot silk with a high waistline, short sleeves, and an ankle-length gored skirt with cord trimming above the scalloped hem. Rather, she *had* felt fine until she caught sight of Lisbet, and then not even the sinfully sensuous feeling of her first silk stockings, or the beautiful necklace that she wore, could pull her up out of the dumps. Lisbet was seduction incarnate in seagreen crepe with a froth of flounces that reached up to her knees. Her décolletage plunged almost that low, providing an admirable setting for her necklace, a series of large colored gemstones, some with diamond or half-pearl borders, the links set with stones of a similar type.

Emily wondered if Ravensclaw had given Lisbet that necklace. If he gave necklaces to every female of his acquaintance. Then she felt ashamed of herself. She was Val's houseguest only, for all their odd communication of minds. Lisbet was clearly more. And it was entirely Val's prerogative to choose to ignore Emily all the blessed night.

Not that there had been much opportunity for conversation even had he wished it. A steady stream of visitors had thronged to their box ever since intermission began. It seemed every gentleman present tonight wished to be introduced to Ravensclaw's houseguest, which was more than odd, and gratifying only in that it put Michael's nose out of joint.

Michael leaned so close his breath stirred the curls around her face. "I tell you, I know what he is."

No question of whom he spoke. "So do I," retorted Emily. "A Romanian count."

Michael was scornful. "You're not that naïve. I can't help but think your papa would be horrified that you're consorting with Ravensclaw, even if he is the old family friend that you claim."

"I'm not consorting with Ravensclaw," Emily retorted

with dignity. *Yet.* And her papa had probably pronounced Val a bosom bow immediately upon being introduced to his library of arcane lore. "Even if Ravensclaw was the Devil's bodyguard, and even were he to lead me up the primrose path, it would hardly be your concern. As I've already pointed out, Michael, we are *not* betrothed."

A muscle twitched in Michael's jaw, above the deep white neckcloth arranged so artistically around his neck, the crisp high collar that brushed his earlobes and framed his chin. Emily had time to admire his dark trousers and jacket, his black velvet vest with its narrow cream satin stripe, before he spoke again.

"Yes we *are* betrothed," Michael murmured. "And if you'll take my advice as your affianced husband, you'll go home. Take your aunt with you. I can't help but be concerned, Emily. You know so little of the world. Ravensclaw could destroy you in less than a heartbeat, and you might even thank him for it, might develop so strong an amorous attraction that you would be willing to do anything he asked for the sake of a mere smile."

Emily adjusted her spectacles, the better to regard her beau. "Have you been reading romantic novels, Michael? Because I can't imagine where else you might have got these jingle-brained ideas." She caught Lady Alberta's warning glance. "That is—thank you, Michael, I appreciate your concern. I assure you that your suspicions are unfounded. Ravensclaw has been a perfect gentleman." Even when she'd rather he was not. Except in her dreams.

Michael opened his mouth to argue. Emily turned her attention to her other admirers before she gave in to the impulse to clout him, which would hardly accord with Lady Alberta's advice on catching flies, or fleas. The theater was noisy with the conversations of the well-dressed ladies and gentlemen in the boxes, and the less prosperous citizens in the galleries and the pit, not that they became noticeably quieter when a performance was under way.

A barrister, a baronet, the younger son of a marquess flocked to pay her fulsome compliments. Emily reflected that she certainly had come up in the world. She felt like a mud hen caught up in a parade of bright peacocks preening in twisted rolls of embroidered gauze and quillings, corkscrew rolls and satin puffs and colored muslin bouillons; and was grateful to have been spared being draped about with festoons of flowers.

Michael glared at his competitors and took pointed possession of Emily's hand. This snail's-pace relationship was not enough to keep his creditors at bay. It had been one thing to have an heiress fiancée safely tucked away in London, another entirely when said fiancée unexpectedly popped up in Edinburgh and showed him no more affection than a gnat. Not that affection was required in a marriage, but people had already remarked that his bride-to-be didn't appear to like him above half.

He squeezed her hand all the harder as she tried to withdraw it from his grasp. "You're such an innocent, Emily, that you don't understand the situation that you're in. A woman, alone and unprotected—"

"Moonshine! I am hardly unprotected." Emily could hardly overlook this provocation, Lady Alberta or no. Michael grew increasingly appalled as she related, with suitable embellishments, and excluding any mention of teeth, her encounter earlier that day. "So you see," she concluded, "you are mistaken in Ravensclaw because he saved me from those thugs."

Gammon! Michael wouldn't have been surprised if Ravensclaw staged the thing himself, so that he could heroically appear in the very nick of time. It was exactly the sort of thing Michael might have done, had he thought of it. Added to Ravensclaw's growing list of sins was the fact that Michael hadn't. "I wonder if this attempt on you has anything to do with your missing knife."

Michael had remembered the athame. Emily couldn't have said why that struck her as ominous. "I don't know why it should. No one knows that the thing has disappeared but you and me. Were you responsible for the attack on me, Michael?"

He stiffened in somewhat dishonest indignation. "Why would I do that?"

"You want to marry me. I refused. You could have hired those brutes to carry me off. Perhaps you intended to force a marriage. We *are* in Scotland, where clandestine unions are legal and binding."

Michael's jaw dropped open. "Hang it, Emily! You can't think so little of me as that."

So much for the use of honey. Emily's nature was clearly less sweet than tart. "I don't, not really. It's just that this patronizing attitude of yours makes me very cross."

Michael clutched both her hands in his and attempted to recover lost ground. "I understand. You're still grieving for the Professor. That's why you're not acting like yourself."

What *was* herself? Emily wasn't sure. But she suspected that Ravensclaw had a better understanding of her already that Michael ever would. Michael found it difficult to follow her thoughts even when she tried explaining them to him.

Not that Emily intended to share her thoughts concerning Ravensclaw.

It was through her negligence that the d'Auvergne athame and the list had disappeared. Now her first act as overseer of the Dinwiddie Society must be to undo the mischief she had done. Or had at least allowed to happen. In the end, it was the same thing.

"This business has me in a puzzle," she admitted. "Why would anyone wish me harm?"

"Perhaps someone wants to discourage you." Michael stared pointedly at Ravensclaw. "Perhaps there is something special about your missing knife. Your family *did* collect artifacts that were somewhat strange."

And still did, if Michael could be considered an artifact. Emily murmured, "The athame's power is not so great as that. Although it *is* said to enable its bearer to summon fairies and find missing objects, and to protect cow's milk from witchcraft."

Michael frowned. "That can't be right."

Of course it wasn't right. Emily was spinning outright clankers just to see his response. She touched the pendant, taking comfort from its warmth against her skin.

Michael's gaze followed her hand. "I haven't seen you wear that necklace before. It looks very old."

Emily stroked the ruby. "It is."

Michael's eyes remained fixed on the necklace. "I suppose the Society has many other treasures hidden away?"

He supposed, wrongly, that he might get his hands on them. "Curiosities, perhaps. However, this necklace has nothing to do with the Society. It was a gift." Let him chew on *that.*

Intermission ended. Reluctantly, Michael rejoined his own party. Emily breathed a sigh of relief and wrinkled her nose at the mingled smells of oil lamps and candle wax and Michael's Macassar Oil.

She was not to be spared further aggravating male company. Cezar slipped into the vacant chair, and Andrei took up a position at the back of the box. Cezar Korzha might not be mentioned on a certain list, but he soon enough would be, once Emily recovered the dratted thing, because she knew exactly what he was. Though their features were not similar, he reminded her of Ravensclaw. Without the slightest apparent effort, Cezar was so starkly handsome that he made Michael's pretensions to fashion seem exactly what they were.

He smiled at her scrutiny. "Are you feeling contentious this evening, Miss Dinwiddie? You are welcome to vent your spleen on me."

His voice was soft, spellbinding, almost overpoweringly seductive. Emily sniffed. "You and Ravensclaw have this beguilement business down to a fine art. The two of you must go back a long way together. To Sarmizegetuza, perhaps?"

"Not so far as that." Cezar studied her in turn. "You are a very bold young woman, Miss Dinwiddie. Or a very foolish one."

"I'm fed up to the teeth with this 'young woman' business," Emily retorted irritably. "You'll excuse my choice of words. My gender is all anybody ever sees. If I was a man, you wouldn't be having this conversation with me."

"Perhaps not." Cezar studied her necklace. "Are you familiar with Sir John Mandeville, a French traveler in the fourteenth century? 'The owner of a remarkable ruby shall enjoy good relations with those around him and shall live his life in peace. He shall escape various disasters.' Provided that he wears his ruby as a ring, bracelet, or brooch, and on his right side."

Emily drew back. "According to legend, the Greek god of war dwelled in rubies, and therefore the gems are full of energy. Rubies are furthermore associated with blood, birth, and death. What is it you want of me, Mr. Korzha?"

"Merely a few moments' conversation. About why you've come to Edinburgh."

All Emily wanted was a few moment's conversation, if conversation she must have, with someone who didn't think she had more hair than wit. "I wished to see more of the world, and reacquaint myself with old friends. Since you are so eager for conversation, you may tell me about Budapest. János Hunyadi. Mátyás and the Black Army. The depredations of the Turks."

Cezar displayed no appreciation of her understanding of Hungarian history. "I could compel you to tell me the truth."

Perhaps he could. It was taking all of Emily's strength to maintain her defenses. Cezar must be very powerful, to affect her as he did.

He leaned closer. "I know the d'Auvergne athame has been in your possession, Miss Dinwiddie. Perhaps it still is."

So this was why Val had asked if she still had the knife! "And perhaps you can turn into a butterfly and waft about the theater. Has it occurred to you, Mr. Korzha, that if I had the athame, I would hardly need Ravensclaw?"

"If you had the athame, what better camouflage than to ensorcel one of us? I warn you, Miss Dinwiddie, I am less gullible than Val."

Emily didn't know which notion was the more absurd, that Ravensclaw was gullible or that she might ensorcel someone. She smiled.

Cezar raised his brows. "I amuse you?"

"You do. Not to put too fine a point on it, if you think I could ensorcel Ravensclaw, you must have windmills in your head." It occurred to Emily that she had just insulted a soulless monster. "That was perhaps too blunt."

"Perhaps." Cezar glanced at Val. "A word to the wise, Miss Dinwiddie. Lisbet Boroi doesn't willingly share what she considers hers."

That might explain why Val had ignored her all evening. "Nor am I gullible, Mr. Korzha. Why are you telling me this?"

"Sometimes one cannot choose one's alliances."
Cezar studied her. "One *can* choose one's friends."

Emily snorted. "Fiddlestick!"

"Fiddlestick?"

"You don't want to be my friend."

"You might be surprised, Miss Dinwiddie, to discover
what I want." His eyes moved again to the ruby necklace. "The fact remains that you have intrigued Val."

It took all Emily's power of will not to flinch away. "I
have no idea what you're talking about."

"Don't try and lie to me. Of course you do. Another
word of warning, Miss Dinwiddie. You're in out of your
depth. Val may be amusing himself with you, but at the
end of the day, he will still be a predator and you, my
pretty"—Cezar flicked Emily's cheek with his cool fingers—"will still be prey."

Emily had endured quite enough male superiority
for one evening. She stared straight into Cezar's inhu-
manly handsome face. "As Mr. Shakespeare puts it,
'The world is grown so bad / That wrens make prey
where eagles dare not perch.' This conversation is at an
end, Mr. Korzha."

"For the moment, perhaps." Cezar's violet eyes pinned
her to the chair. "Be thankful that you amuse me also,
Miss Dinwiddie. You wouldn't wish me for an enemy."
He rose and left the box. Andrei followed. Emily let out
a shaken breath.

She had just defied a master vampire.

Oh, hell.

Chapter Fifteen

As you make your bed, so you must lie on it.
(Romanian proverb)

If Val usually enjoyed the theater—having been privileged to observe its progression from *Gammer Gurton's
Needle* to Edmund Kean's *Hamlet*—he had not done so
tonight, even though he had put into effect his first efforts toward removing Michael Ross from the playing
field, and had for his trouble been awarded with the
sight of that young man's clenched jaw. Now that word
of Miss Dinwiddie's worth had gotten round—and that
worth was not inconsiderable, though Val may have embellished upon it just a bit—there would be considerable competition for her hand. He hoped Emily would
choose someone worthy of her, who held her in regard.
He could interfere only so far.

While it had amused him to watch Michael Ross try
and resume his previous place in Emily's good graces,
Val was not so sanguine regarding Cezar. Cezar might
be his good friend, as well as his *Stăpân*, but Cezar's interest in Emily caused Val a distinct unease. Cezar would
act always for the greater good.

So was Val acting for the greater good, in which case
Emily had no place in his thoughts. Especially since

Lisbet was running her skilled fingers along the contours of his chest, through the thatch of fine auburn hair that trailed down his belly, and below. Her long dark tresses trailed across his skin as she pressed her mouth to his chest, just above his heart.

"Lisbet." His thumb stroked her cheekbone. "It's almost dawn. I must leave."

A speculative gleam flashed in her eye. "You could rest here."

"You know better than that."

She rolled away from him. "Budapest was a bore. You should have come with Cezar. He was surprised to find me there."

"Had I known—" *I would still have stayed a thousand miles away.* "You are a constant surprise, Lisbet."

She smoothed her hand lazily over one full breast. "I wouldn't wish you to grow complacent. They say absence makes the heart grow fonder. Is that true, my Val?"

Val reached for his trousers. "You know I've no patience with these games."

Lisbet leaned back on the pillows, gloriously naked and wholly without shame. Her eyes raked his body. "I wouldn't want you to grow accustomed to my absence."

"There's not much chance of that." *Unfortunately.* Val bent down and slid his fingers around the nape of her neck and brushed his lips across hers. "I must go."

She made no move to stop him. He was almost to the doorway when she spoke again. *"Iubiera ca moartea e de tare.* Love is as strong as death. Remember that, *baĭat."* He didn't answer, but stepped into the hallway and escaped into the night.

Or, rather, the morning, for the city was already astir. By the time the bell of St. Giles had sounded seven times, shop shutters would be flung back on their hinges, the tradesmen leaning over half doors and exchanging gossip; and night soil men would be making their rounds.

The weather was damp and dreary. Fog crept through the dark, narrow wynds and closes, around the tall, forbidding tenements, along the cobbled streets. Easy enough in times like this to expect Major Weir's spectral coach drawn by headless horses to round the next corner, or to hear the ghostly piper that was said to play beneath the stones of the Royal Mile.

Instead, what Val heard was the sound of a footstep; and what he sensed was the presence of a young buck who'd taken too much to drink and was now intent on mayhem. He paused, and let the man stumble into sight. A shock of wheaten hair, a pair of burning if somewhat unfocussed eyes, the smell of fresh blood, as if the fool had recently cut himself, a strong impression of intended threat—

Val fed when he must, discreetly, and made it his habit to provide more pleasure than he caused pain; even were he not already sated, he would have had no interest in such easy prey. Val placed his would-be assailant under a compulsion to present himself naked at the Goblin Halls, caverns said to exist beneath the Calton Hill, where the Fairy Boy of Leith led a horde of fairies every Thursday night to join goblins and elves, witches and ghosts, for feasts and dancing. Let the whelp wear off his aggressions searching for something that didn't exist.

Val wondered if Emily had heard of the Fairy Boy of Leith. It was just the sort of tale that would appeal to her.

She'd actually asked if he was capable of sexual function. Val had come damned close to demonstrating that he was. He wondered if he'd survived all this time only for a primly bespectacled little spinster to drive him mad. Emily constantly surprised him, with her inquisitive little nose and sharp mind, freckled little person and great cloud of frizzy hair which, unbound, must reach down past her hips. Her passionate imagination and appalling store of misinformation. Val wanted to nibble on her neck, as well as other portions of her aggravating little person. To explore her with his lips, and fingers, and tongue. To kiss her until she was wild with longing. And then at last to drink her sweet rich *zână* blood. Intoxicating fairy nectar. One tiny taste of her had left him ravenous with a hunger he hadn't felt in a very long time.

Not that Val would slake his hunger. He wouldn't seduce Emily. Instead he would find her a husband and take himself to Lisbet, let her think she held him enraptured with her pale perfect body and her bedroom skills.

As Emily must also think. He'd seen how she looked at Lisbet, and wished he could explain their history. But he couldn't, any more than he could explain that he'd taken Emily to the theater to show Lisbet that she was of no consequence. Lisbet, and Cezar. Amusement had turned to affection, and Val found himself wishing to keep the exasperating Miss Dinwiddie locked safely away in his curiosity cabinet where she could come to no harm.

His own home loomed before him. Isidore waited at the entrance, armed with an ancient battle axe. In response to Val's questioning look, he shook his head. "Set a cow to catch a hare. Young Jamie's guarding her door. Said if any bajins came around, he'd give them a right clout."

"Well done, Isidore. Get some rest." Val mounted the staircase. Jamie was indeed guarding Emily's doorway, armed with a Scottish claymore almost as big as himself. He and Machka and Drogo were sleeping in a pile. Drogo opened one yellow eye as Val walked up the stair toward them.

He entered his room, locked the door. With the

draperies drawn closed, it was dark as the tomb. Val
pulled off his boots, his coat, his trousers, and stretched
out on the bed. With sunrise, he fell into a stupor, and
though sleep didn't stay long with him, it truly was the
sleep of the dead.

Usually he sank into peaceful darkness. Today the
darkness was broken by a dream. A dream of a woman
with gold-flecked eyes and a wild mass of flaming hair . . .

> *. . . He lowered his face until his lips found hers,
> heard her quick intake of breath. Her hands clutched at
> his shoulders as he traced her mouth with his tongue,
> nibbled gently at her lower lip, teased her with feather
> touches until her lips parted for him.*
>
> *His tongue slipped into her sweet, warm mouth. She
> caught her breath and stiffened, then relaxed against
> him. Her hands tangled in his hair.*
>
> *He lowered his lips to the sensitive flesh of her throat,
> paused to taste her pulse. His lips slid across her silken
> skin to the soft flesh of one small breast. He tormented
> her rosy nipple with his tongue until she cried out for
> more. She shuddered and moaned as he covered every
> inch of her body with small close kisses; teased her slowly,
> mercilessly, with his tongue tip; laved her with long, slow
> strokes. She groaned. Her body pulsed beneath his hands.*
>
> *His teeth scraped the inside of her thigh.*
>
> *He smelled her excitement, felt her heartbeat.*
>
> *His groin grew tight. He wanted her. The hunger
> made him burn. She wound her fingers in his hair, and
> tugged. He raised his head and looked at her. Not car-
> roty hair now, but golden blond. Amber eyes instead of
> brown. Not Emily, but Isabella, and the d'Auvergne
> athame glowed in her hand.*

Val wakened with a start, relieved to find himself back
in his own bed, in the dark bedroom, alone with the

shattered fragments of his dream, and his concern about what it might have meant.

Or was he alone? Val sensed a presence. Not Zizi or Bela or Lilian. Not Emily, Isidore, or Jamie. Machka and Drogo had not yet figured out how to circumvent a locked door.

The presence was not familiar, nor unfamiliar either. Recognition was slow in coming. Accompanying it was regret, another emotion he hadn't experienced in some time. "I hope I'm still dreaming," Val muttered.

If he was, this dream could talk. "Is that any way to greet me after so long?"

Val kept his eyes firmly shut. "Go away. You're not real."

"It's not kind of you to point that out." She sounded sulky. "I still have feelings, Valentin."

Val had feelings also, any number of conflicting ones. "What are you doing here?" he asked, still without looking at her.

She sniffled. "You called me when you told that little *roșcat* my name. Names have power. You might pretend to be just a *little* bit pleased to see me."

He hadn't seen her, yet. "I didn't tell the little redhead your name. She took it from my mind."

"So? You should be careful of that one. She's the keeping kind. I'm amazed you've resisted the temptation to take her this long. I don't recall that you were used to withstanding temptation at all. And since you can't keep her, you'll break her heart, and that wouldn't be well done of you." A pause and another sniffle. "Like you broke mine."

Val knew he'd have to let Emily go. Eventually. "I'm not having this conversation," he said, as he pulled a pillow over his head.

And felt a swat upon his knee. "Yes you are! You might pretend to enjoy it a little bit. Because it's the first of many conversations that you've going to have with me."

Not a dream, but another nightmare. Reluctantly, Val opened his eyes. Quickly, he closed them. Ana was as he remembered her, though unnervingly transparent. "I think I liked it better when you were calling me *trădăto* and *nelegiuit*."

"What did you expect? I'd just seen you dead. And then you returned in the middle of the night and wanted to resume your husbandly rights, just like the legends said." She sighed. "Not that I'd be adverse to a little tupping now."

Val looked at her again. Or, rather, through her. Ana was wearing a great deal of bare flesh and wispy veils, sequins and beads and fringe. "A man can't tup a ghost."

"Tell me about it," she said gloomily. "Do you know what it's *like* to go so long without?" Her eyes moved appreciatively over him. "Of course you don't. You look good enough to eat. Being *vampir* suits you, Valentin."

Being what she was *didn't* suit her. "You can't stay here, Ana. Why haven't you moved on?"

"I don't want to move on," retorted Ana. "You can be sure there's no tupping *there!* You called me and now you're stuck with me until you figure out how to give me what I want."

"What you want?" Ana incorporeal was every bit as provoking as she had been in the flesh. "I don't think *I* want to know what that is."

She thrust out her lower lip. "That's not very nice. Especially since it's your fault that I'm dead."

Val regarded her with reluctant fascination. "How is it my fault that you took up with Teodor?"

Ana twirled a strand of ghostly hair around one ghostly finger. "Because you turned *vampir*. I wouldn't have taken up with Teodor otherwise, or have wound up in the harem of Mürcel the Magnificent, or have been tied up in a sack and dropped into the Bosporus to drown! And all because of a Nubian eunuch, may the snails devour his corpse." She sighed. "Don't dare tell me there is a moral to all this, because now I would give anything— not that I *have* anything, but you know what I mean!— to make love again. That's where I need your help."

"No!" Val said. "I will not—"

"Not you, silly! No offense, but you *are* a vampire. I've seen your stacks of books. Books about sorcery and magic and I don't know what else. I want you to cast a spell and make me solid. Just for a little while." She considered. "Or maybe a long while. I learned a great deal in the harem. The Lovemaking of the Crow was my favorite, I think. Although Splitting the Bamboo was also interesting. The Sultan especially liked the Churning of the Cream."

"Enough!" Val held up a hand. "Ana, I'm no sorcerer."

"Pfft! You raised *me*, didn't you?"

"From what you say, it was Emily who raised you." This was like trying to converse with a wisp of fog. "And I know of no such spell."

"Then I'll just wait until you find one!" Ana settled against the bedpost. "I wonder, since you're dead, and since I'm dead—are we still married, do you think?"

If it wasn't enough that Val must contend with missing athames and inquisitive virgins, now he must also placate the ghost of his dead wife. He groaned and pulled the pillow back over his face.

Chapter Sixteen

It is a dangerous fire that begins in the bed straw.
(Romanian proverb)

Emily paused on the threshold of Val's study, a chamber where she'd never been before. It was a small room with a painted beamed ceiling, a chandelier with iron branches and a central wooden shaft. Near a fine longcase clock hung a piece of seventeenth-century crewel work in the tree of life design. Old oak bookcases were set against the walls. A faded rug lay on the wood floor.

Opposite the fireplace, in front of half-glass shutter windows, sat a long oak table with elaborately turned bulbous legs and square blocked feet. On the table perched an untidy stack of ancient books—*Egyptian Secrets,* the *Grimoire of Honorius,* Frances Barret's *Celestial Intelligence*—a tray bearing an empty teapot and the remnants of cheese scones; a leather portfolio, and an inkstand. Machka lay on her back in a feeble splash of sun. Behind the table, Ravensclaw sprawled in a low-backed armchair. He wore soft breeches, and a shirt open at the neck. His long auburn hair was mussed as if he'd repeatedly raked his fingers through the long strands.

Emily suppressed a strong impulse to run her own

fingers through his hair. She walked further into the room, looked down at the book open before him. Even upside down, she recognized the arcane symbols. "Are you trying to raise the dead?"

"I'm trying *not* to," Val retorted. "But the only banishing spell I can find requires powdered dragon's blood. Why aren't you wearing your pendant?"

Emily was visited by the obscure reflection that a phallus made of amber was considered the ultimate protection against the evil eye. She raised her fingers to the modest neckline of her muslin gown. "I'm not wearing any charms at all. Surely I don't need them in your house. You said the pendant would warn me if I was in the presence of evil. It didn't react to Cezar. Perhaps it has lost its power."

"The pendant *will* warn you. It will grow dark." Val leaned back in his chair. "Has it occurred to you that perhaps Cezar doesn't wish you harm?"

Emily propped her hands on her hips. "Hah!" she said. "How many of your kind *are* there in Edinburgh? Beside yourself and Cezar Korzha and Andrei Torok?"

Val rubbed his temples. "Tell me you didn't accuse Cezar of being *vampir.*"

"I didn't. Not exactly." Emily dragged the toe of her slipper across the faded carpet. "I admit I may have been a little bit foolish. Very well, a large bit foolish! But he was patronizing me."

Val dropped his head into his hands. "Miss Dinwiddie, you are astonishing."

Ravensclaw didn't look astonished. Appalled might be a better word. "Mr. Korzha said I was either very bold or very foolish. And that *you* are gullible. Do you really think I'm running some sort of rig with that dratted athame, Val?"

He raised his head to look at her. "No, elfling, I do not. What else did you tell Cezar?"

Emily sighed. "That he had windmills in his head. Don't stare at me like that. He told *me* that you are a predator and that I am likely your next meal. And that Lisbet Boroi does not willingly share what she considers hers."

Val closed the book in front of him. "I would never harm you, Emily."

She contemplated his wicked mouth. "I don't mind if you do. Or just a little bit. *Are* you Lisbet Boroi's property?"

"The less you have to do with Lisbet the better for all of us."

Emily moved closer to the desk. "Is that why you ignored me last night?"

"You're imagining things." Val wanted to touch her. Instead he reached out and stroked Machka's furry belly. The cat curled herself around his hand.

Emily slapped her own hand down on the table. "Next you'll be telling me that black is white. Don't insult my intelligence, Ravensclaw."

He shifted in his chair, moving slightly away from her. "Let's just say your life would be more pleasant if Lisbet didn't take you in dislike."

"Why? I already dislike *her.* Is she your mistress?" Val glanced up, startled. Emily could have kicked herself. "Forget I said that. Lady Alberta thinks I should agree to marry Michael. Just for a little while. Not marry him for a little while, but pretend that I will."

"Do you think that's wise?"

"No. I think that once Michael has me in his grasp he'll not willingly let me go. On the other hand, he's hardly confiding in me now."

Val studied her. "Perhaps you might be more conciliatory."

"Perhaps you might show me how. I'll pretend to be Michael, you pretend to be me. 'Good God, Emily, don't

off on one of your queer starts now. Be reasonable.
ou must marry me. It's what your father intended. I
ll take your name.' "

"Good God, indeed. I'm surprised you didn't box his
rs. Very well, try this." Val clasped his hands and flut-
red his long lashes. "You do me great honor, sir. I had
ot realized that you held me in such esteem. Pray for-
ve me if I do not give you my answer right away. We
elpless females require some time to focus our vapid
tle minds."

Emily frowned. "But he *doesn't* hold me in esteem.
nd your eyelashes are longer than mine. Ah. I'm pre-
med to be such a nitwit that I think he does."

Val's lips twitched. "Precisely. Go on."

Emily paced the room, trying to remember what
her idiocies Michael had uttered. " 'I had meant to
ve you sufficient time to recover from your grief, but
nce you have followed me to Edinburgh'—that's not
hat he said exactly, but what he meant—'Marry me,
mmit, and I'll help you get back your blasted knife.' "

Val was fascinated. "And you said—"

"I told him he looked very silly kneeling on the floor."
nily glanced at the cat. "And then he discovered
achka had sharpened her claws on his nice beaver
t."

Val smiled. "I see your problem, little one."

Was there ever a smile so devilish, so bewitching, so
ckedly seductive as Ravensclaw's? Emily thought not.
woman could lose her head over a smile like that. Or
r heart.

She leaned against the edge of his desk. "I wish you'd
that thing again."

Val regarded her warily. "Which one?"

"You know." Emily wriggled her foot at him and then
opped it in his lap. Val looked at it for a moment,
en pulled off her sandal and rested her heel on his

strong thigh. Sensation flooded her. Then, abruptly there was nothing. Emily opened her eyes.

Val's thumb pressed into the arch of her foot. "Tha is how it feels when you shut me out."

"But—" Emily paused. Doubtful he felt this bereft.

"I know. You're curious."

Was she being selfish? Emily closed her eyes. Va might have shut his mind to her, but still his touch wa heaven. "Cezar doesn't trust me. Do you?"

Val worked his thumb in a circular motion all the wa from her heel to the base of her toes. "Trust you?"

Emily changed her mind. Heaven could not feel so good as this. "Wish me harm."

He caught her largest toe and tugged it. "What are you talking about, Emily?"

She opened her eyes. "I had the strangest dream You were doing all sorts of interesting things to me And then I had the athame and you were in my power."

That certainly had caught his attention. Val wa frowning as he took Emily's ankle in his hand. "Did you like it? Me being in your power?"

If he had shared her dream, he already knew the an swer. Emily wiggled her toes. "I think I might have, bu then I woke up. I think I would have very much liked to do to you the things you did to me in my dream."

His gaze darkened. "I didn't send you that dream Emily."

"Fustian. I've been dreaming every night since I firs met you, and my dreams are becoming increasingly frustrating because my knowledge of matters amatory i limited and I can't anticipate what happens next." Emily paused. "Are you brooding? I don't think I've seen you brood before."

Val smoothed his hand along her calf. "Before I me you, I didn't have anything to brood about."

Her skin was on fire where he touched it, ever

rough her stockings. Emily experienced a shocking
impulse to yank her skirt up further still. "I thought it
as in the nature of your sort to brood."

"What sort is that?"

"Vampire. *Kudlak. Strigă.*"

He kneaded her calf with his strong fingers. "Why
ould my sort brood?"

"Why shouldn't they?" Emily pushed up her specta-
es. "A nonmortal by his very nature outlives his family
d friends. He must deal with the pain of loss over and
ver again. After a while the continual agony would
rely drive one mad, and there would only be a future
lost loves."

"Not so lost as one might wish," Val murmured, as he
aned back in his chair. "You paint a grim picture, little
e."

"Oh, that's merely the beginning!" Since he appeared
be done with her right foot, Emily presented him
th the left. "Your self-healing abilities may become a
rse, for your body can withstand torture far longer
an your mind. If it was done properly, you could be
rever trapped inside a prison that wouldn't let you es-
pe into death. Then there is the fact that if you are
eprived of, um, sustenance for a prolonged period of
ne, you will rapidly revert to your true age, which in
ost cases would prove not only unpleasant but fatal."

Val pulled off her other slipper. "A pretty thought in-
eed."

Emily exhaled blissfully as his hand cupped her foot.
There you have it. Angst. For which you can hardly
ame me. *Were* you to discover how to animate a corpse,
e could ask Papa exactly what happened that day in
e laboratory, and who took the athame." Which might
ot be such a good idea, because once her mysteries
ere solved, Emily would have no more reason to stay
Edinburgh, and she didn't want to leave. Not the

city, but Ravensclaw. Hardly appropriate behavior for the overseer of the Dinwiddie Society, but there it was. Mercy, Ravensclaw knew his way around a lady's foot. Doubtless Ravensclaw knew his way around a lady's everything. Perhaps he could be persuaded to—

Fortunately, perhaps, Val interrupted her thoughts. "You still haven't told me why you aren't wearing the pendant."

Because she didn't want to be protected, specifically from him. "I thought you said you wouldn't do me harm."

"I won't." Exasperation tinged his voice. "But others might. How am I to convince you that you well may be in danger? Despite your apparent conviction to the opposite, you're not immortal, Emily."

Emily eyed him. "I could be."

"No you couldn't. Even I am not immortal, as you so recently pointed out. I can still die."

"You already did. What was it like?"

Val grimaced. "Painful. You don't want to know the details. I assume you interrupted my studies for a reason. What did you want?"

To press her hands and mouth and body against that golden skin, as she had done in last night's dream. Unfortunately, Val didn't seem to be of a similar frame of mind.

Emily knew he wanted her. She'd felt his desire. *Why* he wanted her she couldn't imagine, but Emily wasn't one to look a gift horse in the mouth.

Or a gift vampire. Rather, he'd wanted her *then*. In this particular moment, Ravensclaw didn't seem to be in the throes of lust. Instead he looked like he wanted to go back to his book.

Appearances could be deceiving. This foot rubbing was pleasant, but not nearly enough. Emily slipped off her spectacles and dropped into his lap.

Val went rigid as a statue. *What are you doing, Emily?*

She wriggled into a more comfortable position. *Sitting in your lap.*

So I see. But why?

Because I wanted to do this. She reached up and kissed the hollow of his throat. Nuzzled the underside of his jaw. Traced patterns on his skin with her damp tongue. *Because I dreamed of you. Because I am exceedingly curious and I'm tired of your acting so infernally coy.*

He caught her face between his hands. "Not coy, but prudent. One of us must be."

He was holding her away from him. Emily scowled. "I don't see why."

"Because of this." Val's voice roughened. The little hairs on Emily's arms tingled. She put her hands on his broad chest and stared straight into his eyes.

His emotions swept over her, hungry and dark. Her blood went thick with wanting as he gently loosened her braid and ran his fingers through her hair. "Emily," he murmured. She moistened her lips.

Val's gaze dropped to her mouth. He clasped her face between his hands and bent his head to take her in a kiss so deep, so carnal, that she forgot to breathe. The feel, the scent, the taste of him burst across her senses. His mouth moved from her cheek to her chin to her cheek again, moved to explore her earlobe with his tongue.

Her skin felt hot. Her heart thudded wildly in her chest. She pressed closer, wanting to wrap herself in him.

He drew back and exhaled sharply. Emily touched her tingling lips. It had been even better than her dreams, that kiss. Now if he would only get on with the rest of it.

He didn't *look* like he meant to get on with anything. Alas. Emily retrieved her spectacles, the better to study his face. Perhaps Val had not shared the intensity of her experience. Hadn't felt the earth move, seen showers of shooting stars. "I've never been kissed before. Did I do it wrong?"

Val smoothed a hand over her carroty curls. "You were perfect, little one."

Emily practically hummed with excitement. Anticipation. Impatience. *"Well?"*

"Well?"

"You said you'd let me *do* things."

"I have. I let you have your first kiss." Briskly Ravensclaw set her on her feet. Emily glowered. He tweaked her nose.

Chapter Seventeen

A thief knows a thief as a wolf knows a wolf.
(Romanian proverb)

The Twitcher was confused. He didn't know what his
companions were havering about, nor why they were
both so sunk in gloom. Here the three of them sat, in
their favorite oyster cellar, which had stone floors and
tallow candles and wooden tables in front of a roaring
fire; and if the air wasn't exactly fresh, a lad still could
get minced collops, rizared haddock or tripe, a roasted
skate and onion, and wash it down with pints of beer.

Oxter and Mowdiewarp—so called because one resembled a mole and the other smelled like an armpit—
looked at each other gloomily. " 'Tis a fashious lass,"
Oxter muttered.

Mowdiewarp looked fair to weep into his beer. "Aye."

Oxter poked his haddock with a fork. "An' she has a
wulf."

Mowdiewarp picked up his mug. "Aye."

"An' t' other un."

Mowdiewarp took a great gulp of his beer.

Mention of a wolf gave Twitcher goosebumps. "What
wulf?" he inquired.

"*Thon* wulf, ye pure mad dafty!" Oxter snarled. Ever

the peacemaker, Mowdiewarp added, "The wulf what wis wi' t' fashious lass." Her that was responsible for Oxter's sore foot, and Mowdiewarp's bruised shin, and the fact that one had been flung onto a rooftop and the other into a wall.

Twitcher regarded his own pint doubtfully. He knew his reasoning wasn't powerful, but—maybe he'd drunk more than he thought.

Or maybe his companions were having one over on him. It wouldn't be the first time. He narrowed his eyes at Oxter. "An' then yer arse fell aff," he said.

"Get off *yer* arse, ye auld weegie bampit!" snapped Oxter, and then recounted the bit of bother they'd encountered while trying to carry out a simple chore, to wit snatching up a certain bit of merchandise and delivering it as arranged, and if one of them wasn't such a gamaleerie, the plan wouldna hae gone agley.

"It wisnae me. I dinna." Twitcher was emphatic. "I wis in t' tavern, drunk as David's sow."

Mowdiewarp frowned. "Who wis David, then?" Twitcher had to confess that he didn't know.

Oxter thumped his fist upon the table. "Ye're goin' doolally. Mayhap it'll all come back if I gie ye a chaup on the heid."

Twitcher wondered if maybe someone had given Oxter a chaup for him to be spinning such tall tales. He glanced at Mowdiewarp, who shook his head. "I wisnae in the tavern, then?"

Mowdiewarp looked as sympathetic as was possible for a man who resembled a mole. "Nay. Ye had the lass tossed o'er yon shoulder like a potato sack." He swallowed. "An' then—"

He'd had a lass tossed over his shoulder? Twitcher was black affronted. True, not many lasses cast their eyes in his direction, but if one had done so, he surely would have better manners than to treat her like a sack of potatoes. "I ne'er!" he said.

Oxter grimaced. "He's aff 'is heid."

"I'm no'!"

"Ye *are* looking a bit peely-wally, son." Mowdiewarp patted his arm. "Let's be done wi' callin' each other names. We've a bit o' work to do, like it or no'."

Twitcher might be a little slow of understanding, but he wasn't altogether a numptie. He squinted at Mowdiewarp. "The lass?"

"The lass wi' the wulf," muttered Oxter. "An' the bogey."

Twitcher was getting a headache. It had something to do with livers being cut out and intestines wrapped around necks. "Hing aff us," he muttered. "There's nae sich thing."

"Hah!" retorted Oxter, and reached for his pint.

"Saw it mesel'," interrupted Mowdiewarp, in an attempt to prevent hostilities from deteriorating into a right rowdy-do. " 'Twas tall as a building—had to be, did it no', t'throw me atop one? Eyes as red as fire. And thon teeth—" He shuddered.

Twitcher shuddered also, at a faint memory of sharp fangs. "Wha' aboot t' lass w' her wulf and her bogey? No' that I believe a word o' it!"

"Believe it." Oxter gestured for another pint. "We're to snatch 'er up agin. An' if we fail this time—" He made a slashing gesture across his throat. "Tha'll be the lot o' us. Unco' deid."

Silence fell, if not in the oyster cellar, where some of the diners had taken it in their heads to attempt to dance, then at the table that was graced by the three associates in crime, at least one of whom was considering abandoning the noble ideals that had thus far prevented him from stooping so low as to rob a cemetery or transport body parts. Scruples were all well and good until one was confronted with building-tall bogeys with wicked sharp teeth.

Mowdiewarp ordered yet another pint. Twitcher muttered, "It'll be the worse for ye," for reasons he couldn't have explained. His companions ignored him. Several pints, and more argie-bargies later, the trio was encouraged to depart the premises. They stumbled out into the street. Twitcher muttered, "Drunk as David's sow."

"Am no'!" protested Oxter, who was. "A wee bit blootered, mayhap."

"Och, ye're right buckled!" said Mowdiewarp, whose own legs weren't functioning altogether properly. Now that he thought on it, he couldn't feel his knees. Twitcher, meanwhile, began to sing.

As I went by the Luckenbooths,
I saw a lady fair.
She had long pendles in her ears
And jewels in her hair . . .

"Shoosh!" If Mowdiewarp couldn't feel his knees, he still knew better than to be singing about ghaisties in the haunted streets of Edinburgh. Or bogeys. Or wulves. Twitcher subsided into sulks.

The night was dark and cold and damp, not fit for man nor beast nor ghaistie. Twitcher might have asked where they were going, were he not so capernoited, and were not Oxter such a carnaptious old deil. Still, he wondered, and finally whispered that very question in Mowdiewarp's ear.

Mowdiewarp shook his head. "I dinna ken." Oxter turned and glared and hissed that anybody with a grain of sense wouldn't choose such a moment to be bumping their gums.

"Sich a moment as wha'?" muttered Twitcher. Mowdiewarp shook his head.

Oxter scowled. Before he could start to scold again, the attention of all three was caught by the sound of a kerfuffle up ahead. They exchanged glances and crept forward to the corner of an ancient tall building. The noises were louder here. Unpleasant noises, thumps and gurgles. Again, they looked at one another, then inched forward to peek around the corner, one above the other, like a tipsy totem pole.

The narrow street ended there in a cul-de-sac, the scene illuminated by a strange red glow that emanated from a knife held in the hand of a man cloaked in black. Impossible to see his face in the shadows of his hood. Impossible not to see what he was doing. Another swish, a thud . . . The man stood up, a bloody knife held in one hand.

"Bogey," said Twitcher, with considerable assurance.

It turned toward the watchers.

As one, they fled.

Chapter Eighteen

Dogs bark but the caravan goes on.
(Romanian proverb)

Val strolled along the cobbled way of Mary King's Close, past the ancient shops and tavern to the dark doorway that he sought. He entered, unaccosted by spectral figures or ghostly groans. Red eyes glowed at him from a dark corner. The rat was a nice touch.

No candles burned in the ancient sconces, not that Val's keen eyes had need of their light. The chamber was as he had last seen it, save that the anatomist's table, and its unfortunate occupant, no longer stood in the middle of the floor. Val avoided a dangling manacle, walked up to the skeleton built in the stone wall, and twisted a certain bone. A section of the wall swung open. Val stepped into a room as different from the one he'd left as chalk was from cheese. Behind him, the wall swung shut.

Here was no filth, no cobwebs, no crimson-eyed rodent. The large chamber was lit with oil lamps and furnished in a Spartan style. No mirrors or portraits adorned the walls, but an ancient oval shield ornamented with a floral device hung there, along with a few pieces of ornamented pottery and a wooden Byzantine cross. Simple benches lined the room, and long-backed chairs with simple carved decoration. It was a room designed for meeting, not for lounging. The members of the Brotherhood were, for the most part, indolent and fond of luxury. Made comfortable enough, they'd never leave. Cezar had cleared a pathway and now stood poised with a long stick and a small leather ball.

At the bottom of the stick had been fastened a piece of wood, flat on one side. The aim of the business, Val had been informed, consisted of propelling the tiny ball through innumerable obstacles to eventually drop it, hopefully with a smaller number of strokes than one's adversary, into a tiny hole in the ground. Cezar claimed to like the game. Val couldn't imagine why. From what he could see, Cezar was no better at it than anybody else, despite his superior coordination and strength, and the fact that he'd been a member of the Honourable Company of Edinburgh Golfers (though they didn't realize it) since their inception in 1744.

Cezar positioned himself, his feet spread at shoulder width, his knees relaxed, bending slightly from the top of his hips. His silver hair fell forward onto his shoulders. He narrowed his eyes at the target, and gently stroked the ball, which then rolled into a little tin cup. "You've been practicing," Val remarked.

Cezar replaced his putting cleek in a bar with other clubs: longnoses, grassed drivers, spoons, and niblets, their shafts fashioned of ash and hazel, the heads from tough wood or hand-forged iron. He bent and picked up the little ball, which was made from tightly compressed feathers stitched into a horsehide sphere. Due to Cezar's enthusiasm, Val knew a great deal more about the game of gowf, or golf, than he wished, including the fact that King Charles I had been on the course at Leith when given news of the Irish rebellion in 1642.

Cezar dropped the ball into his golf bag. "Lisbet doesn't come here, so I do. You may conclude that I've been avoiding her. She's not the easiest of houseguests. It's fallen to Andrei to entertain her today."

Val picked up one of the clubs and hefted it. "I sympathize, having houseguests of my own. One of whom you told that I was Lisbet's property."

Cezar looked contemplative. "I don't think I said that, precisely. Your Miss Dinwiddie is astute."

"I believe you also told her that she was to be my next meal. If you meant to frighten her, you didn't succeed." Val dropped the club back into the bag. "Now she wants to know what it's like to be bitten by one of us. And she doesn't mind if it hurts a little bit."

Cezar moved the golf bag out of Val's reach. "No maiden's gift will make you mortal, *camarad*."

Val wondered at this reference to the folk tales of their youth. "Yes, and witches turn their husbands into horses after sunset and ride them at night." He eyed a Hucul *tshaken*, a beautifully carved stick with an axe-shaped handle, once handed by a bridegroom to his betrothed's brother on her wedding day; and wondered why Cezar had kept the thing.

Cezar added, "You know her lifetime will pass by you in the blinking of an eye."

Val did. He thought of Ana sitting at her spinning wheel, her hair hanging down her back in plaits woven with strands of brightly colored wool. Ana stirring the cooking pot. She'd been a terrible cook, but he hadn't cared. Ana wearing nothing but her striped stockings and sandals with turned up toes.

How long had it been since he'd last thought of Ana? Val felt very old. "No answer is also an answer," Cezar remarked.

"Miss Dinwiddie informs me that our kind fall prey to angst because we outlive everyone we care about.

Not, of course, that we're exactly alive." And not that the past was entirely behind them, though Val wouldn't acquaint Cezar with this news just yet. With Cezar, it was always wise to hold some things in reserve. Perhaps Ana had merely been a bad dream.

Cezar watched him pacing. "Did you explain that our kind care about little but ourselves?"

"I had no wish to disillusion her."

"Disillusionment is one thing. Do you trust her, Val?"

Did he trust Emily? Not entirely. Did it matter? No. "You're determined to see Miss Dinwiddie as a villainess no matter how many times I tell you she's no such thing. I'd know if she was."

"Since I'm your friend, I won't remind you of another Dinwiddie whom you thought you knew. Does this Miss Dinwiddie know the history of the athame, do you think?"

Val didn't know whether ignorance or innocence was a greater evil in Cezar's eyes. "The Dinwiddie Society knows all sorts of things."

"Including what you are. Because of she-whom-we-won't-name."

Rather, she-whom-Cezar-wouldn't-let-him-forget. "I have it on good authority that you have windmills in your head."

"Did Miss Dinwiddie tell you also that she quoted Shakespeare to me? 'Wrens make prey where eagles dare not perch.' " Cezar's violet eyes were cold. "You realize that if you don't deal with her, I must."

Val tensed. "Even think of 'dealing' with her and I'll forget you are *Stăpân*."

Cezar's gaze grew icier still. "You would defy me for this girl and her curiosity? Remember you are *vampir*, Val."

Whatever he was, Val had given Emily her first kiss, and felt as though he'd received his own. Which, along with the reappearance of Ana—which he sincerely hoped had been a nasty dream and very much feared was not— gave him much to think about.

A pity the golf clubs were out of reach. He would have derived considerable satisfaction from breaking one of them.

Instead, Val walked over to an ancient dower chest decorated with symbols of the solar system. "I've decided to find Miss Dinwiddie a husband. Perhaps that will set your suspicions at rest. As for her motivations, why should either of us care what they might be? I know the story of the d'Auvergne athame, if you're curious."

It was a poor attempt at a peace offering. Cezar accepted it with a curt nod.

"Marie d'Auvergne made a pact with the Darkness. At the end of twenty-four years she was to surrender her body and soul. She intended to repent before that time, thinking that the power of Light would prove more powerful than the Dark. Just in case repentance wasn't sufficient, she created the athame to protect herself."

Cezar murmured, "And, I'll wager, the amulet you gave to Miss Dinwiddie. The design on both being the same."

Val had not forgotten Cesar's intimate acquaintance with the d'Auvergne athame. It had, in fact, once been stuck in his back, which was how Val had come into possession of the thing. "The time came for repayment. That night a dreadful storm was heard inside her rooms, and a woman's scream. When her servants dared to look, they found no sign of Marie, but the athame—which never left her possession—was lying on the floor. It's said the Darkness repaid Marie's treachery by imprisoning her in the knife itself, which is why the thing is sometimes called the Hand of the Undead; and that her rage is such she'll destroy any who stink of what Emily calls the supersensible. As for the amulet you mention, it was made to counteract the power of the athame."

"And you know this how?"

"Is—" Val paused, having already learned the folly of bringing the not-so-dearly departed into the conversation. "I researched the matter. Intimately, as it were."

Cezar raised one hand to touch the ancient oval shield. "I dislike repeating myself. However, if Miss Dinwiddie has the thing in her possession, she could do you irreparable harm. And if she *doesn't* have it, have you thought what harm you may be doing her while you entertain yourself?"

Val was silent. Much as he disliked Cezar's accusation, he had to admit its truth. He had already influenced Emily more than he'd intended. Best he find her that bridegroom straightaway.

Cezar put on a pair of dark glasses similar to Val's own. "Come. There's something I want you to see." They exited the chamber through another door, this one known only to the two of them and Andrei, and made their way out into the streets.

The Royal Mile had a fascinating history. The main thoroughfare of the medieval city, it had seen a steady parade of thieves and street entertainers, beggars and soldiers and merchants, regal processions and street fairs. The nobility had made their homes here, alongside the law courts.

Today was market day. Stalls were erected along nearly the whole length of High Street, and some merchants had spread their wares in front of their shops. All sorts of iron and copper wares were offered for sale, along with woolen stuffs and hardware, leather goods and children's toys.

They strolled by grocers and shoemakers and milliners. Curious glances followed them, but those who marked their passing did not remember long. Val paused by a shop and, with a smile and a wink, relieved the baker's lass of a beef pie.

Cezar shook his head. "I don't understand why you eat that offal when you don't need sustenance."

Minced beef, a little suet, and a sprinkling of finely chopped onion wrapped in pastry, brushed with milk and cooked until golden brown— "I like it," Val said.

Cezar regarded the pie with distaste. "You like entirely too many things."

"I don't understand what pleasure *you* get from playing golf. You enjoy that; I enjoy this. It's much the same thing."

Cezar was unconvinced that a beef pastry could compare with golf. Val considered that the pastry won hands down. The disagreement occupied them until they arrived at their destination, a dwelling in Fames Court: the home of Ian Cameron, an anatomist said to be one of the finest surgeons in Europe, who could amputate a leg in twenty-eight seconds, though on one occasion he had also amputated two of his assistant's fingers and the patient's left testicle as well.

Cezar led the way around the side of the building. "In public Ian denounces the resurrectionists. In private he seeks them out and retains their services, encourages them not only to unearth his own patients to see how his handiwork has held up, but also to retrieve colleagues' patients who had interesting anatomical peculiarities." He unlocked a basement entrance. "The good doctor found himself compelled to be elsewhere at the moment or he'd be pleased to show us around."

"I assume he owes you a favor." Along with at least half the city's more influential inhabitants.

"He does. Come."

Val followed. Ian Cameron was no different from others of his kind, back to and including Herophilus, the so-called father of anatomy, the first physician to dissect human bodies, whose enthusiasm had overcome his common sense and led him to cut up live criminals, six hundred by one account, which gave some credence to Hippocratus's theory that the human brain was a mucous-secreting gland.

The private dissecting room was not so bad as Val might have imagined. No skulls bobbed in a boiling pot, no fragments of limbs crunched underfoot, although a nice selection of body parts was preserved in buckets of brine.

Cezar gestured toward the corpse laid out on a dissecting table. "Do you notice anything strange?"

Val pulled off his dark lenses and stepped closer. The body was male, aged, dressed in shabby attire. "Other than that it has no head?"

Cezar pointed. Val looked closer. "A *nefinistat.*"

The *nefinistat,* the unfinished, were those who failed to make a successful conversion and were impaired. The more violent among them were discreetly disposed of, the others allowed to exist. Most drank animal blood, because they couldn't bear to feed off humans, but animal blood lacked sufficient life force to enable them to stay entirely sane.

Cezar moved closer to the corpse. "This one was found in Greyfriars Kirkyard, laid out with his arms across his chest as neat and tidy as can be. As if he was in his coffin, except for the missing head. Do you notice anything else?"

Val looked at the marks left by a several-bladed scarifactor applied by a none-too-skilled hand. "Why would someone drain his blood?"

"To drink it, what else?"

"What sort of fool would drink the blood of a *nefinistat?*"

"A desperate one, I think," said Cezar. "Or one sufficiently deluded to think that by drinking a vampire's blood he'll imbibe a vampire's powers." He paused. "Or, perhaps, someone who wishes it to seem I can't manage matters in Edinburgh."

Politics, damnable politics. "You know that I'll stand with you. You think this has to do with the athame?"

Cezar shrugged. "Whoever did this was interrupted. The body hasn't been staked. I will dispose of it, of course."

"Of course." The Brotherhood dealt with their own, unfinished or whole. If they did not, they were like to find themselves facing an inquisition by the High Council, the *Consiliu.*

Val wasn't deceived by Cezar's seeming insouciance. Apprehension crept over him. Another almost-forgotten emotion. Emily and her bloody angst.

As he thought of her, an image formed in his mind. "Damnation!"

Cezar turned to him. "What now?"

Val was already halfway toward the doorway. "Emily has left the house. Alone."

"You're still convinced of her innocence?"

Val hesitated. Emily wasn't so innocent as she once had been, before he started meddling with her dreams. That hadn't been well done of him. But it had been most enjoyable. And he'd probably do it again unless he managed to put her safely out of reach. Which led him back to that last strange dream, when Emily had turned into Isobella, and held the athame over his head. "It would seem not," Cezar said.

Val shook away his untimely thoughts. "Innocent. Yes."

Cezar studied him. "I'll take your word on it, for the moment. Nonetheless, you're the one who brought her to Edinburgh, and you're the one who lost the athame to her ancestor. If you're mistaken in her, the price will be heavy, Val."

Val looked at the *nefinistat*. The price was already high. "I'll stake my existence on it."

Cezar hesitated, nodded. "Done. Now go. I will deal with this."

Chapter Nineteen

Who spits against the wind, it falls in his face.
(Romanian proverb)

Although it had been her intention, Emily was hardly alone. Arms akimbo, she glowered at Drogo. "You're a wolf. You shouldn't be wandering the streets. People don't like wolves, in case you didn't know." He sat in front of her, tongue lolling, looking as innocent as it was possible for a wolf to be.

Emily sighed. "I'm stuck with you, aren't I?" In truth—not of course that she was frightened—Emily was grateful for the company. If wearing a wolf's tooth would protect her from evil, she was surely triply blessed by the presence of the entire beast.

Emily wasn't deaf to all the warnings she'd been given about being out in the Old Town without a proper escort. However, a proper escort would have gravely interfered with what she meant to do. Which, first of all, involved finding out the truth of Michael's mysteriously disappearing and reappearing *vrajă*. She pulled her cloak more tightly around her and hefted her umbrella. "Very well, then. Come along."

The Lawnmarket was cramped and crowded with a confusion of vendors and shoppers and market stalls.

Well-dressed citizens went about their business in the midst of squalor and poverty. Tall, gloomy houses towered high overhead, many with pillared piazzas on the ground floor, under which were open booths where merchants displayed their wares. Edinburgh Castle constantly appeared and reappeared above the steep gabled roofs and cobbled streets.

Beyond High Street and the Lawnmarket, narrow paths and wynds led out of sight. Emily and her companion—the both of whom had gathered considerable attention from other pedestrians, and more than one sign against the evil eye—passed under an arch and found themselves in a close. Drogo whined.

"You're the one that wished to come along!" snapped Emily, who was feeling none too confident herself. The noise of the street was deadened here by the buildings rising on all sides. None too friendly-looking buildings, but Emily hadn't escaped the house to turn craven now. Umbrella at the ready, she followed the passage between the houses until she arrived in the courtyard. One more glance at the slip of paper in her hand, and she descended a short flight of stone steps that led down to two doors. Emily looked up one last time at the distant sliver of sky, then knocked briskly on the left-hand door.

There was no response. She checked the address one last time, then twisted the door handle. It was unlocked. The door swung open. Emily stepped inside.

It took a moment for her eyes to adjust to the gloom and clutter. Books and bottles and a jumble of merchandise filled innumerable cabinets and shelves. Emily touched her pendant. Drogo bristled and growled. A harsh squawk made them both jump. Emily stared up at the raven on its perch. "Pretty bird," she said.

A white-haired man bustled out of a back room and murmured soothingly to the bird, referring to it as "Styx."

A raven named after the chief river of the underworld? She'd come to the right place. To make doubly certain, Emily said, "Mr. Abercrombie?"

He nodded and bobbed and came closer, revealing himself to be of stout middle age, little taller than Emily, with an unnerving wandering eye. His smile faded when his gaze fell on Drogo. "That's a wolf. We don't allow wolves on the premises." He flapped his hands. "Go away. Scat." Drogo paid no heed to this nonsense, but padded forward and bared his teeth.

Mr. Abercrombie fell back a step. "In this case, perhaps an exception can be made! What can I do for you, miss? Angelica and rosemary for a domination spell? Caraway seed to discourage your poultry from straying? Sage for cleansing, myrrh or sandalwood?"

Emily thought of Val and his studies. "Have you any dragon's blood?"

Alas, Mr. Abercrombie was fresh out. Perhaps he might interest the young lady in Thor's nettles or Job's tears instead. A Love Drawing Oil made with sweet almonds and an infusion of fresh basil leaves. A recipe for Raven's Feather Ink.

Emily shook her head, though she was briefly distracted by the notion of a lust-spell. "I don't mean to pry," said Mr. Abercrombie, "but I might be of more assistance if I knew what it is you need."

Emily drew the *vrajă* from her reticule. "Do you carry charms like this?"

Mr. Abercrombie did indeed. He would have happily showed Emily his entire stock had she not raised her hand. "I don't wish to purchase anything. I *do* wish to know who has recently bought one."

Mr. Abercrombie shook his head. "I can't tell you that. All transactions are private. I must protect the interests of my clients. Confidentiality is my stock in trade."

To start your membership, simply complete and return the Free Book Certificate. You'll receive your Introductory Shipment of FREE Zebra Contemporary Romances, you only pay $1.99 for shipping and handling. Then, each month you will receive the 4 newest Zebra Contemporary Romances. Each shipment will be yours to examine FREE for 10 days. If you decide to keep the books, you'll pay the preferred subscriber price (a savings of up to 30% off the cover price), plus shipping and handling. If you want us to stop sending books, just say the word… it's that simple.

FREE BOOK CERTIFICATE

Yes!

Please send me FREE Zebra Contemporary romance novels. I only pay $1.99 for shipping and handling. I understand that each month thereafter I will be able to preview 4 brand-new Contemporary Romances FREE for 10 days. Then, if I should decide to keep them, I will pay the money-saving preferred subscriber's price (that's a savings of up to 30% off the retail price), plus shipping and handling. I understand I am under no obligation to purchase any books, as explained on this card.

Name _____

Address _____ Apt._____

City _____ State _____ Zip _____

Telephone (____) _____

Signature _____

(If under 18, parent or guardian must sign)

Thank You!

Offer limited to one per household and not to current subscribers. Terms, offer and prices subject to change. Orders subject to acceptance by Zebra Contemporary Book Club. Offer Valid in the U.S. only.

CN095A

ll..l..l.....lll.....ll.l.l..l.l..l..l..l.l.....llll..l..lll..l

Zebra Contemporary Romance Book Club

Zebra Home Subscription Service, Inc.

P.O. Box 5214

Clifton , NJ 07015-5214

From the appearance of the premises, Mr. Abercrombie's clients were few, unless he also sold them dust and cobwebs. "I'm prepared to reimburse you handsomely for any services you might provide me."

Mr. Abercrombie's gaze moved from the reticule Emily was dangling in front of him to the wolf's sharp teeth. "Maybe just this once."

"Excellent! The transaction would have taken place during the past few days. A man of perhaps nine-and-twenty. Dark-haired. Pale. Well dressed. Michael Ross by name."

"Pfft!" Mr. Abercrombie held up a chubby hand. "No names. What a body doesn't know can't hurt him, I always say." He also said that a gentleman of that description had indeed recently purchased a *vrajă*, along with some yarrow, mastic pearls, and bloodstone.

Emily's spirits plummeted, foolishly, because the shopkeeper had only confirmed what she'd already suspected. She opened her reticule. Mr. Abercrombie lit up at the sight of her assorted charms. He especially admired the tiger's eye and the seal of St. Benedict. This was a young lady who knew her talismans. She was well protected.

His attention moved to the pendant. Well protected indeed. Perhaps the young lady might be interested in a spot of trade.

And perhaps the shopkeeper thought he might snatch the pendant off her neck. Emily raised her umbrella. Drogo growled. The raven croaked.

Mr. Abercrombie dropped his hand. "No offense intended, miss."

"None taken." Emily placed a gold coin on the counter. "Should the gentleman return, you won't tell him I was here."

"Mum as an oyster, miss." The shopkeeper radiated sincerity.

Came those flying pigs again. Given sufficient monetary motivation, Mr. Abercrombie's oysters would flap tongues hinged on both ends. Emily could only hope Michael wouldn't soon return here. And what did Ravensclaw mean to do with dragon's blood, which despite its intriguing name, was nothing but an herb? Emily was pondering this as she stepped back out into the close, along with the odd theory that sleeping with a wolf's head under one's pillow protected against nightmares, when she bumped up against a solid and very aromatic bulk.

"Och, now we have ye!" said the bulk, and grabbed her by the arms.

He was overly optimistic. Emily kicked him in the knee, then brought her umbrella down smartly on his head. Drogo leapt out from behind her to sink sharp teeth into the most convenient chunk of flesh.

"Ow! Ow! Ow!" wailed Oxter, and various other indecipherable remarks, interspersed with considerable profanity. "Get 'im aff me arse!" The shopkeeper stuck his head out the door to see what the commotion was about and as quickly retreated, a convenient deafness also being required of one in his line of work.

Emily pulled her little pistol from her pocket. "Well met, gentlemen. I had hoped to speak with the three of you. Drogo, release your captive and make sure none of them escape." Flight was clearly on the mind of at least the twitching man, who was pale as a ghost. "Let us introduce ourselves. As you may or may not know, I am Emily Dinwiddie." She gestured with the pistol. "And you are—?"

"Oxter," groaned Oxter.

"Mowdiewarp."

"Dinna—cannae—" muttered the third. Oxter gave him a clout on the head. "Tha's Twitcher. 'E's a dunderhead."

"Nae need t' be fashious, lass," soothed Mowdiewarp. "We meant ye nae harm."

"Nay." Oxter clutched his bleeding rump and nodded. "We dinna, but somebody else might."

"Awa', ye glaibit bastid!" snapped Mowdiewarp, whose peacemaking tendencies only went so far. " 'Tis but a misunderstanding. We've 'ad a wee drappie. I widna wonder if we was no' richt smeekit. No hard feelings. We'll just be on our way."

"No, you won't." Emily aimed the pistol at Oxter. "Not without telling me why the three of you are so set on accosting me."

Twitcher moaned. "It wis no' me, I dinna."

Oxter smacked him again. "The de'il will get ye for tellin' lies."

"Tha's enow clishmaclaver!" Mowdiewarp interrupted sternly, one eye fixed on Drogo, and the other on Emily's gun. "Twitcher's in a richt pelter, lass. Not t' mention he's a windae-licker. Pay nae mind t' anything he says. Noo aboot this wee stooshie—"

Twitcher might be embarrassed at having tossed the lass over his shoulder like a sack of potatoes, and also terrified by the vague notion that it would go the worse for him if he lay a hand on her; but there was only so much abuse a lad could take. "Wha ye callin' a windae-licker, ye eejit?" he demanded, and popped Mowdiewarp smack in the nose. Caught off guard, Mowdiewarp fell on his own arse, blood streaming down his face.

"Haud on, ye sumph!" snarled Oxter, and grabbed Twitcher by the arm. Twitcher took offense at being grabbed. Mowdiewarp climbed to his feet. A right stremach ensued. Emily and Drogo watched. Both came to the conclusion that Jamie's bajins were fools.

Fools with a mission. Emily raised her voice. "Stop that at once or I'll be forced to shoot one of you!"

Twitcher pointed at Oxter. Before he could voice the

suggestion that danced on the tip of his tongue, a tall figure appeared at the end of the close. Tall as a building, eyes as red as fire. A reluctant closer inspection, and Twitcher conceded that the eyes *weren't* red as fire. Yet.

The face was unnervingly familiar. Twitcher had a terrifying memory of sharp fangs. Threats involving livers and intestines. "Ah dinna ken ocht aboot it," he moaned, and sank into a swoon.

Emily was more interested in the newcomer than in her accostors, the other two of whom were cowering in the shadows of a building. She scowled at Drogo. "Traitor," she said.

Val clamped a strong hand on her shoulder, and squeezed. Emily dropped both pistol and umbrella. "I told you to pretend to be a nitwit, not to act like one," he snapped.

There was some justification for his comment. Not that Emily would admit it. She jerked her chin at the pendant. "I wasn't in any real danger. Look, it hasn't turned dark."

Twitcher stirred. Drogo, who was sitting guard, licked his face. Twitcher opened one eye, moaned, and scurried to join his comrades by the wall. All three were talking at once. Emily retrieved her pistol. "Now see what you've done!"

"What I've done is nothing like what I'd like to do. To you!" Ungently, Val tucked her under his arm.

A second figure appeared at the opening of the close. In the blink of an eye he was beside them. Oxter goggled and gasped as Cezar picked him up with one hand. "Wrens making prey, Miss Dinwiddie? Shall I pinch off this one's head?"

"Um." Emily was distracted. Val's body was solid against hers. Almost as solid as when she'd sat on his lap and licked his skin.

When he'd given her her first real kiss.

And then had tweaked her nose.

Emily kicked him. "No! Why is it you must meddle? I wished to speak with these men and find out who sent them after me—clearly someone did because they haven't a brain among them! There was no need for you to interfere."

Val released her to rub his shin. "How inconsiderate of us. And just when things were going so well."

Cezar gave the gibbering Oxter a shake. "You thought they would confide in you?"

Emily bent to pick up her umbrella and her pistol. "Don't bother to point out I can only shoot one of them."

"Oxter!" gasped Mowdiewarp. Twitcher agreed. Oxter struggled all the harder in Cezar's grasp.

Cezar tightened his fingers until the man's eyes bulged. "Perhaps you will allow us to assist you."

"*You* assist her," Val said coolly. "I'm still sulking. She called me a meddling male."

Emily frowned at him. "You're enjoying this too much."

"On the contrary, Miss Dinwiddie." Ravensclaw's smile was feral. "I'm not enjoying this at all."

He was truly angry with her. Emily felt like she'd been frozen by a blast of frigid arctic air. "Then go to the devil! I didn't invite you here." She turned to Cezar. "Yes, please."

Cezar loosened his grip so that Oxter could breathe, then fixed the man with his violet gaze. Oxter's face went blank and slack. His eyes rolled back in his head. A moment passed and Cezar released him. Twitcher moaned as Oxter flopped to the ground.

Emily bit her lip. "Will he be all right?"

"No, but he'll be no worse than we found him. This one knows nothing, not even how his instructions were received. He experienced them as a compulsion in his mind."

"Which is hardly a surprise." Val looked at the other two. "They know even less."

Emily disliked the look on Val's face. "Don't hurt them. As you say, they're merely dupes, and they did me no real harm." She glanced at Cezar. "Perhaps a strong suggestion that they find another line of work?"

"It's hardly that simple. I suspect their employer won't be happy that his plans were foiled." Oxter had wakened, and Cezar contemplated the quivering trio. "Perhaps we should implant some suggestions of our own."

"Such as that this never happened?" Val glanced at Twitcher. "I already tried that."

Twitcher clasped the top of his head. "Ye'll no' chop it off!"

Emily pushed up her spectacles. "No one's going to chop off your head. Why would you think that?"

"Bogeys!" wailed Twitcher, and buried his face in Mowdiewarp's coat.

Mowdiewarp patted him. " 'Twas no' these lads. Look ye, Twitcher, they're tae tall." His eyes narrowed. "Lest they can shrink themselves. *Thon* bogey wis shorter, smaller. We couldnae see his face, bein' as he wis wrapt in a dark cloak. An he glowed. Something in his hand."

"The athame," murmured Emily. Val and Cezar exchanged a glance. She opened her mouth, but Val frowned at her, and she closed it with a snap. If only he would tuck her up against him again. She was feeling unaccountably cold.

Cezar asked questions. They were answered. Unfortunately, the trio knew only that they had interrupted what they called a bogey at his work not far from there. Cezar sent them on their way with the understanding that they had neither seen Emily nor had this encounter, that they weren't going to see Emily again even if they fell smack on top of her. Looking even more than usually slack-jawed, the three of them shambled on down the close.

Cezar turned. "Perhaps you will explain how is that *you* can close your mind to us, Miss Dinwiddie."

Emily was feeling ill-used. "Perhaps I won't."

Two pairs of cold eyes rested on her. Drogo bumped against her knee. "Oh, very well! My papa taught me from the cradle how to shield my thoughts." She glared at Val. "So that no supersensible creature could make me his dupe."

"Enough." Val moved, and somehow the pistol was no longer in her hand, and her arm was in his grasp. Emily tried to jerk away from him. His fingers were like iron. "We're going home now, Miss Dinwiddie. Where I may very well lock you in the dungeon if you further annoy me."

Emily paused in her struggles to peer up into his face. Val looked as if he might well carry out his threat. "I've never experienced a real dungeon," she said, with genuine curiosity. "Does yours have a torture chamber? A scavenger's daughter? Thumbscrews?"

Val stared at her as if she had suddenly sprouted horns. Cezar murmured, " 'Where eagles dare not perch.' "

Chapter Twenty

Better some of a pudding than none of a pie.
(Romanian proverb)

Lady Alberta frowned at Val over the top of her teacup. "Tsk!" she said.

Val closed his eyes against the pain of the first headache he'd had in decades. "Tsk?"

Lady Alberta selected another piece of shortbread. "It was not well done of you to make Emily cry, Ravensclaw."

Granted Val had lost his temper, also for the first time in decades. Granted he had said things perhaps better left unsaid. Even so, surely the most critical of observers must admit he'd had sufficient provocation to test the patience of a saint.

Apparently not. The various members of his household were treating him as if he carried the plague. Zizi, Bela, and Lilian had given him a collective cold shoulder, while Isidore informed him sternly that no garden was without its weeds. Jamie had damn near dumped the tea tray in his lap. All this despite the fact they had all been so caught up in helping—or in the case of Lady Alberta, hindering—Mrs. MacCamish create a hotchpotch that Emily had been able to slip away unnoticed.

Lady Alberta was still glowering. Val bowed to the inevitable. "Where is she?"

"In your study." Lady Alberta pushed the tea tray toward him. "A peace offering might be in order. I know for a certainty Emily has had nothing to eat today."

Val picked up the tray. Now Emily's refusal to take sustenance was his responsibility. He supposed he would also be blamed for whatever folly she might next commit.

Not that he could fairly fault her for impatience. It must seem to Emily that he'd done little, though she'd begged for his help. Life—or his existence—had been simple once, before Miss Dinwiddie came knocking at his castle gate. Val climbed the stair and pushed open the study door.

Emily sat at the long oak table, the *Grimorium Verum* open before her. Sunlight struggling through the ancient windows turned her untidy hair into a fiery halo. Machka was curled up by her elbow. Drogo sprawled at her feet.

Even the animals regarded him with disfavor. Val set down the tea tray. "Out," he said. Drogo padded toward the doorway, giving him a wide berth.

"You, too." Val picked up Machka and deposited her in the stairway. When he turned back Emily had risen from the chair. "Not you," he said. She sat back down. He closed and locked the door.

"Lady Alberta thought you might care for some tea." Emily shook her head, her gaze fixed firmly on the grimoire.

She was a picture of misery, her eyes shadowed behind her spectacles, her cheeks so pale her freckles stood out like ink spots, her nose reddened by weeping. As Val watched, a tear trickled down her cheek.

He moved toward her. Emily looked up with a combination of defiance and dread. Val plucked her up out of the chair and sat down, holding her on his lap. She was stiff as a fence post. He set aside her glasses and pulled her against his chest.

Gradually, she relaxed against him. He waited patiently. Finally a gruff little voice said, "It wasn't an accident, was it. Papa's death."

It wasn't a question. Val said, "Your father was ordinarily a very careful man."

Emily was silent for a moment. "You don't have a dungeon. You lied to me again."

"I do have a dungeon. It just isn't here." If only he could take her back to Corby Castle and lock her in the dungeon and let the rest of the world go and be damned.

Though Emily had her feelings firmly closed to him, she moved one hand to rest against Val's chest. "I suppose you expect me to apologize."

"For what?"

"You said I was a nitwit. Among other things."

"I said you *acted* like a nitwit. As for those other things—" Val rested his chin on the top of her head. "I was frightened for you."

A pause while Emily considered this. "Were you, really?"

"Yes."

Emily hesitated. Val felt her reach out to touch his mind. He lowered his guard and let her in. She was cautious, like a babe taking its first steps, exploring the parameters of this new world. It was charming and almost unbearably sensual. Val tamped down his emotions, and let her poke around.

She withdrew, shifted in his lap so that she might see his face. "I'm not supposed to be able to do that, am I?"

"No." Her soft little bottom was snuggled against him. Val stroked one hand along her spine.

His touch was immensely soothing, and Emily leaned back against him. "I know from my reading that for each *vampir* there is an *ailaltă*, one destined other, who must be proven worthy by meeting a challenge, a *provocare*. Rather like a knight of old slaying a dragon for his lady. Which I used to think so much poppycock." She paused. How to delicately phrase it? "Since you and I have a special affinity, I wonder ... perhaps I am your *ailaltă*."

The idea of Emily slaying dragons for him chilled Val to his toes. "I suspect this 'affinity' you mention is more likely because your ancestress and I—well."

Emily had expected it would take him some time to become accustomed to the notion. However—

She squirmed around to stare at him. "You and Is—"

"Don't say that name! I'm afraid we did. Curiosity seems to run rampant in the female members of your family."

"I suppose it does." And what better moment in which to indulge it? Emily reached out and tentatively touched his lower lip; ran the tips of her fingers over his cheeks, along his jaw, drifting low over his throat.

Val held very still, and contemplated thwarted lust. If she didn't soon stop caressing him, Miss Dinwiddie would find out for herself if vampires wept tears of blood.

Before he realized what she was about, Emily sat up, grabbed his letter opener and slashed her arm. Val stared at the red ribbon flowing across her pale skin. "I have come to the conclusion that if one wants something, one shouldn't sit about waiting for it to fall into one's lap. Taste me," she said.

He truly didn't wish to. Rather, he wished to—Val hadn't experienced this ravening a thirst in all his countless years—but he tried very hard to refrain. And then Emily raised her bleeding arm to his lips, and the barriers between them came crashing down.

Val groaned and surrendered to his nature. Emily

watched wide-eyed as he licked away the blood, then pressed his mouth against her flesh.

Her pleasure curled through him, her heat. Her heart sped up as his hunger shot through her, shocking and intense.

He bent to kiss her. Emily's mouth was soft beneath his, eager, warm. Val bit gently at her lip. Nuzzled at her neck. His teeth found her pulse—

I am willing. Drink from me.

Those simple words stopped him. Val drew back, appalled at what he'd almost done.

Emily's disappointment washed over him. She looked bereft. Val ran his thumb over her soft lower lip. "You don't want to do this."

"Why can't you understand? Of course I do." Emily caught his hand. "I may not be experienced, but I know from my own reading that for you to drink the blood of another is the ultimate intimacy. *Dissertation on the Bloodsucking Dead,* 1732."

Val was stunned. She trusted him. He couldn't remember how long it had been since he'd been given someone's trust.

Not something he'd missed, trust, and the responsibility that accompanied it. Val clamped his teeth together and his sharp fangs nicked his lip.

"You're bleeding." Emily caught the trickling liquid on her fingers and raised them to her mouth.

Val *was* a blood-drinker, albeit a regretful (at least in this moment) one, and it was beyond his power to stop Emily from this highly erotic act. It was barely within his power to stop himself from leaping on her and sinking his fangs into her tender throat. "You don't know what you're asking," he growled.

"Piffle!" said Emily. "You're being noble again. I wish you wouldn't do that."

Val looked at his blood smeared on her lips. Watched her pink little tongue lick it away. Looked into her gold-flecked eyes. Lovely eyes without her glasses. She blinked owlishly at him and he felt himself falling into those warm, gold-flecked depths.

Had she somehow ensnared him?

He knew the folly of underestimating a Dinwiddie. Emily was a Dinwiddie, after all.

The devil with it. Val touched his fingers to the pulse beating so rapidly, so richly, at the base of her throat. Emily clasped his shoulders, arched her neck. Val leaned closer, and—

A throat cleared: "Ahem!" Emily's eyes jerked open to stare at the apparition that had appeared atop the desk. Val bit back a curse.

Emily fumbled for her spectacles. "You didn't tell me that this house was haunted. Why ever not?"

She sounded cross, as if he'd withheld some great treat. "Because it wasn't," Val replied. "Until recently."

Emily studied the apparition. "Did one of the castle ghosts follow you here? It doesn't look like a Gowkit Gordie or a Kiuttlin' Kate."

Val's headache had returned, threefold. "Meet Ana," he said.

Emily's eyes widened. "Your wife?"

Ana jiggled one faint foot. "Where are your manners, girl? Don't you know it's rude to talk about me as if I weren't here? Not to mention sitting on my husband's lap."

Emily was exactly where he wanted her. Val tightened his grip. She squirmed. He winced.

Emily glanced reproachfully at him then returned her attention to Ana. "You poor thing! Doomed to wander through eternity until your death is avenged."

"Avenged?" Ana attempted, unsuccessfully, to filch a

piece of shortbread. "Oh, I took care of *that*! Oko was set upon by wild dogs on his way to the *souk,* may he fester in his grave."

Emily realized she was hungry, and snagged a piece of shortbread for herself. "Then why are you still here?"

"Everyone wants to get rid of me! Well, you shan't. Not until I've been tupped." Ana considered. "And maybe not even then."

"Tupped?"

"You know. Tup. Swive. Dance at the buttock ball." Ana caught Emily's blank look. "How simple can I make it? A man has a pizzle. A manroot. Like a maid has—"

"Don't say it!" Emily's sensibilities were far from delicate, but some things really shouldn't be said out loud. "I understand."

Ana tilted her head. "It appears to me, Valentin, that you've lost your touch. Mayhap vampires don't—"

"I assure you vampires *do*. Unless uninvited guests take it into their heads to interfere." For which he should probably be grateful, but frustration had him in its claws.

Emily was still mulling over possibilities. "You *are* referring to the amorous congress?"

"Call it what you wish! You're welcome to him, miss whoever-you-are, as soon as he gives me what I want. And until he *does*—" Ana shook a ghostly finger. "I intend to see there's no tupping hereabouts."

Emily looked at Val. *This is why you wanted the dragon's blood.*

It is.

But just think what we can learn from her!

"Bloody hell!" muttered Val.

Chapter Twenty-One

A crow is never whiter for washing herself often.
(Romanian proverb)

Emily was very eager to have further conversation with her first ghost. She had many questions to ask. For example, where had Ana been between the time of her demise and her reappearance in Ravensclaw's study? What had she been doing, and who with? Not that—the hereafter being doubtless a very large place—Emily imagined Ana had come across her Papa. And if all that was not enough to occupy her mind, there was the revelation that Ravensclaw and Isobella Dinwiddie had had intimate relations of some sort.

Isobella had had intimate relations with any number of gentlemen, from all accounts. Emily supposed she should have guessed that Ravensclaw might have been among them. However, she hadn't, and the discovery made her cross.

Gaining Ravensclaw's cooperation had been her original purpose. Cooperation concerning the matter of the vanished athame. Now, however, Emily preferred that he cooperate with her in this neck-nibbling business.

Maybe she wasn't womanly enough to keep his interest. Although she had caught it briefly, and what a revelation that had been. Then she had as abruptly lost it. Emily retitled her adventure. *The Perplexing Problem of the Prudent Fiend.*

What in heaven was she thinking? Ravensclaw was a vampire. A vampire who in this particular moment was very gracefully waltzing with Lisbet Boroi. Lisbet wore a gown made from a cashmere scarf, with a scalloped bottom and split oversleeves, and a broad, low neckline which left most of her shoulders bare. Perhaps it was Lisbet who was Val's *ailaltă*, in which case Emily had made a cake of herself. Cezar and his shadow, Andrei, were nowhere in sight. She hoped they were searching for the athame. Lady Alberta rapped Emily's wrist with her fan. "You're staring, dear."

So she was, and why shouldn't she? Every other female in the Assembly Rooms was doing the same thing. Val's dark coat was molded to his broad shoulders, and his breeches to his thighs. His auburn hair, tied back with its velvet thong, gleamed in the candlelight. Add golden skin, high cheekbones, deep blue eyes, and that passionate mouth . . . he looked handsome as Adonis, and wicked as sin.

He was also smiling at Lisbet in an annoyingly intimate manner. "Tell me, Lady Alberta, what do you see when you look at Ravensclaw?"

Lady Alberta glanced at the dancers. "An extraordinarily handsome gentleman who has every female in the vicinity panting after him. We can hardly fault him for enjoying it. Dear, do you feel quite well?"

Ravensclaw was as he was without the use of *glamour,* unless he knew how to alter perception on a monumental scale, and the overseer of the Dinwiddie Society was no different from any other female. Or perhaps a little different: she *had* offered herself up to Ravensclaw like a plump piglet on a platter, and he'd turned her down. Although perhaps he might not have, if not for the interference of his dead wife.

Tupping, indeed. Emily's education was proceeding in leaps and bounds. She knew she wasn't the sort of female to attract a gentleman's attention in the normal way of things, and since the man, if not gentle—and, for that matter, not a man—was the most gloriously masculine creature she'd ever set eyes upon, and since he could cause her to practically dissolve in pleasure by merely looking at her—

Lady Alberta nudged her. "Emily?"

"Oh. I'm quite well, thank you. Merely a little overwhelmed. There are so many people here." Emily gestured vaguely at the glittering throng. Lady Alberta glittered a bit herself tonight in a gown with gold banding, additional gold rope trim on her neckline, the scooped edges of her overskirt, and the ends of her short sleeves. Assured that Emily wasn't going to swoon amid the crush of bodies, Lady Alberta resumed her lecture on Edinburgh, which had been founded nine hundred and ninety years before the birth of Christ, or alternately in 330 B.C., and had definitely been given a Royal Charter in 1329. Emily wondered just how long Ravensclaw had made his home there.

She surveyed the ballroom. Sparkling crystal chandeliers reflected in mirrors at each end of the long chamber. A sea of dancers dipped and swayed to the music of the orchestra, and an astonishing number of young men had already asked Emily to dance, or if they might escort her to dinner, or call on her tomorrow, or at the very least fetch her a glass of lemonade, all of whom she'd sent away with the excuse that she was still in mourning, and therefore it wouldn't be fitting for her to engage in such frivolity.

"Gracious!" murmured Lady Alberta, as one more suitor was sent to the rightabout. "You are all the crack. How strange. I mean—"

"I know exactly what you mean," retorted Emily. "And it is."

Lady Alberta watched as yet another gentleman prepared to assault the citadel. "Unless they have all heard a certain rumor."

"What rumor?"

Lady Alberta leaned closer. "Fifty thousand pounds."

"Damn and blast!" said Emily, then lowered her voice, not that it was necessary: what in a mere miss would have been considered uncommonly rude was in a considerable heiress thought refreshingly frank. "No wonder everyone is emptying the butter dish over me. I think I shall strangle Ravensclaw, because I can't imagine Michael let the cat out of the bag, and who else would know?"

Michael Ross might well have put about any number of rumors if he sought relief from impatient creditors. Lady Alberta murmured, "You're certain you'll find him here?"

Emily frowned so severely at a hopeful young gentleman that he abruptly changed direction and headed for the refreshment table, where he sought solace for his failure to recite a poem he'd composed in honor of the heiress's eyebrows. "Michael must marry well, I think, for all his fine appearance. He will have a contingency plan in case he can't bring me to the sticking point."

"And what better place to survey the field than the Assembly Rooms." Lady Alberta turned her head, causing the plume in her turban to quiver as if wafting in a gentle breeze. It had been a most interesting evening thus far, with Emily advising one admirer to stop talking like a nodcock, and another to pray not stare like a stuck pig. "Forgive my presumption, but you *are* wealthy, then?"

"Less wealthy than before Ravensclaw started buying my clothing—and I shall repay him, so don't raise your eyebrows at me." Tonight Emily wore another of Val's selections, a dark gown with a draped bodice, and an underskirt peeping out from the knees down. Ravensclaw possessed excellent taste, which wasn't surprising, considering how long he'd had to develop his aesthetic sense.

Folly, to contemplate Val's experience with women's wardrobes, especially now when Emily strove to appear brisk and businesslike. "The Society—that is, my family has done well on the Exchange. We invested in a company that financed Sir Francis Drake's piratical attacks on Spanish commerce. We also made a fortune in tulip stocks and at the same time obtained some splendid specimens, including an Admiral Kiefken and a Semper Augustus, and most precious of all, the Viceroy. Even more important, we were fortunate enough to avoid the South Sea Bubble." Lady Alberta's expression was astonished, so Emily didn't go on to explain that she herself knew a great deal about Interest, Discounts and Transfers; Tables and Debentures and Shares. Her feet in their pretty slippers ached.

The waltz gave way to Scottish country dances, and still Val remained on the dance floor. Set to and turn corners . . . Emily wished she might see Lisbet strike her hands and give three jumps. Even more, she wished she might see Lisbet jump off the Castle Rock.

Lady Alberta broke off complaining about a gasworks in the Canongate that had a chimney more than three hundred feet high. "Here comes your friend. I believe I shall visit the supper room." She whisked herself away.

Michael looked quite the fashionable young gentleman. Emily wondered who his tailor was, and if the poor man had been paid.

He made a stiff little bow. "Emily. You are still in mourning, so I won't ask if you care to dance."

Emily glanced at the dancers, who were now attempting to bump elbows together, first the right and then the left. Lisbet and Val were no longer in sight. Emily hoped they too had gone to the supper room instead of discreetly retiring for a different sort of snack. "You haven't yet told me what brought you home to Edinburgh."

Nor was Michael about to tell her, since it had to do with his creditors, who were partially appeased by the rumor of his fiancée's wealth, though some took leave to doubt she *was* his fiancée, while others were laying wagers on whether he could bring her up to snuff. "Family business. A small disagreement. It has been resolved."

Emily took his arm. "I distinctly remember you telling Papa you don't have a family."

"I don't, in the usual sense of the word. What does it matter? I'm here, you're here. What did you want to talk about?" She was acting entirely too much like a proper young lady. Michael didn't trust this unusually sweet-tempered Emily one inch.

The man grew more and more annoying. Emily wished she might punch him, like Twitcher had punched Mowdiewarp, right in the nose. Then she wondered about the troublesome trio, and hoped they'd come to no harm on her account.

Michael tried to draw away. Emily tightened her grip. Michael was shorter than both Val and Cezar. She could hardly ask if he was going around removing heads. However, she *could* ask if he was acquainted with Oxter, Twitcher, and Mowdiewarp, and did.

Just as Michael had suspected, Emily was in one of her

odd humors. "What maggot have you taken into your head?"

Emily thought perhaps he was telling the truth, although it was impossible to tell. Most women had to avert their gaze when lying. Men could look a person right in the eye. "Never mind. You look tired, Michael. Have you been burning the candle at both ends?"

"What would it matter if I did?" he snapped, then forced an apologetic smile. "Maybe you do care for me a little, if you're concerned about my welfare. I've been having abominable headaches."

Emily was also concerned about the welfare of the three corkbrains who were so determined to abduct her. She didn't point this out. Michael didn't appear eager to broach the matter of their union, so she said, "Do you still wish to marry me, Michael?"

He gaped at her. "Have you finally come to your senses, then?"

Emily pinched him. "That was hardly romantic."

"I'm not—" Michael paused, and took a breath. "Emily, be my wife."

Emily had already known she was not the sort of female to inspire ardent declarations. Why, then, was she suddenly depressed?

On with business! Emily fluttered her eyelashes and recalled her practice session with Val. "You do me great honor, Michael. I hadn't realized you held me in such esteem. Pray forgive me if I don't give you my answer right away. We helpless—Um! I will require some time to focus my mind."

Michael was still staring at her. "How could you not know how I feel about you? And you've never required any time to focus your mind before. Why are you blinking like that? Is there something in your eye?"

So much for lash-fluttering. "*And* I know you purchased a *vrajă* from Mr. Abercrombie! Perhaps you might like to explain?"

Now they came down to it. "No, I wouldn't! I suppose you still think I had something to do with that attack on you."

Emily studied him. "Actually, I don't."

Michael felt bewildered, a not unusual condition for him when dealing with Emily. "Have you found your knife?" he asked. "I'm still not sure about that cow's milk bit."

Emily for her part was sure of nothing. She was relieved when Lady Alberta rejoined them, and drew Michael into conversation about Arthur's Seat and the old Tolbooth, the Luckenbooths and the Krames. Emily gripped Michael's arm all the harder when she saw Lisbet and Val making their way toward them.

Michael glanced irritably at her. "Why are you clutching at me?" His eyes narrowed. "Your pendant has turned dark."

Emily lowered her head and squinted down her nose. So the pendant had. It had also grown warm. Neither of which were particularly helpful since she was in the middle of a large crowd. "Gracious!" said Lady Alberta. "Does that mean something, dear?"

It meant she was indeed a nitwit for being without her pistol. Emily would have to rely on her wits. Precisely how, she wasn't certain. She adjusted her spectacles.

Lisbet's voice reached them. "You've been neglecting me. Leaving me too much to my own devices. You know how much I dislike that, Val."

"I haven't entirely neglected you." Val smiled down at her. "May I remind you of the other night? As for abandoning you to your own devices, some bothersome details have taken up my time."

So she was a bothersome detail? Emily's cheeks

burned. When she thought of how she'd behaved . . . although he *had* been the one to set her in his lap.

Emily imagined Val had done a great deal more to Lisbet than set her in his lap. There was little question of what "haven't entirely" meant. Val's glance flickered indifferently over her and away.

It felt as if he'd plunged a knife into her heart.

Peawit! Cabbagehead! Beetlebrain!

Michael frowned at her. "Emily?"

"Michael, I've made my decision. I will marry you."

Emily had spoken loudly enough that everyone in the vicinity overheard. Lisbet appeared mildly interested. Val looked distinctly annoyed. Michael recovered from his astonishment to raise her hands to his lips.

Oh, Lord, what had she done? Lady Alberta poked her with a discreet elbow and whispered, "Smile!"

Chapter Twenty-Two

When you are an anvil, hold you still;
When you are a hammer, strike your fill.
(Romanian proverb)

The skirt of Emily's voluminous dressing gown swished across the bedroom carpet. Late though the hour was—or, more precisely, early—she was unable to sleep. She had tried to pass the time in reading, had learned that to protect herself from danger she should carry the tip of a calf's tongue; that safety in battle was achieved by rubbing oneself all over with leeks; that one's home might be protected from witches by hanging the diseased leg of a calf near the hearth, or keeping a bull's heart stuck with pins in the chimneypiece; had finally flung the book into the fireplace and with some satisfaction watched it burn. That would show Val. *What* it would show him was uncertain, unless that it was that Emily could behave as badly as anyone.

The rest of the household had long since retired, after she had bid them to the devil for their protectiveness. Only Machka remained, less to keep vigil, Emily suspected, than because the cat was loath to give up her warm spot in the center of the bed. She walked to the window. Dawn would soon be nigh. Emily most definitely didn't want to think about Ravensclaw and what he might be doing in the hours since they'd left the Assembly Rooms.

Didn't want to think about it, but couldn't help herself. Emily indulged in a string of oaths that would have distracted even her papa from his studies. Machka twitched one ear and buried her nose beneath her tail.

Men! What blessed use were they? *Vampir* or not, in that regard Ravensclaw was very much a man. Emily no sooner suggested she was his *ailaltă* than he decided to marry her off to someone else, because what other reason could he have had to noise her fortune about? And where had he come up with the figure of fifty thousand pounds? Which, truth be told, somewhat understated the case. Emily picked up a pillow and threw it at the wall, then plopped down in a chair and glared at her open door. She was determined to waylay Val the moment he set foot upon the stair.

Unaware of the freckled fury awaiting him—although he surely would have been, had he opened his mind to her, which he had no intention of doing, because he was very cross—Val walked through the late-night streets. First Emily had declared herself his *ailaltă*, then betrothed herself to Michael Ross. Val didn't know which made him more out of charity with her.

Yes, he'd wanted her to marry. He'd even thought he might influence her choice. Although, now that he'd looked over the prospects, he had to admit the field of eligibles was thin. One of Emily's new admirers was a close-fisted clunch, another a corny-faced cod's head, a third a lascivious old goat. The unmarried gentlemen of Edinburgh might have been astonished to discover that Ravensclaw considered them all twiddle-poops, beau nastys, and jaw-me-deads. Val might have been amused to discover himself so high a stickler, had not his sense of humor abandoned him.

The air was chill, not that the weather concerned him much. Though Val's senses were acute, he was largely impervious to extremes of heat and cold, the latter most common to this city, which lay a scant mile from the sea. On a rainy night like this, Edinburgh seemed a strange piling up of rocks, with roads rushing downhill like rivers, and buildings soaring up to the sky as if spit out by the old volcano on which the city had been built. Val remembered when Heriot's Hospital had been erected, the first stone laid for the North Bridge. When the Old Town had been a fashionable address, instead of the dangerous and overcrowded slum it was now becoming, the muddy, crowded closes sloping away from the High Street home to poverty-stricken immigrants. When the narrow passages between the tall medieval houses had doubled as sewers and cess-pits, and it had been forbidden to empty waste into the street until the curfew bell rang at ten o'clock.

Sometimes progress was for the better. Val was unlikely to forget how Edinburgh had smelled. "The Athens of the North," they called it now. Auld Reekie the city had been, and to Val always would be.

As for progress, perhaps gangs of apprentices, the youngest of them as little as twelve years old, no longer roamed the streets at night, to bludgeon and rob anyone unlucky enough to cross their path. Instead, factory boys had their earlobes nailed to a board if too many of the spikes they produced were bent, while in the Lothian mines young women hauled coal carts through the suffocating darkness using harnesses that twisted them into hunchbacks. Val hadn't needed Emily to tell him of the plight of chimneysweeps. He could hardly be unaware of the vast injustices in the world, having had more than ample time to observe them all. However, he didn't know what he might do about such things. It had not previously occurred to him that he *should* do something, his kind surely being exempt from any other civic responsibility than not draining away the life of one of mankind's benefactors.

He doubted Emily would agree. Which, since Val was at the moment in huge disagreement with Emily, only seemed fair.

What the devil had she been thinking, to betroth herself to Michael Ross? Oh, he knew *what* she'd been thinking, because he'd heard it clearly, although he was uncertain whether "peawit," "cabbagehead," and "beetle-brain" applied to her or to himself. He even understood her reasoning; she thought her fiancé might be persuaded to confide in her.

He also understood her motivation. Emily had overheard the excuses he made to Lisbet. Val's expression was grim as he opened his front door and found no one standing guard. It turned even grimmer when Emily popped up in the stairwell like a ghost. Val was somewhat sensitive on the subject of ghosts at the moment. And surely he hadn't spent good money on that shroud of a night-rail.

She got in the first blow. "Pray tell me what the *devil* were you thinking when you put it out that I'm an heiress, you—you toad!"

Val found his own mood perversely improving: Emily was fit to murder him. He picked her up and carried her, mightily protesting, into her room. There he dropped her in the middle of the bed. Machka opened one eye, glared at the pair of them, and went back to sleep.

Emily pushed up her glasses. Ravensclaw was in her bedchamber. The novel experience of a male in her bedchamber cooled her ire a little bit.

Only a little bit, however. Emily struggled upright among her pillows. "I passed *such* a charming evening, thanks to you. Have you any idea what it's like to be besieged by lovesick swains—sick of love for my pocketbook, that is! I am very displeased, Ravensclaw. I think I shall scream until I am purple in the face."

"Please don't." Val seated himself a prudent distance from her in the chair. "Think what Isidore would say."

She was being childish, and enjoying every moment of it. Emily wondered why it was so much more pleasant to misbehave than the opposite. "Isidore informed me earlier that those who eat cherries with great persons must expect to have their eyes squirted out with the stones. *Why* did you do it, Val?"

He wasn't entirely certain. What had seemed a splendid notion at the time seemed remarkably wrongheaded now. "Perhaps I wished to see you comfortably bestowed?"

"And perhaps you wished to entertain yourself." Emily pointed an accusing finger. "I understand you, Ravensclaw."

Val wasn't so lackwitted as to answer that accusation. "Speaking of cork-brained behavior, you're the one who's on the verge of being leg-shackled to Michael Ross."

"That was because—" Emily broke off.

"I know what it was because of," retorted Val. "And it makes me fit to murder *you*. I told you already that Lisbet is of no consequence."

No consequence, was it? So where had he spent the evening? Emily sniffed. And then she fervently hoped that in that moment Val hadn't glimpsed her thoughts. "I'm not going to marry Michael," she said, in an attempt to reclaim her dignity. "I just wanted him to think I was. Perhaps he will confide in me if he believes I'm to be his wife."

Cezar thought Emily was using Michael Ross as a diversionary tactic, a smoke screen of sorts. Val did not. If Emily couldn't draw the young man out—Val wouldn't further insult her by denying her the opportunity, even if he could, a point that was debatable—then Val would take steps of his own.

She was regarding him suspiciously. "Did you flutter your eyelashes?" Val asked.

"And simper like a ninny? I'm afraid I did nothing the way we rehearsed it. I merely said I'd marry him. Poor Michael was no little bit shocked."

Poor Michael, indeed. Within grasp of a tidy fortune, only to have it snatched away. And it *would* be snatched away. If Emily didn't break off the betrothal, Val would do it for her.

Val marveled at himself. From whence had come this dog-in-the-manger attitude? This feeling of protective possessiveness? He could not remember when he'd last felt this way. Not for Ana, certainly; and sometime in the countless years since then, he had ceased to care. One willing body had been much like another, and although he enjoyed them all, he had also known that any interaction would be temporary, because of what he was.

Emily was broadening his horizons. Pillowy breasts and quivering thighs were all fine in their place, but in time a man grew hungry for something different. Specifically, a stubborn, brown-eyed, redheaded temptress whom he couldn't have. Whom he would have taken anyway, and the consequences be damned, if not for the interference of a certain ghost.

Val supposed he should be grateful to Ana. He wasn't. Val was in charity with no one. He rose from his chair.

Emily looked very small perched on the edge of the bed. The sight of her would have tugged at his heartstrings, had he any, which he didn't. At least, he wasn't supposed to. Val took her cold fingers in his. "I apologize for my high-handedness. In the future, I promise not to act in what I consider your best interests without consulting you first."

Emily eyed him warily. "Very well. Then I suppose I must apologize also, for calling you a toad."

"Toad is the least of the things I have been called, elfling." Val patted her hand, then released it. "Now I will bid you a good night."

Emily watched him walk out of the room and close the door behind him, then lay back beside Machka on the bed. She could imagine what Val had been called, and how often, for aberrations had been lurking in the shadows of mankind ever since Adam's first wife coupled with fallen angels near the Red Sea.

How very strange it was. An entire other race of beings lived side-by-side with humans, and still the authorities didn't believe such things existed outside the pages of Mr. Polidori's sensational story. Despite the evidence right beneath their noses. Gilles de Rais, Eszsébet Bathoy, Vlad Tempes: it was much easier to believe in human evil than in vampires. Humankind was very good at believing what it wished.

Including herself. Emily crawled beneath the covers and chose to believe that Ravensclaw would in time come to realize that she was indeed his *ailaltă*, his eternal consort. She was smiling as she fell asleep.

Chapter Twenty-Three

Two sparrows on one ear of corn make an ill agreement.
(Romanian proverb)

Princes Street—named for the sons of King George III when His Majesty had objected to christening it after the patron saint of the city, St. Giles—divided the Old Town from the New, below it the filled-in Nor' Loch. Only the wealthy lived here, on the one side of the street where building was permitted: the residents could afford to insure nothing spoiled their panoramic view. Cezar Korzha was among those residents, his home a surprisingly plain house of three stories and a basement with a small garden behind where he had constructed a conservatory in which he experimented with exotic plants. Stables and a coach-house entered from the mews lane at the rear.

Lisbet slipped out of the house into the dark and dismal day. She seldom had a chance to be alone, and wanted no company on her current errand. Princes Street to the intersection at Lothian Way, past St. Cuthbert's Kirkyard with its lichen-encrusted markers and trees, the round tower erected for the watchers who attempted to protect the place from resurrectionists; towering Edinburgh Castle, another reminder of the mortality of man, for a hill-fort settlement had been built on that summit as long ago as 850 B.C. . . . how dreary it all was. Lisbet disliked this filthy, stinking city of stones and lime and dung, where ancient buildings shut out the light of heaven, and tall rocks frowned all around; where well-dressed, seemingly respectable women walked barefoot in the street, among laborers recently arrived from country villages, still reeking of the animals with which they cohabited, and remarkably ugly fishwives sang as they tramped to market carrying enormous loads across their chest. It was vastly different from Budapest, Vienna, Moscow.

However, circumstances required that she instead be in Edinburgh, where she was being sadly overlooked. Her host had more interest in his conservatory than in her, Cezar's current enthusiasm being cycads, an ancient group of plants (so he had informed her) that were growing when dinosaurs ruled the planet; although he also had a curiosity about Gesneriaceae and Zingiberaceae. Lisbet had left him with his nose deep in *The Botanical Register: or, Ornamental flower-garden and shrubbery; consisting of coloured figures of plants and shrubs, cultivated in British gardens; accompanied by their history, best method of treatment in cultivation, propagation, etc.*, a golf club propped against his chair. Andrei had little more conversation than a turtle, though he was immensely prettier to observe. His main interest was in warfare. Lisbet knew far more than she wished about the battle strategies of ancient China, including "Hide the Dagger Behind a Smile," "Lure Your Enemy Onto the Roof, Then Take Away the Ladder," and "Tie Silk Blossoms to the Dead Tree." Their preoccupations she didn't mind. However, Lisbet felt far differently about Val, whose passion was for pleasure, and whose enthusiasm had been sadly lacking of late.

Only a fool would expect fidelity from Ravensclaw.

Lisbet was no fool, nor was she in the practice of fidelity herself. However, that Val should neglect her for a dab of a girl put her hugely out of humor. It had been plain as the perfect nose on Lisbet's face that news of Emily Dinwiddie's betrothal had struck him a blow.

Lisbet arrived at her destination, a certain *modiste*'s establishment. She pushed open the shop door and stepped inside, interrupting the dressmaker in the totting-up of her monthly accounts, an undertaking that was not turning out at all well.

Astonishing, how one's outgo could outpace one's income, despite one's best efforts. If matters continued as they were going, Mme. Fanchon—*née* simple Franny Brown—would be forced to make severe economies. Just *what* economies, she was uncertain, since she had already given up chocolate and having butter on her bread. Therefore, when the shop door opened to admit an elegant visitor in a stone-colored walking dress trimmed with swansdown and a black sealskin hat, black kid half-boots, and York tan gloves, carrying a huge matching sealskin muff, her spirits greatly improved. She shoved her post-obit bills into a drawer, pushed back her chair, and rose to greet her visitor with a smile.

That smile continued, broadened even, through an inspection of silks and muslins and cambrics, a perusal of hand-colored fashion-plates. Indeed, so great was her excitement that Franny almost forgot her accent, and had to fan herself.

Lisbet leaned back in her chair. Persons of this sort were easy to manage. It only required a clever mind, a degree of guile, and the lure of a handsome profit. She felt rather like she was dangling a bunch of carrots in front of a hungry rabbit. "Now I will give you the word with no bark on it," she said, interrupting Franny's paean to jaconet and lutestring. "You shall turn me out in the first stare of fashion on one condition. Tell me how it came about that you are dressing Emily Dinwiddie, for of course you *are* dressing her. I recognized your handiwork. And I know you are costuming Lady Alberta Tait as well."

Franny's brief spurt of optimism faded. Good fortune had not smiled on her of late, Ravensclaw's generous patronage having only gone so far toward defraying her expenses. She had been optimistic in thinking it might smile on her today.

"Mademoiselle Dinwiddie," she echoed, in an effort to buy time, her clients not being in the habit of liking their business bandied about town. Especially the gentlemen. Ravensclaw's generosity would only go so far.

Franny did not wish to make him cross. The opposite, in fact. Ravensclaw made her almost wish she was a dollymop instead of a respectable woman of business, so that he might perhaps express his generosity in another way. Were Ravensclaw the type of gentleman to take a woman into his keeping—and why should he when he had only to look at a female to have her petticoats up around her ears?—Franny might have been tempted to toss her own bonnet over the windmill.

But he wasn't, and she wouldn't, and Lisbet Boroi sat in her salon, looking lovely, and determined, and dangerous as a snake poised to strike. *"Je m'excuse?"*

Lisbet revised her opinion. Mme. Fanchon was not a rabbit, but a fox. "I am not at all stupid, *madame*. Tell me what I wish to know or not only will you not gain my patronage, you will lose your other customers as well."

Franny knew when to cut her losses. *"Ah ça!* Now I recall. Ravensclaw summoned me to his house. The *demoiselle* required an entire wardrobe. Morning dresses, evening dresses, walking dresses. Petticoats and stockings, shawls and scarves, half-boots and satin slippers, an entire rainbow of gloves." Franny sighed in memory of her commission, and reflected shrewdly that it was Ravensclaw's interest in Emily Dinwiddie that was causing her visitor to have fits.

"It must have quite a challenge for you," murmured Lisbet. "That hair. Those freckles. While not precisely an antidote, or fubsy faced, the chit is merely passable."

Franny thought Mme. Boroi was perhaps a trifle severe. Wisely she kept this reflection to herself. "Ravensclaw said he wished to make her 'presentable.' Although he also said he already considered her to be perfection. Ravensclaw is a most polite gentleman, *n'est ce pas?*"

Her visitor shot her a sharp glance. Franny picked up a length of ribbon and ran it through her fingers. "*Moi-même,* I'd the impression there might have been another gentleman whose interest Mademoiselle wished to attract. Lady Alberta seemed to think Mademoiselle might set a new style."

Lisbet wished she might wrap that ribbon around the *modiste*'s neck and tie it tightly. "She may indeed. A style for freckle-faced little nobodies with portions of fifty thousand pounds."

Fifty thousand pounds? Franny almost dropped her ribbon. Perhaps Miss Dinwiddie might be interested to see the new fashion plates just arrived from Paris. A rose-colored shawl. Some lovely pearl embroidery.

Lisbet saw the greed on the modiste's face, as well as the slight sheen of perspiration that gleamed on her brow. "And your impression of Lady Alberta Tait?"

Franny returned abruptly to the present. "An excellent creature, *enfin.*"

Lisbet gave her a level look. "You will have to do considerably better than that. This is all very proper, but I wish to know a great deal more. Ravensclaw called you to his house. Lady Alberta and Miss Dinwiddie were there.

Did you have any impression of a relationship between them?"

Franny stared. "Between Lady Alberta and Ravensclaw? *C'est moi!*"

"No, you ninny! Between Alberta and Miss Dinwiddie."

"*Eh bien.*" A ninny, was she? Franny strove for an expression of bewilderment. "I don't think they had met previously. Is one permitted to inquire why you ask?"

"One is not." So much for the tale that Lady Alberta was Miss Dinwiddie's aunt. What manner of rig was Val running? Had that snippety chit snared him so well and good that he'd actually taken her under his protection, and set up Lady Alberta as a convenient chaperone?

Mme. Fanchon was regarding her speculatively. Lisbet felt like giving the woman a good shake. "Tell me everything that transpired. From the moment you arrived at Ravensclaw's house until you left. Don't just sit there like a block!"

Perhaps she should have stayed Franny Brown and worked as a simple seamstress, instead of aspiring to a shop of her own, where people could walk in and insult and threaten her. Franny didn't doubt for a moment that Lisbet could make good on every one of her threats. At least she had already made sure the door to the workroom was closed, so her employees couldn't catch her at her accounts, and thereby be reminded that they also wished to be paid. "*Comment?*"

Lisbet was wholly out of patience. She slapped the *modiste* smartly across the cheek. Mme. Fanchon gasped in astonishment. "I'm waiting," Lisbet said.

Franny was tempted to tell this fine lady that she might wait until hell froze over. One look at that furious face caused her to change her mind. Franny recounted, as best she could, her dealings with Emily Dinwiddie and Ravensclaw.

Satisfied—or if not satisfied precisely, because she

was still in a temper, at least certain she'd drained the *modiste* of every bit of knowledge she possessed—Lisbet rose to take her leave. Franny watched her warily.

So might the mongoose look before the cobra ate it. Lisbet smiled unpleasantly. "Now that we have enjoyed our *tête à tête*, Mme. Fanchon, I find that you shan't suit me, after all," she said, and sailed out the door.

Franny touched her hand to her stinging cheek. If she'd ever spent a worse half hour, it had slipped her mind. She reached into the desk drawer for the bottle of medicinal brandy that she kept on hand. It was empty. Mme. Fanchon said, with considerable justification, *"Merde!"*

Chapter Twenty-Four

A word and a stone let go cannot be called back.
(Romanian proverb)

When it came to bridge-building Edinburgh had no equal, which was perhaps not surprising since there was a mountain in the middle of the city, causing unexpected alternations of heights and depths.

Bridges blended into existing streets. The gaps they spanned were filled in, developed, and built up, buildings constructed above and on either side until the mighty structures were almost concealed. Bricked in and built around, the vaults formed by the arches of the South Bridge were a warren of nooks, crannies, and tunnels used for wine storage, leather works, and a multitude of small businesses, as well as living quarters for the city's unwanted and unseen poor. Also stored there were cadavers either dug from fresh graves or plucked from the streets and sold to Edinburgh's Medical School.

Drogo whined, sensing his master's mood. Val touched the wolf's sleek head. *Dog*, he reminded himself. *Rare Carpathian copoi. Believe that and I'll sell you a fine barren moor.* It was due to the ungrateful Miss Dinwiddie that they were out and about so early, Val's dark spectacles set firmly on his nose. If sunlight posed his flesh no danger after so long a time, it still caused discomfort to his eyes. Perhaps after several hundred more years had passed, he would be able to put the spectacles aside.

Several hundred more years. Val felt like crushing the spectacles in his bare hands. Several hundred years ago he had married Ana, in a ceremony that began when his spokesman, Cezar, had gone to her family's home to woo her with the tale of a young emperor and a flower which couldn't bear fruit until it was planted in the proper soil. Then Val had been obliged to solve a series of riddles to prove his cleverness. Following had been three days of ceremonies, ending with a dance of masks. Ana had worn a traditional costume and flowers in her hair. Val wondered how Andrei would react to the discovery that his sister had returned, and why. What use Cezar might make of a ghost. Val was putting off telling them, perhaps in an attempt to protect Ana, and more likely himself.

Time had passed more quickly than he could have imagined. Several hundred years from now, when perhaps he could venture into the sunlight without dark glasses, Emily would have long since shuffled off the mortal coil. Have gone the way of all flesh. Would be dead as mutton, and Val very much feared he would still be missing her. Perhaps Emily would haunt him then, as Ana was doing now. Demand he make her corporeal so she could tup someone, but not him, because he was *vampir.*

Vampir. Condemned to lifetimes of loneliness. Yearning to live and love like an ordinary man. Feeling bloody mortal. How damnably trite of him.

Had any of Ravensclaw's acquaintance been out and about so early (which was unlikely), and had they encountered him in this particular part of the Old Town (which was even more unlikely), they would have deduced from his expression merely that he was appalled to find himself so far from his bed. Drogo knew better. He pressed closer, and whined again.

"You're right," Val said aloud, and rubbed the wolf's ears. "I'm as addle-brained as those three fools we sent to the docks." Because Emily had been worried about her inept assailants, he'd volunteered them for a sealing expedition sailing from the Port of Leith, thereby hopefully removing them from underfoot without doing lasting harm. Val didn't delude himself that Emily would be grateful. Were she apprised of his solution to the problem, she would probably demand he rescue the seals.

He would not oblige her. The addition of a sticky-fingered chimneysweep to his retinue was sufficient. Val refused to introduce any marine life with webbed flippers into his household.

These ruminations took him past High Street and the Lawnmarket, along a passage between two houses, into a dark courtyard surrounded by ancient high buildings. As Emily had before him, Val glanced up at the distant sliver of sky before he descended the short flight of stone steps that led down to two doors. Drogo pushed a shoulder against the left. The door swung open. Val stepped inside. It occurred to him that he was acting in Emily's best interests without consulting her, again.

This place was not unfamiliar to him, though its present owner was. Val looked down at the little man who bustled out of a back room. "Mr. Abercrombie, I presume. I see you have not changed the décor. Hello, Styx." The raven flew down from its perch to alight on his shoulder and mutter in his ear. Mr. Abercrombie's wandering eye moved from Val to the raven and then to Drogo, who immediately padded forward and rested his damp nose against the little man's thigh. Mr. Abercrombie squeaked, "And may I know who you are, sir?"

"Certainly." Val took off his dark glasses. "I am Ravensclaw."

If Mr. Abercrombie didn't know exactly who Ravens-claw was, or what, he realized he was dealing with a person of substance. Had he a forelock he would have tugged it. Instead he smoothed a hand over his balding pate and professed his desire to be of service. Would the gentleman be interested in a crescent-shaped charm made from a boar's tusk, or a chicken's wishing bone? A cure for the ague? No? A pity. He had in stock an especially fine batch of bull's-horn plantain. Some alchemical supplies, perhaps?

Val was accustomed to reading the thoughts of others. There were as many cobwebs in this little man's mind as on his overladen shelves. Not that the cobwebs deceived him. Things of power rested in this room, amid the clutter and dust. "A young woman came here recently. Red-haired. Freckled. Inquisitive."

Mr. Abercrombie glanced at Drogo, who hadn't budged an inch. "Aye. I recognize her, er, companion." Then he looked startled, as if he'd meant to lie.

"You will tell me what you told her."

Looking even more astonished, Mr. Abercrombie did so. Val was briefly distracted by the notion of Emily in conjunction with a Love Drawing Oil. "The young woman was very well protected," the shopkeeper added. "Maybe you might know where she found that pendant, sir?"

Val raised an eyebrow. "What pendant?"

"Ah. Yes, indeed. What pendant." Mr. Abercrombie shuffled his feet. "Perhaps I might interest you in a recipe for Raven's Feather Ink?" Styx shifted on Val's shoulder and muttered darkly.

"I think not." Val lifted the raven back up on its perch, moved around the cluttered shop, inspecting the jumble of books and bottles, the muddle of merchandise in the cabinets and on the shelves. "Tell me what you know about Michael Ross."

Mr. Abercrombie opened his mouth, perhaps to protest, then looked at Drogo. The wolf's jaws were uncomfortably close to his most vulnerable parts. "Like I told the young lady, he bought a *vrajă*, along with some mastic pearls, yarrow, and bloodstone. That's all I know. I swear."

The shopkeeper appeared as innocent as a babe newborn. Ravensclaw wasn't deceived. *Tell me everything you know of Michael Ross. Now. Do not waste my time.*

In the end, it was not so much. Michael Ross had sold the shopkeeper a number of books—the English translation of the *Rosarium Philosophorum; Geber's Discovery of Secrets; An Hundred Aphorisms Containing the Whole Body of Magic, 1321;* though Mr. Abercrombie had passed on a tattered copy of *The Hermaphrodite Child of the Sun and Moon*—and had in turn been most anxious to procure a copy of *The Book of Thoth.* Not that Mr. Abercrombie had such a treasure lying around. In ancient Egypt, the lunar god Thoth had been credited with the invention of both magic and writing, revered as the patron of magicians and scribes. The book was believed to hold the secrets of the universe. To possess a copy was to command and control destiny itself. Were Mr. Abercrombie in possession of such a treasure, he would hardly be here in this dusty little shop. He had sent the young man off with *The Book of Raziel* instead.

So. Michael Ross had sold a number of volumes concerning the manipulation of natural forces and powers to achieve a desired end. Sorcery, in a word. Just the manner of volumes that might be found in the library of the Dinwiddie Society. But if Michael was a mere thief, what business had he reading such stuff himself?

Val had a sense that time was running short. However, since he was here . . . "Tell me, what would you recommend as the best way to rid oneself of a ghost?"

Mr. Abercrombie ruminated. Had the gentleman tried

stuffing his keyholes full of fennel? Burning powdered bistort? Throwing beans at the apparition? Alternately, one could place three peeled cloves of garlic in a bowl with a handful of sea salt and fresh rosemary leaves, grind and mash them together, and sprinkle the result to create a boundary. Val doubted anything so mundane would inspire Ana to join the choir invisible. He took his leave.

The Book of Raziel, he mused, as he put on his spectacles and climbed the stair. Written by a sympathetic angel and given to Adam to compensate for his exile from Eden. Val was familiar with the tome. For that matter, he also had in his possession *The Book of Thoth,* although he had no sense of controlling destiny, not even his own. Miss Dinwiddie had seen to that.

Even as he thought of her, Val felt Emily's presence, some distance away.

She was frightened. Val reached out with his senses and found her, backed into a dark dead-end alleyway by an amorphous blob that sometimes seemed to be a snake and sometimes to have wings. She was holding the pendant out in front of her and muttering beneath her breath. The gem was black as coal.

Jamie was supposed to have been guarding Emily. Jamie and Lady Alberta. Yet with the added efforts of Zizi and Bela, Lilian and Isidore, they had been unable to keep her safely within doors. Cursing fluently in several different languages, Val set out to the rescue.

Chapter Twenty-Five

Believe nothing of what you hear, and only half of what you see.
(Romanian proverb)

Emily did not lack the means to defend herself. However, all her assorted charms were proving no more useful in this moment than her sharp-pointed umbrella, or her little gun. Only Marie d'Auvergne's pendant kept the thing before her from gulping her down like a tasty snack.

No question that it had been foolish to come out alone. But the note slipped to Emily had demanded secrecy and stealth, and promised she would be given information concerning the whereabouts of the athame if she complied. *Not only foolish, but gullible,* she amended, clutching the pendant so tightly that her fingers hurt.

The thing, whatever it was—most likely a demon—constantly changed shape. In one instant it was snake-like, then winged with cloven hooves; a manlike figure with too many fingers and something monstrous about its mouth and teeth; a pillar of smoke, or wavering lights. In all its configurations piercing dark eyes nailed her to the ground. It advanced, retreated, circled, writhed.

If only she might free herself of this paralysis. Emily wasn't so foolish as to wish to do battle with an otherworldly creature; she wanted to run away. At least, that's what she thought she wanted. It was difficult to concentrate her mind. She even thought she heard the howling of a wolf. The monster must have shared her auditory hallucination; it turned away. In that instant, as its focus wavered, Emily saw through the illusion. Her assailant was a winged manlike being of terrible beauty. She had only a brief glimpse before he changed again, into a great scaled fire-breathing dragon with long curved talons like those of a bird of prey.

Demons, Emily told herself: *Concentrate*. To name a demon was to lessen its power. But there were 4,601,200 demons, according to the *Egyptian Book of the Dead*. Or 7,409,127 commanded by seventy-nine princes, if one preferred the sixteenth-century physician Jean Weir. On the other hand, according to legend, King Solomon of Israel shut up seventy-two rebellious kings into a brass vessel and threw it into a deep lake. In an attempt to locate great treasure, the Babylonians had broken open the vessel, allowing the demons to escape into the world.

Concentrate, you ninny! "Glasyalabolas," she murmured. "Raum. Flauros. Seere, Andromalius, Balaam." Now that the demon's attention was no longer fixed on her, Emily found that she could move.

A scuffle behind her, the sound of struggle, a snarl and yelp. Emily spun around. Drogo sprawled on the filthy pavement, blood streaming from a deep gash in his flank. Emily fell to her knees beside the wolf, her hands pulling at his thick fur as if she could hold the edges of the wound together and staunch the flow of blood. Drogo whined. *Emily!* came Val's voice in her mind. *Leave this place, at once!*

Val? Emily raised her head. Her thoughts moved slowly as molasses in wintertime.

This was not Val as she knew him. His face was leaner,

harsher, his fangs fully extended; he seemed taller, broader in build. Sharp claws extended from his finger-tips. His eyes bled black fire. *Go!* he said again.

I won't! Emily took a firmer grip on Drogo's sodden fur, gasped as the demon slashed at Val and drew blood. Emily was no stranger (though she should have been) to the gentlemanly art of fisticuffs, but in a struggle be-tween vampire and demon, the ordinary rules did not apply. Here was no boxing in Mendoza's scientific style, no cross-and-jostle work or application of Jack Broughton's favorite hard right to the abdomen. This was a struggle to the death with talons and fangs. Val caught the demon and flung it against the side of a building with such force that, had the thing hit, the ancient structure might have tumbled down. Instead the demon dissolved into mist, and reformed itself as a huge apelike creature with long powerful arms and huge hands and a coat of long silver-yellow hair. Val slammed the beast to the ground. It was mobile again in an instant, and delivered a rib-breaking blow. Val grunted. The demon raked him again with its claws, severing tendon and sinew.

Emily winced. This wasn't going well. "Cimeries, Sytyr, Vassago—" Drogo whined. Emily glanced down at him and glimpsed her reticule, its chain still wrapped around her wrist. Her mind was clearing. The demon knelt on Val's back with an arm wrapped around his neck, pre-pared to twist.

The literature claimed a vampire would die if its spine was snapped. Emily thrust her hand into her reticule, brought out a handful of salt and flung it. The demon burst into flames.

The ape-thing disappeared. Emily was gazing again at the beautiful manlike being with his vast wings and red hair. He appeared annoyed. He also looked a trifle singed.

Red hair. A great serpent with twelve wings who flew like a bird. "Samael!"

The demon released Val and turned its eyes on her. Before that terrible gaze could again ensnare her, Emily held up her little mirror and captured its reflection. "Samael, angel of death, prince of the fifth heaven, genii of fire. Samael, accuser, seducer, destroyer. Who interfered with Abraham, wrestled with Jacob, took part in the affair of Tamar—"

The demon unfurled a sooty wing and examined it. "You've made your point."

"Samael, angel of death, prince of air, demon who tempted Eve. Samael, lord of demons, leader of the angels who married the daughters of men. Tremble, O Demon, enemy of mankind, source of avarice, seducer of man, root of evil, discord and envy—"

"You do me too much credit. And that should be seducer of *woman*kind." Samael plucked out a singed feather and eyed Emily. "Perhaps—"

Emily gripped the mirror tighter. "In the name of Yod, Cados, Eloym, Saboath, and Yeshua the Anointed One, I command you to return from whence you came."

"As you will." The demon spread his great wings and disappeared.

Emily exhaled in relief. One could never be certain of the outcome when dealing with a demon of such strength.

Cezar spoke from behind her. "Well done, Miss Dinwiddie. I wouldn't have expected banishing demons to be one of your skills."

Emily twisted around to frown at him. "I don't know why you should be surprised. Papa *did* teach me things, even if he didn't let me practice them. How long have you been here?"

"Long enough." Cezar moved closer. If Val's head

was still where it belonged, the pavement around his body was slick and dark. "Our friend doesn't look well."

Emily's hands tightened in Drogo's fur. "I thought your kind could heal yourselves. And don't insult me by saying you don't know what I'm talking about!"

"I wouldn't wish to insult you, Miss Dinwiddie. We do have remarkable regenerative powers. However, that *was* a demon. And we cannot replenish our own blood."

Val lay unnervingly quiet and still. Emily would have gone to him if Cezar had not stopped her with a single sharp command.

Emily uttered several words unsuited to young ladies. "How can you just stand there? Why *did* you just stand there when you might have helped?"

"It wasn't my battle. I couldn't influence the outcome. Move your hands." Cezar knelt and touched elegant fingers to Drogo's wound. The wolf whined.

Emily watched. The damage looked no less. "I thought werewolves—"

"Could heal themselves? It would seem, Miss Dinwiddie, that there is no end to what you believe."

Emily sniffed. "If not for my beliefs, you'd still be standing there watching a demon destroy Ravensclaw. And speaking of Val—"

"That was no ordinary demon." Cezar pressed the edges of Drogo's wound together. "It couldn't have been called up by ordinary means. Which returns us to the matter of the d'Auvergne athame."

Emily fumbled for her spectacles. Was it a trick of the shadows that made it seem as if the gash had begun to mend? "Oh, bugger the blasted athame! You're healing Drogo. Can you heal Val?"

"Drogo is a dumb animal." The dumb animal growled. "Apologies, my old friend. Val can heal himself, Miss Dinwiddie, as you've already guessed. But he won't survive without blood."

Emily stared at Cezar in dawning horror. "Then give him some!"

"Our kind cannot derive sustenance from one another."

"Then bugger you too!" snapped Emily, and looked frantically about for something sharp.

Nothing came to hand. She crossed the pavement to kneel by Val. He opened his eyes. They were merely sapphire now, but his face retained its feral cast.

He needed her. Gingerly, Emily touched his cheek. Val's coldness frightened her more than a hundred demons ever could. "I'm so sorry. Forgive me."

No need. His eyes closed.

It's my fault you've been injured. Let me help you. Drink from me.

I cannot.

He was as stubborn as any mule. Action was required. Gingerly, Emily settled her body atop his, pulled back her hair and bared her throat. *I know you would prefer somewhere else—breasts, groin, and the like—but I refuse to disrobe in front of* him. She glared at Cezar.

Val hesitated. Emily raised herself to peer down into his pale face. *Don't tell me you're shy!*

His pale lips twitched. *Are you afraid of nothing?*

I'm afraid I won't please you. Val, let me give you the gift of blood.

Cezar said, "Do it, Val."

A moment passed. Then Val's fingers moved to the neckline of Emily's dress. He tugged the material aside, wrapped one hand in her hair and drew her head back. Emily felt his lips on her skin, his teeth; gasped as his fangs sank into her flesh. The smell of copper flooded the air.

Pleasure rolled over Emily, Val's pleasure in tasting her, in taking her blood. Her own pleasure, raw and sensual, as she felt her heat and warmth pulse through his veins. And then his hunger was upon her, sweeping like a sweet narcotic through her veins. *Open to me, Emily. We feed on emotions as well as blood.*

Her body sang with strange sensations. Bright colors danced behind her eyes. Emily gave herself to Val, and knew nothing but a deepening velvet darkness, heard not even the hammering of her own heart.

Chapter Twenty-Six

Of two evils choose the least.
(Romanian proverb)

Val was dreaming. Of Emily.

She sprawled on top of him, her small body burning hot. She felt like all he would ever wish to know of heaven, sweet and soft and unbearably innocent. He longed to accept the gift she offered, and take her innocence. To slide his lips across her bare skin, to feel her thrum with anticipation; to drop his head to her breast, lick her belly, and the inside of her knees; to tease her with his tongue until she gasped and wept and moaned, and screamed out her satisfaction at the end.

But slowly, slowly. Val would not rush her pleasure, or his own. His hands caressed her as he bit gently at her lower lip, kissed the pulse beating at her temple, breathed her in. She pressed closer, as if she wished to crawl inside his skin. Well, then, he would let her. Val pressed his teeth to the soft flesh where neck met jaw . . .

. . . and wakened abruptly, to find himself alone in one of several stone-walled chambers kept for the use of the Brotherhood. Val had never had need for one of these small rooms before. He wondered why he did now. He moved, and grimaced as he felt the soreness in his ribs. His body healed quickly, but not overnight. Just as the fresh scars on his body would fade in time.

Scars? Broken bones? Val raised his hands to his head. He felt as he had in the old days after celebrating the feast of Dionysus. He recalled a proverb of his youth. " 'Three glasses of wine are just enough: the first for your health, the second for your delight, and the third for a good rest. A fourth will bring shame on you, a fifth will make you scream. And to go on drinking will drive you mad.' "

Val had no use for liquor, and certainly not for chewing ivy leaves. The only thing that could affect him this way was overindulgence in blood.

He touched his tongue to his lips. So vivid had been his dream that the scent of Emily still clung to him. He could taste her in his mouth. She had been intoxicating in her purity. No wonder he felt drunk.

Val reached out for her. He should have been able to sense her emotions, her response to the dream; he should have been able to feel the aftermath of pleasure still curling through her, lazy and sweet. Having once tasted her, he should be able to touch her mind, to know her thoughts, to hear her heart beat.

Instead he felt nothing. She had again closed herself to him. Val swung his legs over the side of the bed and walked unsteadily into the main meeting room. Cezar was there, addressing a golf ball. Judging from the other balls scattered around the room, his efforts today had not met with much success.

Cezar glanced up at Val. "Our people believe that a corpse found with one eye open and one closed is in the process of transforming into a *vampir*."

Val squinted both eyes at the bright light of the candles. " 'What does the Romanian like? Fresh bread, old wine, and a young wife.' I don't suppose you have some tea."

Cezar returned his attention to his putter. "Zalmoxis taught that men don't die, but go to a place where they'll live forever and have all good things." The ball rolled off the shank of his club and bounced into a wall. "Like I do."

Cezar was in a strange mood, to be mentioning old Dacian gods. Val saw a teapot sitting on a table, and poured himself a cup. "What's the matter with you today?"

Cezar retrieved the golf ball. "Andrei is keeping Lisbet occupied. He may well supplant you in her affections before long."

"He may have her with my blessing." Although Val needed tea no more than wine, the beverage's pleasant taste left him feeling revived. "Since we are both aware that Andrei is no fool, I assume he's sacrificing himself for the greater good."

Cezar moved in the sudden way of his kind, which was of no use whatsoever to him in the game of golf. The ball rolled forward a few inches and came to a stop. Cezar dropped his putter on the floor. "How much do you recall about the events of yesterday?"

Val put down his teacup. "I went to the sorcerer's shop, which is now in the hands of a man named Abercrombie. I questioned him about Michael Ross. He didn't know much. Then I realized Emily was in trouble." He closed his eyes. "Did I really do battle with the Darkness?"

"Miss Dinwiddie sent him home. It was all very polite, other than the fact you lost."

Val looked at Cezar. "Tell me I didn't drink from her."

"Very well. You didn't drink from her. You didn't enjoy drinking from her so much that you refused to stop. You didn't attempt to break my neck when I tried to stop you. I wasn't forced to summon Andrei for assistance. Nor did it take both Andrei and me to get you here. Yes, it was all a dream."

Val eyed his friend warily. "What have you done with Emily? If you dared switch her memories around—"

"I've done nothing. Miss Dinwiddie is your responsibility. I suggest you don't tarry much longer in assuming it. Not, like I said, that it's any of my affair."

Nothing was Cezar's affair unless he chose it. Val had no illusion about Cezar's current choice. "I'll ask you once more. What have you done with Emily?"

"And I'll tell you once more, I've done nothing. Come with me. See for yourself." Cezar led the way down a narrow hall and into another cell, where Emily lay on a cot. Drogo was stretched out beside her. As Val stepped into the chamber, the wolf lifted his head and growled.

Val moved closer to the bed where Emily lay motionless, her tangled hair spread out on the pillow. One hand rested limply atop the blanket. There was dirt beneath her fingernails, dark stains on her gown. Unnerving to see Emily so still, so quiet, as if the pointed little face, the generous mouth, had no more life force than a stone.

Life force. Memory crashed over him. Emily's body sprawled atop his had not been a dream. He took her dirty hands in his. Her fingers were ice cold. Still, he felt a faint heartbeat. *Emily.* There was no response.

He felt Cezar behind him. Grimly, Val said, "You let me take too much from her."

Cezar raised his eyebrows. "Since when am I your conscience? At any event you were in no condition to heed the voice of reason, as I have already pointed out. I did warn Miss Dinwiddie, if you'll recall, that she was likely to be your next meal."

Val touched his fingers to the small marks on Emily's neck. Conscience rose up and smote him, another almost-forgotten and most painful sensation. Emily had trusted him, and he had failed to protect her, despite his wish to keep her from harm. He was indeed a soulless fiend.

"Self-loathing," observed Cezar. "I recognize the signs. The responsibility is not entirely yours, Val. Miss Din-widdie would not be swayed from her intended path."

Val stroked her pale cheek. "You tried to do so? How unlike you, then."

"I did not. It would have been futile. She was deter-mined that you should drink from her." Drogo looked from one of them to the other, then dropped his head protectively on Emily's thigh. "And you did."

Val chafed Emily's cold hands. This was not the way the stories went. The hero was not supposed to require that the heroine make a blood sacrifice of herself. "She thinks she is my *ailaltă.*"

Cezar touched Drogo's fur. "How goes the husband hunt?"

"*Dudevite dracului!* You could heal her."

"I could, but then she would be mine. You don't want that, I think."

What Val wanted was his existence as it was before Emily arrived to turn him lunatic. Cezar added, "She hasn't much time left. Don't glare at me. I didn't make the rules."

"No, but you enforce them. I don't suppose you'd care to turn a blind eye."

"No. However—" Cezar held out an ornate silver knife. "I don't believe it suits me that the secrets the Dinwiddie Society has collected over the centuries be set loose on the world. Therefore, our little wren must not be allowed to fly away from us just yet."

"*Our* little wren?"

"Are we not comrades?"

Val looked at the knife. Impossible to know the consequences of feeding a mortal their mingled blood. What would it do to Emily? What would it do to them? Not to mention that such a thing was so far beyond the rules that the mere thought was staggering. The vampire population was regulated. No newcomers were created without serious forethought; and even forethought was not sufficient to prevent such mistake as the *nefinistats*.

Best not to think of making monsters, but instead of saving lives. "You absolve Emily of duplicity?"

"At least regarding the d'Auvergne athame. As for the rest, only time will tell. She risked her life to save you, Val, knowing full well what you are. That sort of courage is rare. Too, I have never seen you so besotted. Now, will you remedy the situation, or shall I?"

Friend Cezar might be, and *Stăpân*, but Val mistrusted his motives all the same. Perhaps Cezar suspected, as Val did, that this spate of killings was intended to undermine the authority of the Brotherhood.

"Or perhaps they're merely a distraction. Perhaps our opponent is more subtle than we think. Perhaps I value Miss Dinwiddie simply because you do." Cezar brushed his fingertips against her tangled curls. "You must trust someone sometime, Val. Why should it not be me?"

Why, indeed? And what choice, truly, did he have?

If Cezar chose to share the repercussions of this forbidden act, so be it; but it would not be Cezar's blood that Emily tasted first, not Cezar's blood that forced the bond. Val grasped the knife and slashed the vein on the inside of his elbow. With all his force of will, and Cezar's will behind him, he focused on her mind. *Emily.*

Her eyes fluttered open. His conscience wept again at the emptiness he saw there.

He pushed his regrets aside. *Emily, drink.*

Chapter Twenty-Seven

Beware of a silent dog and still water.
(Romanian proverb)

Lady Alberta wore a morning frock of sprigged India muslin with a back fastening and a double ruff, full sleeves with vandyked edging at the wrists, and scalloped flounces at the hemline. If the gown was more suited to someone half her age, as Mme. Fanchon had suggested, Alberta really didn't care a whit. Machka rubbed against her ankles, an act Alberta might have found more comforting if not for a suspicion that the creature was marking her as prey.

The drawing room was quiet save for the tapping of Alberta's fingers on the arms of her hardwood chair, the rustling pages of her magazine, the pit-pattering of Machka's paws upon the floor. On a nearby table sat a tea tray with remnants of a feast that had included apple gingerbread, Dundee cake, and petticoat tarts.

Alberta shifted in her chair, and wondered if a youthful shape was worth the discomfort of stays. Not that she would think of leaving the house without her corset—and not that she meant to leave the house, but couldn't help thinking each time she dressed of her dear mama's maxim about making sure to wear clean undergarments in fear of being turned topsy-turvy in a carriage accident—but she was most ambivalent about those odd garments known as drawers. Today she had encased herself in a long elastic stay intended to give its wearer a true Grecian form by lending an agreeable and graceful shape to the shoulders, reducing the bosom if too embonpoint, or increasing its natural appearance if too diminutive. Alberta glanced down at her own bosom, and brushed off a couple of crumbs resting there. At least fashion no longer decreed that one's hips be squeezed into a circumference little more than one's waist, and one's bosom be shoved up into a fleshy shelf reaching almost to one's chin. As her own hips might do if she didn't soon stop eating. Alberta eyed the desecrated tea tray. Today she had felt an even more than usual need to fortify herself.

Emily had eluded them. Ravensclaw would *not* be pleased. Even now Zizi, Bela, and Lilian were scouring the Old Town, accompanied by Jamie, who had refused to be left sittin' on his behouchie when some bajins might dare meddle wi' his Miss Emily. Jamie was a continual revelation. Alberta had not previously known that a mixter-master was an untidy jumbled condition, or that something tapsalteerie was upside down, or that a centipede was a meggy mony-feet.

Isidore interrupted these reflections. He was short of breath. "Mr. Michael Ross to see Miss Emily," he announced, with a meaningful wriggle of his eyebrows.

Alberta's eyebrows being averse to wriggling, she gave the smallest of shrugs before turning to the newcomer with as much enthusiasm as she could muster. A young man come a-wooing would expect to see the object of his affection, if affection he had for her, which Alberta took leave to doubt. "More roses! How lovely!

You know what to do with them, Isidore. What a pleasant surprise, Mr. Ross. I was feeling a trifle moped. Now you can tell me who's doing what, and to whom!"

Michael stepped into the room. "I don't know why it should be a surprise. Emily and I are betrothed."

"So you are!" Alberta wagered it wouldn't be for long. Were *she* to have been privileged to share Ravensclaw's bed—not that Alberta thought Emily had actually shared it (in the biblical sense, that was, although perhaps the Good Book hadn't couched the matter in quite those terms), not the act of a well-brought-up young woman of course, but Alberta had realized early on that Emily was hardly that—and all the better for it, in Alberta's opinion—but if she hadn't yet, she would. Emily, that was. Alberta had no illusion about that sort of thing regarding herself, and didn't mind a bit, well recalling how very exhausting was the dance of love. Or lust. At her age—and what *that* was would remain a secret she would take with her to her grave—Alberta was surely old enough to call a spade a spade.

Michael Ross, she had to call a pigeonheart. He was peering about him as if he expected a hobgoblin to pop out from behind a chair. As well it might, if Machka might be considered one. Alberta tsk'd at the cat. Machka gave her tail an irritated twitch.

Alberta would have done so also, if she had a tail. Since she didn't, she pasted a polite smile on her face. "Emily has gone shopping. A young woman on the verge of entering into matrimony requires a great many things. Just because you are betrothed, young man, doesn't mean you may expect your fiancée to hang upon your sleeve. You frown, Mr. Ross. What exercises your mind? I am hardly qualified to counsel a young man on the verge of matrimony, but if you wish it, I will try! Gracious, where are my manners? Do sit down!"

Michael did so, keeping a wary eye on Machka as he placed his hat on a nearby table. "Surely you haven't let Emily go out alone!"

"Of course not." Which wasn't really a taradiddle, because Alberta hadn't *let* Emily go anywhere, and furthermore it was unlikely that Emily was alone, which might or might not be a good thing. "I see what it is: you fear you'll dwell under the hen's foot. Not that anyone can call Emily hen-hearted! I daresay she has more steel in her backbone than is needed for a dozen swords. Still, she may knuckle under in time. You'll just have to put your foot firmly down. Or try to, at any rate!"

Machka jumped onto the table. Michael snatched up his hat. "When do you expect Emily to return?"

"A few minutes, a few hours. One never knows with shopping excursions such as this." Alberta picked up her magazine. "In the meantime we contrive to entertain ourselves. Are you familiar with *The Vampyre*, Mr. Ross? 'There was no colour upon her cheek, not even upon her lip; yet there was a stillness about her face that seemed almost as attaching as the life that once dwelt there: upon her neck and breast was blood, and upon her throat were the marks of teeth having opened the vein . . .' I must say, I have certain reservations about Lord Ruthven's relationship with Aubrey. Lord Ruthven being Mr. Polidori's vampire, and Aubrey a silly young man with somewhat ambivalent preferences." She hesitated. "If you know what I mean."

Anger flashed in Michael's eyes. "Emily says you disapprove of the supersensible."

" 'Disapprove' may be too strong a word. I have been doing some reading"—Alberta gestured toward the pile of books—"and find I am quite taken with the notion of staving off insomnia with a violet wreath, breaking a hex with stinging nettle, making a wish on a sunflower seed."

Michael didn't respond, but watched Machka inch closer. The expression on his face reminded Alberta of a certain invisibility spell in the *Grand Grimoire* that involved boiling a black cat in a covered pot. "Let us speak frankly, Mr. Ross. What are your prospects? Forgive my asking, but as Emily's aunt, I do stand *in loco parentis,* as it were."

His prospects were bleak indeed if Emily eluded him, and since Michael had no notion why she had suddenly decided she wanted to be leg-shackled, he wouldn't put it past her to cry off. "Emily will want for nothing. I shall see to that."

Alberta barely refrained from snorting. Instead, she picked up a gingerbread crumb and popped it in her mouth. Her own discreet inquiries about this young man had led to the conclusion that he was as poor as a church mouse. An odd expression, surely; were there wealthy mice? "Where do you plan to reside once you are wed? Surely not here in Edinburgh. Dear Emily will want to continue her papa's work." Her newly acquired niece's claims to the contrary, Alberta's hearing was quite keen, and she considered the young woman fit to head up any number of societies. Miss Dinwiddie was so very capable that she even understood the mysteries of the 'Change.

Emily was also a very aggravating young woman, and Alberta had grown fond of her despite her oddities. And her tendency to go missing. "What was that you said?"

Michael had said nothing, although his face darkened with temper. "I haven't yet decided where we will reside."

He had not decided. Alberta repressed a smile. "Do

call me Aunt Bertie! We are almost kin." Not, she suspected, that they were like to be, even if they could be, which they couldn't, because Emily had been telling clankers—not that it was any of her affair!

Or perhaps it was a little bit, because Emily had taken her advice regarding the catching of fleas. Alberta wasn't accustomed to people taking her advice. She relented and offered Michael a cup of tea.

Michael accepted the tepid beverage. "Where is Ravensclaw?"

"Val isn't in the habit of explaining his activities to me."

"Yet you dwell beneath his roof."

"So I do." Alberta gestured with her teacup. "Dear boy, surely you aren't jealous of Ravensclaw. One might as well envy the moon."

Michael opened his mouth and closed it, fidgeted a moment, plucked a cat hair off his boots. Machka leapt down from the table to crouch beneath his chair and give one ear a good scratch.

Alberta watched them both. She didn't know when she had so enjoyed herself as during her sojourn under Ravensclaw's roof. Aside from the fact that Emily had gone missing again, which meant that Val would become cross again, and thunder about the house like Thor in a tantrum. "And the item that was stolen?" Michael asked. "Has Emily learned anything about it yet?"

Alberta felt a pang of hunger. Or perhaps it was indigestion. "What item might that be?"

Michael's fingers curled around the arms of his chair. "I'm concerned about Emily's well-being. She can only suffer from prolonged exposure to Ravensclaw. He is the devil's spawn."

Lady Alberta tittered. "All men are the devil's spawn, my dear Mr. Ross! They are put on this earth entirely to beleaguer us poor females. Ravensclaw may be one of the more singular examples, perhaps, so very handsome as he is, but I hope you don't mean to infer that he would do any of us harm."

"You know him so well?"

"Ah, that is the question, isn't it?" Lady Alberta clasped her hands to her now crumb-free bosom. "Who among us ever knows another well? Look at Lord Aubrey and Lord Ruthven. I have just finished reading the *Dissertation on the Appearance of Angels, Demons and Spirits; and on the Revenant Vampires of Hungary, Bohemia, Moravia, and Silesia.* Written in 1647. I'm personally partial to the Celtic Dearg-dhu, the Red Blood Witch, who rises once a year from her grave to seduce men into her embrace and drain them dry of blood—patently absurd, of course, once a year being entirely too seldom for any creature to feed." Especially herself, as the straining confines of her corset could attest. "Are you familiar, Mr. Ross, with the 58 blood-drinking deities listed in *The Tibetan Book of the Dead?*"

Michael decided his hostess was two groats short of a guinea. "This is a very serious matter, Lady Alberta. Emily came into grave danger the instant she took up residence in this house."

"Aunt Bertie, dear. You're suffering wedding nerves, poor boy. Where do you plan to be wed? Dear Emily will want an elaborate ceremony."

Michael flinched. "Emily is in mourning," he protested.

"She won't be by then. I hope you don't mean the marriage to be a havey-cavey affair! What month will you choose? 'Marry in May and you'll live to rue the day; marry in Lent, live to repent.' And what day? 'Monday for wealth, Tuesday for health, Wednesday the best day of all; Thursday for losses, Friday for crosses, Saturday for no luck at all.' Emily will toss her garter to the gentlemen, unless they grow so inebriated as to try and take it from her, in which case you'll have to intervene. Perhaps we shall release a pair of doves to symbolize your undying love." Alberta paused. The young man looked so appalled that she almost pitied him.

Almost, but not quite. "Also, we must consider your wedding trip. In Ireland, a laying hen is tied to the bed on the first night of the honeymoon in hope some of its fertility will be passed on, which is to my mind an odd way of thinking, because all that clucking and fluttering about would surely interfere with the task at hand. Or perhaps not. As a spinster, I don't know a great deal about these things!"

Michael snatched up his hat. "You mock me. I hope you may not be disillusioned, 'Aunt Bertie,' in your precious Ravensclaw."

Alberta lifted her teacup. "You haven't been listening, Mr. Ross. He's not my Ravensclaw."

Michael stood abruptly, thereby annoying Machka, who had been admiring her reflection in his shiny boot. She pounced and dug her claws into the glossy leather, not ready for her mirror to migrate.

Michael swore and shook his foot. Machka clung all the harder, and climbed higher still, until her sharp claws shredded not only leather but skin. Michael howled. Alberta tried so hard to suppress her laughter that her corseted sides creaked.

She rose from her chair, plucked the cat off Michael's thigh and held her at a prudent distance. The fur on Machka's back stood straight out about her, making her look twice her size. Her ears were flat against her head.

Michael scowled at his shredded footwear, then plopped his hat upon his head. "Pray tell Emily I am anxious to speak with her!" Favoring his damaged leg, he limped out of the room.

Machka bared sharp little teeth. Alberta dropped the cat down on the floor, then descended the stairway to the kitchen, where Mrs. MacCamish kept on hand stimulant considerably stronger than tea.

Chapter Twenty-Eight

Honey is sweet, but the bee stings.
(Romanian proverb)

Emily opened her eyes to find herself in a small stone-walled room. A rather crowded stone-walled room, which held both Cezar and Val as well, and Drogo stretched out beside her on the narrow cot. The terrible gash in the wolf's flank had completely healed, leaving only a smooth scar.

She surveyed her Spartan surroundings doubtfully. "Is *this* the secret meeting place of the Brotherhood?"

Cezar moved to the foot of the bed. "Not all of us are sensualists like Val."

Emily glanced back at Val, whose auburn hair tumbled loose over his shoulders. He had removed his ruined clothing, and wore only a pair of breeches, in which he appeared even more delicious than Mrs. MacCamish's Paradise Cake. Narrow waist, chest covered with soft curls that she wished to rub her cheek against, muscles that rippled under golden skin on which the new scars had already formed: he was so beautiful he hurt her eyes.

And he was watching her watch him. Emily felt a little giddy. "I take it I'm still alive."

Val sat down on the bed. Drogo snarled softly and scrunched into a smaller ball. "You are."

"And I'm not a vampire."

"No, elfling, you are not." Val's bare skin brushed against hers, and little sparks fizzed up her arm.

Animal magnetism. Magnetic friction. Emily had only glimpsed Val's chest before, and now to see him almost in a state of nature . . . "Um."

Cezar was holding a golf club. He gave it a gentle swing. "Nor are you altogether mortal, because both Val's blood and mine have mixed with yours. Which leaves you, Miss Dinwiddie, somewhere betwixt and between."

Emily contemplated the coverlet. *Both* of them! That had indeed been the ultimate intimacy. She wished she could remember more of it.

"I don't," murmured Val.

Colors seemed brighter. Val's voice seemed to stroke her skin. Emily raised one hand to study it, wriggled her fingers, touched them to her lips. "Just what am I, then?"

Cezar's smile was, for him, gentle. "Yourself, Miss Dinwiddie, and probably a good bit more."

"But what does that mean?"

"I honestly don't know. We'll have to wait and see."

See? Emily's eyes widened. "I'm not wearing my spectacles, and yet I can *see* you! You're not just a blur."

Cezar exchanged a glance with Val. "Miss Dinwiddie may hold other surprises in store than merely sending the Darkness away."

Emily blinked and blinked again, but the bright colors didn't fade. "Don't talk about me as if I wasn't here. By the Darkness, do you mean Samael? It was pure luck that I remembered his name."

Cezar rested his golf club on his shoulder. "Samael is leader of the Fallen Ones. Otherwise known as the Venom of God. If you had not been wearing Marie d'Auvergne's amulet, we would not be having this conversation, for all your demon-banishing skills."

Emily touched the pendant, bright now against her breast. Her first demon, and she hadn't had a chance to enjoy meeting it.

"You are undeniably your father's daughter, Miss Dinwiddie." Cezar resumed his putting stance.

"You knew my papa?"

"By reputation only." Cezar swung.

As Emily contemplated her papa's reputation, Val settled more comfortably, his thigh pressed against hers. "Samael wasn't merely out for an early morning stroll. It might be helpful, Emily, if you could tell us who might wish you harm."

The sound of Val's voice made Emily quiver. The warmth of his strong thigh. The sight of all that lovely gold skin.

Definitely she was a little giddy. Emily tried hard to concentrate on the here and now. "Not Michael, I think. What reason would he have, even if he possessed the power to call up demons, a notion that is altogether absurd? I'd just said I'd marry him, thereby giving him access to all my lovely money, which is all he wants. And which he wouldn't have if something happened to me before we were wed. *After* perhaps, but since I've no intention of really marrying him, that is a moot point."

Came a brief silence while Cezar and Val seemed to be having a silent conversation. Emily's curiosity resurfaced. A brief temptation to try and eavesdrop was abandoned when Cezar speared her with a glance, and she mused instead upon the possibility that she might now grow fangs. Develop a craving for raw meat. Perhaps she would become irresistibly charming. The thought made her smile.

You are already irresistibly charming, little one. Val's voice in her mind was a caress. *You charmed me on our first meet-*

ing, with your umbrella and your garlic and your assorted talismans.

Now Ravensclaw was emptying the butter boat over her. Emily had never in all her life charmed anyone. She narrowed her eyes at Cezar. "The literature claims that your kind can strike one dumb, rob one of one's strength and beauty, and steal milk from nursing mothers, although I don't know why you would. Your senses are so greatly heightened that you can hear a liar's heartbeat, and smell the faintest fear. I wonder how you can stop yourself from eavesdropping."

Cesar looked up from his imaginary golf ball. "Val didn't mean *you* were a bothersome detail. Bothersome, perhaps, but considerably more than a detail."

Emily stroked Drogo. "That was rather more than eavesdropping. I hope this doesn't mean that now I'll also have *you* in my mind."

No, little one. Nor will Cezar invade your dreams. Val took her hand in his.

Emily relaxed, a little bit. She still felt most unlike herself, perhaps because of what she'd done. Or what had been done to her. "I fear I've been somewhat precipitous. Again."

Cezar murmured, "I believe I'll leave the two of you alone. Drogo?" The wolf growled softly and refused to budge. "It seems you've acquired a champion, Miss Dinwiddie. Or a chaperone."

Emily watched Cezar leave the room. "I hope he's going to search for the athame."

Val rubbed his thumb across her knuckles. "More likely Cezar's going to rescue Andrei from Lisbet. Or exercise his golf swing."

Perhaps Cezar might exercise his golf swing on Lisbet. Not knowing how clearly Val could read her now, Emily shoved all thought of the other woman from her mind, and said, "Are you going to scold?"

Val wound his fingers through hers. "Would you listen if I did?"

"Papa used to say the same thing." Emily studied their interlaced hands. "Val, I *must* retrieve the athame."

"We will." Val put a knuckle under Emily's chin and tipped her face up to his.

She felt as if she were drowning in his eyes. *Be sensible!* she told herself. "Just how closely *are* we bound together now?"

"So closely that I feel your heart beating as if it were my own." His fingers brushed her breast. "As Cezar, Andrei, and I are bound to our maker, you are bound to Cezar and myself. Not as strongly, certainly, but if something happens to one of us, you'll experience some of it. And the opposite."

Curious as Emily might have been about Val's maker at another time, she was in this moment appalled. *Cezar knows what we're doing now?!*

It's not so close a bond as that.

Emily lowered her gaze to Val's bare chest. Her body grew warmer, her heartbeat erratic. She touched the faint traces of dried blood that still stained his satin flesh.

Val stiffened. *You don't want to be like me, Emily.*

She wanted to be *with* him. For eternity. Which was something he clearly was not prepared to hear.

Emily wriggled around to thrust her hand into her pocket. Val winced and closed his eyes, thus putting the lie to any impression that he didn't want her, because it was more than obvious he did. Emily retrieved the dirty crumpled note that had led her to Samael.

Val studied it. Emily wondered if his preternatural senses were at work. Perhaps some aura of its writer still clung to the paper. Some scent. Emily sniffed but could smell nothing but herself. She needed a bath.

He remained silent. "Have you learned something from the note?" she asked impatiently.

"No. I was just trying to decipher what it says."

Why was it that the males of any species were so reluctant to ask the females for assistance? Emily snatched the note from him and read it aloud.

"That's ambiguous enough," Val said, when she concluded. "How could the writer be so certain you would take his bait?"

"Papa used to say I have the curiosity of a cat combined with the good sense of a pudding. Don't look at me like that. You know it's true."

Val didn't argue, but drew her back against him. "I wish you'd stop scaring me half out of my wits."

Emily felt so astonishingly unlike herself that she grinned at the notion Ravensclaw might become a half-wit, too.

Val's breath ruffled her hair as he drew her closer. *I am forever in your debt, elfling. You risked your life for me.*

Piffle! Emily snuggled against him. *You and I and Cezar . . . I've never heard of such a thing.*

Val was determined to do penance. *I'll never forgive myself for taking too much from you.*

There is a way you may repay me. Emily drew back and rested her hands against Val's bare chest and looked into his face. *You did say you'd let me do things.*

She *was* going to drive him mad. Still, Val could not refuse her. *What would you like to do to me?*

Emily moistened her lips. Words were beyond her. She slid her hands over his strong arms to his shoulders and tugged.

She felt Val's resistance, then passion flared as his mouth touched hers. He caught her lower lip gently between his teeth, spread a line of teasing kisses along the curve of her cheek, sampled the taste and texture of her earlobe. Her breath caught in her throat as Val nuzzled her neck. *Yes.*

No teeth.

He kissed her, really kissed her, then. Need quivered deep in her belly as his tongue twined with hers in a way that even Emily recognized as a mating dance. He felt like silk beneath her hands.

Emily was afloat on a river of sensation. She shivered as Val's fingers caressed the small wound on her throat. She wanted—Emily didn't know what she wanted, but she wanted it ferociously.

Val wasn't laughing now. He kissed her with deep hunger. Emily pressed against him, her fingers digging into his shoulders, her hands fisting in his hair . . .

Drogo growled. Val froze. Emily bit back a shriek of frustration and opened her eyes to see Ana hovering unnervingly in midair.

The ghost wafted closer. "So here you are, Val, and doing what you shouldn't! You pledged yourself to me, remember, until death did us part? And though it did, it didn't, so you're stuck with me until—"

Emily said, in wonder, "It's not your house that's haunted, but you, Val!"

Ana's attention turned to Emily. "What happened to you? Really, Val, you should take better care of her. Although, now I think on it, you didn't take very good care of *me*!"

"He didn't?" said Emily.

"I did so," retorted Val.

"Then where were you when Oko stuck me in that burlap sack? Nowhere to be found, that's where!"

Emily felt Val contemplating violence. Fascinating, this glimpse of married life. Equally fascinating, her own desire to strangle Ana with one of her veils.

Veils? Burlap sacks? "You were a concubine!"

"I was an odalisque!" Ana snapped. "A favored one. The sultan liked my way with the *dance du ventre*." She struck a pose, and began to dance.

Never could Emily have imagined anything like this.

Or anything like Ana, for that matter. Emily wasn't accustomed to seeing a female so scantily dressed. True she couldn't see Ana as much as see through her, but there was no question that Ana wasn't wearing much, and all of that was in movement as she writhed and shimmied with a good deal of stomach play and twisting of her body, fell upon her knees and bent backward til her hair swept the floor. Every muscle and both shoulders were made to quiver. She concluded with a final suggestive wriggle of her hips, and a two-handed finger snap.

"Astonishing!" said Emily. "I wish I could do that."

"No you don't," retorted Ana. "Being fancied by the Sultan wasn't all that great a treat, particularly when he was in the mood for the Fixing of a Nail, because he wasn't altogether perky, even with the help of a special paste made of forty-one different spices, honey, and herbs. The eunuchs, on the other hand—"

"I beg you," interrupted Val. "No more."

Ana huffed and plopped down at the foot of Emily's cot on top of Drogo, who whined. "Have you found my spell yet?"

"We've been a little busy. Although Abercrombie informs me that if I burn acorns, mistletoe, and oak bark, at the same time murmuring my ardent desire for you to do so, you might leave."

"No!" protested Emily. "Not yet. I wish her to find my papa."

Ana looked doubtful. "I don't think we stay around without good reason. I wasn't here myself until Valentin called me back."

"I didn't call you back. That was Emily. In case there's any doubt, I don't want you here."

Ana's lower lip quivered. "This, after all those vows you swore to me? I think you just broke my heart."

Val snorted. Emily poked him with her elbow. "Where were you before we called you back?"

Ana was still sulking. "I don't know. Somewhere *other*. And I also don't know why you're not working on finding a spell to make me solid, because the sooner you find it, then the sooner you can tup yourselves!" She reconsidered. "I don't think that's exactly what I meant."

Though the notion of tupping oneself was intriguing, albeit somewhat perplexing, Emily was preoccupied. "*Can* you contact other spirits?"

Ana sniffed. "I'm sure I don't know."

Chapter Twenty-Nine

Never choose your women or your linen by candlelight.
(Romanian proverb)

Dusk had darkened into night by the time Val escorted Emily up the stair to his front door. That portal was opened by Isidore, who so forgot himself at sight of them that his lips twitched into a faint approximation of a smile, despite the flood of flowers and invitations and *billets-doux* that had been arriving ever since word of Emily's fortune had gotten round. Isidore's reaction was shared, rather more enthusiastically, by the other members of the household, Mrs. MacCamish becoming inspired by Miss Dinwiddie's return to prepare a Cullen Skink. Jamie nicely summed up everyone's feelings when he said, "Lor', Miss Emily, ye gie us an awfu fricht!"

Once assured of Emily's well-being, Zizi, Bela, and Lilian rushed off to prepare her a nice bath, and a fresh change of clothes. Jamie scurried to fetch his master a sustaining pot of tea. On, then, to the drawing room, where Machka marched up to Drogo and swatted him on the nose, then twined herself around his legs with a rumbling purr.

Lady Alberta sat in an upholstered chair, on the table beside her a stack of books. She wore a gown that flattered her, and so it should have, considering the cost. Not that Val begrudged a penny. Lady Alberta was worth her weight in gold, a weight that had noticeably increased since she'd taken up residence beneath his roof.

She watched Drogo settle on the hearth. "I don't believe I've noticed that scar before."

"It's of fairly recent origin." Machka was twining about his own legs now, and Val picked up the cat. "Nothing to concern yourself about."

Emily nudged him. *Due to Cezar. He's a healer, isn't he? I'm not the only one full of surprises, I think.*

Val placed Machka on his shoulder and took Emily's hand in his. Cezar was indeed a healer, a gift rare among their kind. Impossible to tell the long-term effects of what they had done.

Emily seemed quite lively at the moment. So lively that, had Val not known better, he might think she'd been into his port.

Lady Alberta didn't know better. She eyed him disapprovingly. "I don't know what's going on with the two of you—and mind you, I don't want to!—but there's definitely something in the air."

Emily sniffed. "I think it's me."

Val smiled. *There's nothing more enflaming to a male than a female's natural scent.* Emily wrinkled her nose at him.

Lady Alberta said, "Whatever it is, it seems to agree with you. Have you lost your glasses, dear?"

"I have. But it doesn't matter. I don't need the silly things." Emily snatched up a small volume and held it up before her nose to read aloud.

From my grave to wander I am forc'd,
Still to seek The Good's long sever'd link
Still to love the bridegroom I have lost
And the life-blood of his Heart to drink . . .

She tossed the book aside. "What poppycock."

Lady Alberta regarded her with interest. "Johann Wolfgang Von Goethe's *Bride of Corinth* is poppycock?"

"The heroine is poppycock. A lovestruck young maiden who dies when her parents refuse to allow her to marry her paramour, then returns from the grave to consummate her love, as beautiful as she was in life mind you, only to end up burning on a funeral pyre." Emily raised her free hand to brush her tangled hair back from her forehead. "To die of love, indeed!"

Val paid little attention to the conversation. He didn't know quite what to make of this hey-go-mad Emily. What he wished to *do* with her was simpler. He wanted to give her slow, sweet kisses until her toes curled. Until his own toes curled. To discover what little cries she would make at the height of passion, when he introduced her to *la petite mort*.

Emily tugged him down on the sofa. Val tucked an errant curl behind her ear. Machka leapt down from his shoulder to curl up in his lap.

Val dropped his hand to the cat's soft fur and wondered at his own reckless frame of mind. Somehow, when he wasn't paying attention, Emily had stolen past his guard.

Or had crawled under his skin. Damned if it didn't feel like she was inspecting him from the inside out. From the inside of his elbows to the outside of his knees. His shoulders to his thighs. His—

Val focused his attention on Emily and felt her body warm, her heartbeat speed up. His own body warmed apace until Machka growled and bit his hand, and Val recalled that they were not alone in the drawing room.

Emily. Stop staring at my mouth. She blinked at him and touched her fingers to his lips.

"It seems I must be blunt!" Lady Alberta crossed her arms and tried to look stern. "Whatever else the two of you have been doing, Val, I trust that you haven't given Emily the Kiss."

He had given her any number of kisses. Val found himself at an unusual loss for words. Emily murmured, "That's rather a personal question, Lady Alberta, don't you think?"

Lady Alberta was briefly distracted by the arrival of Jamie with a tea tray bearing Tantallon cakes, border tarts, and raspberry buns, sent from the kitchen to sustain them until more hearty fare had been prepared. After informing them that Isidore had said that an army of stags led by a lion would be more formidable than one of lions led by a stag, Jamie was persuaded to depart.

Once she had performed the tea-pouring ritual and in the process snatched several delicacies for herself, Lady Alberta returned to the attack. "Don't be obtuse, Emily. I refer to *the* Kiss. The Dark Kiss. The Kiss of Souls."

Emily took a bite of border tart. "I didn't know kisses had names."

"Indeed they do, my dear! There are the basic sort, which include the Peck, which I think of as the Chicken Kiss, the Lip and Nip, the Neck Nibble, and the Butterfly. Among the more advanced varieties are the Buzzing Kiss, and the Tickle Kiss, and the Reverse Lips. And we mustn't forget the French, and its variant, Sucking the Tongue."

"Hmm," said Emily thoughtfully.

Val sipped his tea. She would require demonstrations. Miss Dinwiddie's thirst for knowledge was unquenchable.

As had been Val's thirst for her. Emily was making him remember what it was like to have life, and be in love. Although love as Val remembered it had been a simple emotion, nothing like the complex muddle of

emotions he felt for Emily. Did he regret the compli-
cated tangle she had made of his existence? Val thought
he did not.

He did regret, however, his appalling lack of control.
As he had begun to suspect was usual for her, Emily had
gotten what she wanted. He had bitten her. More than a
little bit.

Val wondered why Cezar had acted as he had, and
what the consequences would be.

Perhaps Cezar simply liked Emily.

Unlikely. Cezar didn't "simply" do anything.

Lady Alberta's voice interrupted Val's thoughts. "Not
that I should be speaking to you of *that*! Mr. Ross came
to call during your absence. According to the gabble-
grinders, he has been selling off everything he owns,
and attempting to borrow money besides, none of which
is likely to save him drowning in the River Tick." Over
the edge of her teacup, she studied Val. "He anticipates
that you shall disillusion us."

"How shall I do that, I wonder?" said Val.

"You would have to try very hard." Emily licked cake
crumbs from her fingers. "Lady Alberta, do you believe
in the undead?"

"Well you might ask." Lady Alberta gestured toward
the stack of books at her elbow. "I've been reading all
sorts of curious material, since I had to do something to
distract myself from worrying."

Emily was startled. "You worried about me?"

"Of course I did! As did Isidore. Jamie and the girls
scoured the town in search of you." Lady Alberta's hand
hovered over the remnants of the Tantallon cake. "Why
do you find it such an odd notion that someone should
be concerned on your behalf?"

Emily considered. "I suppose because no one ever
has been. Oh, Mama worried that I would behave inap-
propriately, with some justification, I admit. But she

never worried about *me*. I was entirely too 'capable' for her taste. As for Papa, he simply refused to let me do anything that might have become worrying." She selected another raspberry bun. "So that he wouldn't be distracted from his experiments."

In that case, the Professor must be spinning in his grave. And if he were not, Val might give him a good kick.

Lady Alberta sat up straighter. "I see! As I was saying, my own efforts at distraction led me to reading, and I have consequently discovered that there are apparently a great many more things than hitherto dreamt of in my philosophy! I know now that if a gentleman pricks an orange all over and sleeps with it under his armpit, then presents it the next day to the object of his affections, and if the lady eats it, she will return his regard. Unless instead she eats lizards dipped in urine. It hardly requires a leap of faith to also credit the existence of Mr. Polidori's vampires." Lady Alberta reached for the teapot.

Not for the first time Val wished Polidori to perdition, as he watched Emily lick jam off her lower lip and squelched an all-too-mortal urge to turn her tap-salteerie and acquaint every freckle on her little body with the Besotted Vampire kiss. Instead he gave Lady Alberta a brief, expurgated summary of recent events, to wit that Emily had been set upon and rescued in the very nick of time, omitting any mention of demons and ghosts lest he try her astonishing tolerance too far.

"Good gracious!" Lady Alberta gasped. "How very romantic! You rescued dear Emily in the nick of time!"

"How very paper-skulled, you mean. Emily could have been killed." No matter how many years he studied, Val would never comprehend the workings of the female mind.

"But I wasn't, was I? Because of you. My hero." Emily twinkled at him.

Damnation. If not for the presence of Lady Alberta, Val would have had his wicked way with Emily there and then. And then he remembered that he mustn't have his wicked way with her then or ever, and was suddenly cross.

And about to become more so. Steps sounded in the stairway. Isidore's irritable tones intertwined with familiar sultry tones. Val cursed beneath his breath as he rose from the sofa, and saw Emily's hands clench into fists. Machka padded across the carpet to curl beside Drogo on the hearth.

Lisbet pushed past Isidore and walked into the room, elegant in a gown of embroidered silk gauze with a sarsenet slip and very likely nothing underneath. Her hair was drawn up in an Apollo knot. Around her shoulders was a velvet mantelet trimmed and lined with white swansdown. "*Mea amant,* I was wondering what had become of you, and was so worried I couldn't stay away. You *do* recall that you are engaged to me tonight, for the theater and after, Val?" She linked her arm possessively with his. "*Zău!* Lady Alberta, you have grown quite plump! My dear Miss Dinwiddie, has the cat got your tongue? You will forgive my plain speaking, I know, when I say that you look like something that animal dragged in!"

Lady Alberta spoke before Emily could respond in kind. "Least said, soonest mended! Dear Miss Dinwiddie has been having quite an adventure, but we shan't bore you with that, not lacking for manners, unlike some I know. Really, to present oneself at a gentleman's house without an invitation . . . In my day, we would never have dared do such a thing. Yes, I know, you needn't point out times have changed. But not that much, I think. What an interesting gown *you* are wearing, ma'am, but I fear you have left part of it behind. It is unwise to bare your chest in this climate, lest you catch your death of cold!"

Never had Val been so grateful for Lady Alberta's chatter. *Elfling—*

She turned her face away from him. *Go to the devil, Ravensclaw!*

Chapter Thirty-One

Good words cool more than cold water.
(Romanian proverb)

It was a sunny morning in Auld Reekie, a rare enough occasion at this time of year to draw the Old Town's residents out of doors to enjoy the clement weather. The narrow streets were crowded with all manner of pedestrians, from children escaping orphanages and the slums beneath the city to judges in their satin robes and the occasional constable, as well as street vendors of everything from herbs to hardware, perambulating pickpockets, and dissolute lordlings en route to their beds after yet another night of determined debauchery.

Among those savoring the sunlight was Lady Alberta, though not after any night-long dissipation, it having been a very long time since she enjoyed anything any more depraved than Mrs. MacCamish's Honey and Whiskey Cake. Her pale purple redingote was a joy to snuggle into, with its gold cord and grey fur trim, and the curly plume of her plum velvet turban perfectly matched her tar-black hair. Next to her Emily felt like a drab little wren, even though her ankle-length pelisse of grey shot sarsenet, clasped at regular distances from the throat to the hem, was of the finest quality, as was the straw and muslin capote with a stiffened brim that framed her face and hid her curls. Jamie trailed importantly after them.

"What a lovely day!" Lady Alberta beamed with approval upon the cerulean blue sky. "For once the rain isn't pouring down like cats and dogs. Wherever did that expression come from, do you think? Because no matter how hard it may rain, I cannot imagine little Drogos and Machkas descending from the heavens. Why not ducks, I wonder? Or perhaps, frogs? At least they have some passing acquaintance with water. Although I did know a cat once that enjoyed being bathed. Put the silly creature in a basin of water and it would purr." Her smile slipped a little. "Ah well, that was long ago and in another country, so to speak." Neither of her companions made a comment, though Jamie might well have, had he not grown fond of the auld bletherskate, and didnae Miss Emily look bonnie without her spentacles, and wisna he quite the lad o' pairts in his finery? Alberta gave Emily a sideways glance. "He really doesn't care for her, you know. Lisbet Boroi."

Emily made no pretense at misunderstanding the identity of that "he." Had she not lain awake all the night waiting for Ravensclaw to return home so that she could either kiss him or kick him or rip off his jacket and do all three at once? "Then why spend so much time with her?" she snapped.

Lady Alberta glanced back at Jamie, who strove to look cherubic, with a marked lack of success, and lowered her voice. "Sometimes gentlemen find it difficult to remove themselves from their little entanglements."

Emily suspected Val wouldn't find it difficult to remove himself from anything or anywhere. As he had so effortlessly removed himself from her. In which case he might have removed himself from Lisbet, and therefore one could only conclude he didn't wish to, which was most perplexing, since Emily had a very clear impression that Val didn't like Lisbet above half.

Perhaps liking wasn't of especial importance in matters amatory. "I'm sure I don't care."

"Doing it rather too brown, my dear, but never mind! I believe it's time you left off those somber colors and adapted a more dashing style. In a word, we shall fight fire with fire!"

Emily wondered how Val would react if she wore her gown cut down to her navel, not that a bold décolletage would display anything of particular interest. Probably he'd be amused. Emily wanted to see Val lose his dratted self-control. As he had already done once, but she'd been too overwhelmed to remember much.

Emily intended to have her wits about her the next time. If there was a next time. Perhaps she *should* let Lady Alberta take her in hand.

First, Emily had a stop of her own to make. She led her companions down the stone stairs at the foot of Lothian Road into St. Cuthbert's Kirkyard.

"A cemetery?" Lady Alberta contemplated a mossy grave marker. "Might one know what you are looking for, dear?"

Emily bent to read an inscription. "Dirt from the grave of an innocent."

"I had to ask, didn't I?" Lady Alberta murmured.

Some little time passed while Emily poked and peered among the lichen-covered monuments—*Here lyes Elizabeth Shile, spouse to Baillie James Adamson, Brewer and Portioner of Portsburgh, who died October 25th, 1731*—and Jamie aided in her efforts, while Lady Alberta remained prudently on less soggy ground. It was Jamie who at last found treasure, a lass who expired at seven years of age, and a hundred years earlier, most likely being unkenand. Emily scooped up some dirt into a twist of paper, and tucked it in her reticule. As a reward to Alberta for her forbearance, shopping they would go.

As the trio made their way through the crowded town to their destination, Lady Alberta pointed out places of interest: the spot in High Street that had once marked the end of Edinburgh, the Canongate having been a separate town envied for its gardens and orchards; Brodie's Close, home to a Town Council member whose penchant for midnight burglaries climaxed in an abortive armed raid upon the Excise Office in the Royal Mile, and who was consequently hanged; John Knox's House and the street well near the door which at one time had been the only source of water in the neighborhood. Jamie added his own observations, of a somewhat more ghoulish nature, concerning Fleshmarket Close, and Coffin Lane, Greyfriars cemetery with its corpse mountain of executed Covenanters and plague victims dumped to rot in unmarked graves. Emily ignored both of her companions to ponder the various permutations of what Val and Lisbet might have done to one another during the long night, and whether teeth might have been involved, and by the time their destination was arrived at had worked herself into no small snit.

Lady Alberta paused at the bottom of a small shop-lined street, inhaled deeply, and quivered like a hound on the scent. And then Emily was caught up in a veritable orgy of shopping that involved shoemakers and woolen-drapers, modistes and milliners and manufacturers of fine lace.

Having declared he'd be struck down deid afore he set foot in a ladies' emporium, Jamie waited in the street outside, for which the ladies were grateful, due to his tarry-fingert tendencies. In no time at all, Emily found herself in possession of a morning cap trimmed with white work embroidery, and an evening cap con-

fection of colored satin trimmed with ribbons and lace;
a fichu of fine sheer white muslin embroidered with a
continuous band of purple flowers and shaded green
leaves, the edges scalloped and embroidered with green
silk; ivory satin garters to hold up her stockings; a pretty
pair of slippers in robin's egg blue, another of green
leather with blue-green silk ribbon trim and ties, and
half-boots of brown kid leather embellished with silk
rosettes at the toe. No one had a greater appreciation
of shopping than Alberta because, as she admitted, she
had been purse-pinched for so long.

Jamie attempted to balance the pyramid of purchases, and observed that since he was packed up like a
donkey, Lady Alberta might want to bewaur 'is teeth.

"Don't sham it so, you cheeky wee rapscallion!" Lady
Alberta caught a package in mid-tumble and tucked it
back beneath his chin. Then nothing would do but that
Emily must have a Kashmir shawl, not the sort made on
hand looms in Edinburgh, or heaven forbid Paisley, but
the genuine article woven in a twill tapestry technique
with goat's fleece taken from beneath the coarse outer
hair of the underbelly of wild central Asian goats, the
result being a light, smooth shawl with a natural sheen.

Lady Alberta was unstoppable. Her questing eye was
next caught by a chemist's shop and she shepherded
Emily inside to sample Improved Gowland's Lotion,
Royal Tincture of Peach Kernels, and Olympia Dew. Did
Emily know that the juice of green pineapples would
take away wrinkles and give the complexion an air of
youth, and that if pineapples were not available, onions
would do as well?

Emily did not. Nor was she aware that powdered
parsley seed was believed to prevent baldness, or that
grated horseradish immersed in sour milk would get rid
of freckles, though this latter she took leave to doubt. If
her recent adventures had left her freckles unaffected,

then they were with her for life, in their vast numbers and various hues. Not that Emily had ever tried to count them. Perhaps Val would do so. If she ever spoke to him again.

Having concluded her business with the chemist, Lady Alberta waited for the bundle to be made up. "I don't wish to pry into your business, dear, but I'm concerned about Mr. Ross. He wishes to live in clover, and no one can blame him, because to do so would be highly preferable to being in the basket, but I cannot like this business of attempted assaults, and things gone missing. When did you first notice that he'd set his cap at you?"

Emily cast back in her mind. Had it been during the inspection of the Perpetuum Mobile? The Personal Astrolabe? On the occasion of the unveiling of the Phantasmagoria Machine? "I think it was the day we were discussing the Rule of Gradation, and he seemed quite taken by my comment that though the variations seemed interminable, it was questionable whether they wouldn't delay rather than defy detection. *I* in turn was quite taken with his admiration. Prior to that I'd thought of Michael only as another of the young men who came round out of curiosity, Papa's reputation being what it was. Papa used to spin them the most astonishing yarns. Afterward it seemed Michael was everywhere I went, asking my opinion on all manner of things, and flattering the quality of my mind. No one had ever courted me before. I should've realized it was all moonshine."

"Why?" inquired Lady Alberta. "Forgive me for saying so, but a young woman with your upbringing could hardly be expected to understand the game of hearts."

Emily fingered the chain of her reticule. "A game, is it? With rules? I wish you'd tell me what they are."

"How should I know? I am a mere spinster. But were I to guess I'd say there are no rules save follow your own heart."

Their transactions finally completed—Emily having at the last minute been inspired, or coerced, to purchase some Pomade de Nerole for her unruly hair—the ladies returned to the street and added yet another packet to Jamie's pile, which now reached to his nose. Lady Alberta declared that she was in need of refreshment, specifically a dish of savory mussels cooked with bacon and eggs coddled in cream.

Emily had just suggested they might go home when Jamie gestured to the opposite side of the street. Outside the Penny Post Office, from which letters and small parcels were dispatched eight times a day to Leith, stood Michael Ross. Lady Alberta murmured, "Speak of the devil and he will appear!"

As Emily wondered what Michael might be posting, and to whom, he spied them and hurried across the street. "Emily! I almost didn't recognize you without your spectacles. Have you broken them again?" A dark glance at Lady Alberta. "I must speak with you alone."

Lady Alberta drew herself up to her full height. "I trust you jest, young man! Anything you wish to say to my niece may be said in front of me. I caution you, however, that I shan't have her upset by more of your dark mutterings!"

Emily winced as Michael's fingers dug into her arm. Deep into her bravura performance, Lady Alberta didn't seem to notice that Michael looked strange. Very strange, feverish almost, and it was clear from the condition of his clothing and the aroma that surrounded him—a great deal less pleasant even than Macassar Oil—that it had been some time since he bathed, which led Emily to the conclusion that females must be very different from males in their likings, because Michael's natural scent didn't enflame her one little bit.

Lady Alberta concluded: "I trust I make my meaning

clear. You may be as private as you wish with Emily *after* you are wed."

Michael didn't argue. Instead he punched Lady Alberta on the chin. She toppled over with a screech and a flurry of petticoats, landing on top of Jamie and his mountain of packages. The event went not unnoticed by other passersby, who quickly gathered round to gawk and offer advice and try to snatch away some of the parcels that lay scattered on the cobblestones. Jamie further proved himself a lad of parts by kicking one would-be thief in the knee and elbowing another in the groin and demanding to know what had given anyone the idea he was a chuntyheid?

Confusion reigned. Emily didn't observe the outcome. Michael pulled her away.

She took firmer hold on her bonnet and her reticule and let him. Time she found out what the deuce was going on.

A total lack of protest would put him on his guard, however. "I'll go with you willingly, Michael, if only you stop pawing me about!"

Michael gripped her all the tighter. "You haven't gone anywhere willingly with me since you came to Edinburgh. If only you'd stayed at home!"

Through a labyrinth of dark, crooked closes he dragged her, deliberately she thought, so that even if she wished she couldn't find the way again. If Emily's sense of direction had not entirely deserted her, they came at last to the warren of vaults formed by the arches of the South Bridge. Michael plunged through a crumbling doorway, down a dark pathway so narrow that Emily could have laid a hand on either side, so steep that in bad weather the ground would be as treacherous as ice.

They were in the underground city. The atmosphere was dense with open fires for heat and cooking, the stink of human excrement, the reek of the fish-oil lamps that provided what little light there was. The broken pavements were littered with loiterers, unkempt bare-foot children, ragged men, women wearing tattered flannel petticoats and ancient tartan shawls. Some were sleeping, some were drunk. Some would never venture out into daylight. The smell and sight of the under-ground dwellers made Emily draw nearer to Michael as they entered a series of gloomy, abandoned tunnels. He was muttering beneath his breath.

Around one last corner, down a steep and slippery pathway, until an ancient door loomed ahead. Michael inserted a key into the lock, and pushed. The vault gaped open before them like an open tomb. Michael stepped inside, hauling Emily along with him, then shoved her to the ground.

The hard ground. Emily yelped as her hands encountered stone so rough it tore the soft kid of her gloves. Her bonnet slid forward to rest on her nose. Behind her, the door slammed shut.

A lamp glowed in the darkness. A lamp that burned fish oil, from the stink of it. Fish oil and Michael's un-washed body were not the worst smells in this place. The scent of pungent herbs burning in a brazier added to the general stench. Carefully, Emily climbed to her feet. Her hands still stung. She pulled off her torn gloves and pushed her bonnet back in place.

The lamp hung from a rusted hook set high in the old wall. Its dim light gleamed on a collection of instru-ments on a small rickety table. Spring-loaded lancets, fleams, a scarifier with a series of twelve spring-driven blades that when cocked and released caused many shallow cuts, a sharp curved sword—

In one corner was a grisly display of severed heads. Emily swallowed and wished for her pistol, which had been lost in the encounter with Samael. Or even her umbrella, which Lady Alberta had insisted be left behind, because to carry it in such lovely weather would seem odd indeed.

Emily hadn't wished to appear odd. Now she heartily regretted her lapse into vanity. "What is this place, Michael? Why have you brought me here?"

"You didn't leave me much choice, did you?" Michael rubbed his forehead. "Deuce take it, Emily, you're determined to be a thorn in my flesh."

How unwell he looked. Emily wondered if she truly could have shot him. "How?" she asked.

Michael stared at her in confusion. "How what?"

"How am I a thorn in your flesh?"

"By not agreeing to marry me when you should have. It's your fault I was forced to steal those things. If I *hadn't* stolen those things, we wouldn't be here now. And then you had to follow me and refuse to return home."

Emily didn't waste time with pointless questions. "You stole the athame. Were you also responsible for Papa's accident?"

"I don't know what you're talking about. And if you weren't so damned unreasonable you'd admit I had no choice."

Emily saw that she had been unreasonable in giving Michael the benefit of the doubt. "You admit you stole the knife. Now you must give it back. Along with the list."

"I must, must I?" scoffed Michael. "You have windmills in your head. What I *must* have is your necklace. Give it to me."

Emily wasn't sure if the pendant would nullify the athame or enhance it, but this was no moment in which to experiment. "I'm not wearing it today."

"Liar. You always wear it." The blade of the athame

gleamed in Michael's hand. Emily felt the pendant tucked away from view inside her pelisse. It was burning hot. She glanced again at the severed heads.

Ravensclaw might have *her* head for putting herself in this position. "Was it you who called Samael?" Having sent away the demon once, Emily could do it again. She hoped. At any event she'd prefer to be in Samael's presence than Michael's, which gave rise to the question of which was the greater fiend.

"You're trying to distract me." Michael started forward. Emily stepped back, stumbled over something lying on the floor. A large something, lean and muscular, with chestnut hair half-hiding a harsh, scarred face. She knelt beside him, saw no obvious injuries. "Andrei?"

"All cats are grey in the dark. Even cats as old as Ravensclaw." Michael moved closer. "I'm sorry it has to be like this, Emily, but I really have no choice."

"Stuff and nonsense. There's always a choice."

"The devil there is." Michael raised the knife. "If you don't willingly give me the necklace, I'll be forced to persuade you."

Independence and so forth were all well and good but it was clearly time to call in the cavalry. Even though she wasn't speaking to him. *Val!* Truly, it was less a thought than a shout.

Meanwhile, she must try for a diversion. Emily fluttered her eyelashes. "Does this mean you no longer wish to marry me, Michael?"

Chapter Thirty-One

Curses, like chickens, come home to roost.
(Romanian proverb)

Val would have been first to admit that he was very old. Only recently he had attempted to reckon his own age, using human lifetimes as a measuring stick: if he counted four generations to a century, he could be Emily's grandfather how many times removed?

The resulting answer caused him to swear off higher mathematics. Val and Emily weren't May and December, they were this century and the dawn of time, and why was he thinking such nonsense anyway? He couldn't have Emily, and that was the end of it. And he certainly couldn't let her have him. And he'd be eternally damned before he allowed anyone to do her harm.

Not that he probably wasn't already eternally damned. Damn Lisbet as well for appearing before he'd found an opportunity for explanations and then keeping him with her until well past dawn.

He'd left her now, and without a word of explanation. Let Lisbet make of that what she would. She was already displeased with his performance, or his lack thereof.

Emily was frightened. Val felt her emotions as if they

were his own, and with them a great rage. Emily was his—well, not really, but if he wasn't what he was she surely would have been—and if anyone was going to frighten her, it should be him. Not that he wished to frighten her. He *did* wish to shake her until her teeth rattled in her head.

She served as his beacon. In less than the time it took to think his angry thoughts, Val was in the vaults beneath the South Bridge. The dwellers in the underground city didn't see him pass.

Into the gloomy abandoned tunnels, where his keen eyesight and heightened senses more than compensated for the absence of light, around one last corner, down a steep and slippery pathway . . . Emily's presence was so vivid Val could almost touch her. Her voice came to him through an ancient barred door.

She sounded very reasonable, all things considered. "You can't have all my lovely money unless you marry me, Michael. And you can hardly marry me if I'm dead."

Val paused, poised to break down the door, as Michael spoke. "I'm not going to dwell under the hen's foot, so don't think it, Emily!" His voice lowered. "Anyway, I'm not the one who wants you dead."

"Then who?"

"I can't tell you that."

A moment's silence, while Emily ruminated. Her thoughts were vivid in Val's mind. Through her eyes he saw the small stone chamber, the table with its grisly instruments, the grim corner display. Emily appeared to be in no immediate danger, so Val waited to hear what she would say next.

Emily said, "Do you remember the Phantasmagoria, Michael?"

"The Magic Lantern. Adjustable lenses and ventriloquism and moving slides. I remember everything, Emily." A pause. "Almost."

"Then you may also remember that people believed the forces of darkness and sorcery were responsible for projecting images where none had been previously. Which was so much poppycock. Whatever *you* believe, Michael, the athame must be returned to the Society."

Val felt the athame, stronger now than he remembered, even more dangerous. It was the nature of the thing to feed off the person who wielded it. Michael Ross was no longer the young man who had courted Emily.

"The knife belongs to whoever holds it, and I'm holding it now. Look, Emily. See how it gleams in the lamplight. Feel how sharp it is."

Val felt the sting of the blade as it pierced her skin. Furious with himself for waiting, he kicked in the door.

Emily glanced at him. Her wrist was bleeding. *I apologize for wishing you to the devil. Thank you for coming anyway.* Michael took advantage of Emily's distraction to slip his knife under the clasps of her pelisse. They melted like soft butter, exposing the pendant to his view.

Michael reached out. Emily clasped her hand protectively around the ruby and backed away.

Marie d'Auvergne's athame and her pendant in one place again. How long had it been? Power was thick in the room. Val felt as though his feet were mired in sludge.

He couldn't move. Not only power, but something else had him in its grip. In the brazier burned pungent herbs. As Val tried to identify them, Michael sprang at him, athame upraised to strike.

Val! Emily hurled herself in front of Michael. He flung her aside. She slammed against the instrument-laden table. It collapsed on top of her.

Val recognized the unfamiliar smell then, as his limbs refused to obey him, and Michael feinted and jabbed with the athame. "You walked into the trap. That wasn't very clever of you, Ravensclaw."

Mr. Ross was fortunate that Val couldn't catch up with him, else he would have snapped the bastard's neck. As it was, he could only stand frozen while Michael slashed at him with the athame, and the sharp blade drew blood.

One hand emerged from the wreckage of the table, then a leg. Emily was swearing, fulsomely, in his head. *Dammit, Ravensclaw, what's wrong with you?*

The herb burning in the brazier. It renders us helpless. See if you can rouse Andrei.

Emily climbed cautiously to her feet. Val was further angered to see that her scalp was bleeding now as well as her wrist.

Michael was oblivious as Emily removed herself from the wreckage of the table. He was intent on taunting Val. The adder's tongue hadn't affected Val's vision, or his appreciation of the sight of Emily's sweetly upturned bottom as she crawled across the floor. If this was to be his last sight, it was at least a pleasant one. He regretted both his prudence and his forbearance, now that it was too late.

Emily glanced back at him. *Never did I think to hear such drivel from the great Ravensclaw.* As Michael brought down the knife again, she opened her reticule, uncorked her vinaigrette, and stuck it under Andrei's nose. Andrei sniffed and stirred. Michael was too caught up in his mad frenzy to notice the addition of vinegar to the other odors in the room.

He danced around, slicing and chanting until Val felt like a maypole being wound about with ribbons of blood. "Stinking motherwort grows upon dunghills. Moonwort will open locks and unshoe such horses as tread upon it. Dead nettle—I forget what dead nettle does, but it will come back to me."

Emily said crossly, "Stop this foolishness, Michael."

Michael ignored her, gave Val another poke with the

athame. Val concentrated all his effort on keeping Michael's attention fixed on him as Emily reached for the sword. "How do you like your adder's tongue, Ravensclaw? The juice of the leaves, drunk with the distilled water of horse-bait, is a singular remedy for all manner of wounds. The leaves infused with the oil of unripe olives, set in the sun four certain days, makes an excellent green balsam. Not that either will help you now. Your fate is sealed." Michael's voice covered the sound of Andrei getting unsteadily to his feet.

Emily propped Andrei up, shoved the sword at him, and pressed the vinaigrette into his other hand. Andrei looked disheveled and disreputable, and no whit less dangerous for the vinaigrette held to his nose. Flickering lamplight lent his scarred face a somewhat diabolic cast as he stared Val dead in the eye and smiled. Andrei's smile at the best of times was chilling. In this moment he resembled the Grim Reaper responding to a bad joke.

Michael hadn't glanced away from Ravensclaw. "What do you think, Emily? I could pour boiling oil on him, make a paste of his flesh and feed on it, cut off his toes."

Emily moved closer to them. "Cook his heart with vinegar, oil, and wine? Prevent him from straying by stabbing nine spindles into his grave? Really, Michael, you're carrying this nonsense too far."

Michael reached out for Emily, grabbed her wounded wrist. "If you drink the lifeblood of your enemy, you will gain his powers. Perhaps you and I should drink the blood of Ravensclaw."

"I already have," retorted Emily. "It was quite tasty." As Michael gaped at her, she raised her other hand and threw the contents of a paper packet into his eyes.

"Gaaah!" Blinded, Michael raised the athame. Emily wrenched it from his hand and dropped to her knees as

Andrei swung. The sword connected with a gratifying thud.

It was less a fight than an assassination. When curiosity became too much for her to bear, Emily opened her eyes to peek. Bloodied but not beaten, Michael crawled across the floor to the broken table of instruments. Emily scrunched her eyes shut as Andrei swung the sword again, and once more for good measure, and then again.

The fresh air—"fresh" being a relative term in a place like this—had begun to sweep away the poisonous smoke. Val found that he could speak. "You can open your eyes now," he said weakly, as Andrei—still holding the vinaigrette to his nose—extinguished the brazier and carried its contents outside.

Emily dropped to the floor beside Val. She had lost her bonnet, and her hair stuck out every which way, and she was the loveliest thing he had ever seen. "You've rescued me again, elfling. What was that you threw into his eyes?"

"Dirt from the grave of an innocent. I had meant it for another use, but it turns out to be very handy stuff." She eyed his numerous cuts. "You're not healing."

"It's the adder's blood."

Emily pulled her sleeve away from her still-bleeding wrist. Val tried to turn his head. She threaded her fingers through his hair and made him look at her. "Yes, I know. You don't trust yourself to take me again without taking me too far. Well, *I* trust you. Don't be so stubborn, Val."

Val had meant to keep Emily safe, at least until he was certain she suffered no ill effects from what had been done to her. Truthfully, if Val were honest with himself, he wanted to keep her safe longer than that. For Emily, forever wouldn't be enough time.

But he didn't have forever. Or if he did, Emily did

not. He thought. What she did have were both the d'Auvergne athame and its matching pendant. Val could no more have resisted her than the earth could have refused to orbit the sun.

Not that he wanted to resist her. *This is becoming a habit, little one.*

A pleasant one. She drew him closer. *Pleasure me, Val.*

The warmth of her skin was sweet against his lips. Val pressed his mouth to her pulse, gently licked. Magic sizzled in the taste of her in his mouth. He felt her blood race in his own veins.

The hunger, when it struck, was overwhelming in its strength. Her blood scent rolled over him, through him. He, who had the power to make a woman beg, was helpless before it. Before her.

Admit it. You want me. Emily lay sprawled across his chest. *And I want you. I want to feel you against my bare skin. I want you to show me all the things I don't yet know.* Words dissolved into images of racing hearts and tangled limbs.

The adder's tongue had worn off. Val could have moved, had he the inclination. Emily's riotous curls were tickling his nose.

He knew he should stop. He didn't want to. Val needed Emily. He licked at her, caught her flesh between his teeth and gently sucked. She moaned.

That little sound undid him. Rules be damned. Val would take Emily home and make love to her as she deserved. Flesh to flesh. Heart to heart. He would introduce her to all the forms of loving that he knew, and then make up some more. He would—

She thumped him in the ribs. *Val.*

He groaned. *What now?* If Ana had interrupted them again he'd find a way to make her corporeal long enough that he could wrap his hands around her throat.

It was not Ana, but Andrei's ruined voice that spoke. "Valentin. The *Stăpanâ.*"

All the warmth left Val's body. Gently, he pushed Emily off himself and sat up.

Lisbet stood in the doorway. "*Iubiera ca moartea e de tare.* I warned you, *baiat.*"

Chapter Thirty-Two

Women are the devil's nets.
(Romanian proverb)

Lisbet threw back the Persian shawl she'd draped over her head. Dark hair tumbled loose over the shoulders of her muslin morning gown. Her pale skin was luminous in the lamplight. "What a cozy gathering. All we need is Cezar. How prudent of him to stay away." She glanced at Andrei, who bowed his head.

Val stepped in front of Emily. Lisbet's dark eyes fixed on him. He stood watching her, his expression as unreadable as her own, as Emily climbed slowly to her feet.

Tension was thick in the room. Tension and dark energy. Emily tucked the pendant inside her bodice and slid the athame into the small pocket of her pelisse.

Lisbet prodded Michael's lifeless body with her toe. "A faulty tool, but useful for a time." She raised her eyes to Emily. "Troublesome chit, you've been playing with my toys. It makes me very cross."

Emily was also feeling cross, at having her amorous education interrupted once again. "Your toy seems to have been going about killing people. Or perhaps that was your wish?"

Lisbet walked further into the room. "You misunderstand, Miss Dimwiddie. I was speaking of Ravensclaw."

Emily glanced at Val. His thoughts were closed to her, his face impassive. He said, "Lisbet. Let her go."

"No." Her tone was sharp as a whip's lash. "You disobeyed me. Perhaps I will take your little English miss away from you. There would be no better punishment, I think."

Val couldn't shut Emily out entirely, try though he might. She realized that he didn't want Lisbet to know of the bond they shared. "You can't possibly think Val is your toy."

"I don't think it, I know it." Lisbet circled Andrei, trailed her hand along his arm, removed the sword from his hand. He didn't try and stop her. "Val, Andrei, and Cezar. Pretty boys, aren't they? I chose only the best."

They were hardly boys. Lisbet was as mad as Michael. A madwoman whose power hammered against Emily. What manner of creature was she? A sorceress?

Emily had never spoken with a sorceress before. A pity the conversation wasn't more amiable.

She gripped the handle of the athame so hard that it hurt her fingers. "Why would anyone wish to destroy their toys?"

"That flaw which drew me to each one no longer intrigues me now. Cezar's failing is arrogance, Andrei's pride, while Val cares for nothing but himself and his pleasure." Lisbet's smile was chilling. "I wonder, Miss Dinwiddie, how well he's pleasured you."

Not well enough, not yet. Deliberately, Emily didn't look at Val.

Lisbet balanced the sword in her hand. "Don't try and protect him. I know he's set his mark on you, as I know Cezar has gathered a formidable amount of influence. I should have destroyed them myself."

Was Emily the only one capable of speech? "Why didn't you?"

"It would have been too simple." Lisbet ran her finger along the sword's sharp blade, watched blood well from the cut. "I preferred to watch them fret. Val was first on my list but he proved clever, so we moved on to Andrei. Michael lured him here so simply it might have been child's play."

Val hadn't stirred. Andrei stood impassively. Emily felt like a rabbit hopping about in a forest of tall trees. "Weren't you afraid they'd realize what you were doing and retaliate?"

Lisbet moved closer to Andrei, raised her bleeding finger to his lips. "They can't. Give me the pendant."

The sight of Andrei licking Lisbet's blood was beyond unsettling. "I can't. Perhaps you should tell me what you want it for."

Lisbet threw back her head and laughed. "You can't seriously think to challenge me."

Emily thought that someone should challenge Lisbet, and she appeared to be the only one so inclined. Brave little bunny that she was. Though her earlier exhilaration had left her, she still felt the combined power of the pendant and the athame.

Neither of which she intended to give Lisbet. "I do, rather," Emily said.

Lisbet moved away from Andrei. Her dark, bottomless gaze pulled at Emily with tangible force. Emily stared back, caught up in that slumberous, seductive spell. Lisbet's dark eyes were mysterious, mesmerizing . . .

As bottomless as the pit, came Cezar's voice in her mind. *And as dangerous. Draw back, Emily. Now!*

Emily blinked. Lisbet stroked a cool finger down her cheek. "Come to me. You know you want to."

"The devil I do!" retorted Emily, and reached out for

Cezar, and struck back with all their combined mental strength.

Lisbet recoiled. The force of her fury sent Emily to her knees.

It was like being buffeted by a storm. A very angry storm that shrieked and raged with a force strong enough to pull her skin right off her bones. Emily squared her shoulders and opened her eyes.

There was truly nothing to focus one's concentration like glimpsing a set of fangs. Lisbet's fangs, to be precise. Emily whispered, "You're *vampir.*"

Lisbet gripped her shoulder. "I am Val's *Stăpană.* His mistress. Do you understand what that means?"

Emily had thought she did. Now she wondered.

Lisbet shook her. "I made him, you little fool. I made them all. Now they try to find a way to escape my hold, though truly there is none."

"Fustian!" Emily grasped a piece of the broken table and thwacked Lisbet on the knee. Lisbet released her. Emily stood up. "Where there's a will, there's a way."

"How very unoriginal," snapped Lisbet.

Emily felt Val, then, and less clearly Cezar and Andrei. *Believe me, there's a will. Don't let her have the pendant.*

Lisbet flicked her hand across Emily's face, a movement so quick that Emily barely saw it coming before she tasted blood. "Stop this foolishness. I know you have the ruby. I can feel it. Give it to me."

Emily pressed her hand against the pendant. Perhaps it was due to the athame that Val and Andrei were both so still. Or perhaps it was because, according to the literature, a vampire could not kill its maker. Not that the literature had been right about much yet.

And not that Emily could take the chance. "Why do you want the pendant?"

"Power, of course." Lisbet struck Emily another

sharp blow. "Give me the thing and perhaps I'll let you go."

Emily believed that no more than she believed in flying pigs. "No."

"Then I shall simply take it." A concussive surge of current, and Lisbet stood transformed into a creature straight from nightmare, all fangs and claws and dead black eyes.

"Goodness!" said Emily. "Perhaps you should try the juice of green pineapple. I'm told it takes away wrinkles and imparts the air of youth."

Snarling, Lisbet leapt. Val moved forward in a blur of speed and placed himself in front of Emily. He, too, had changed, into the fanged, clawed creature Emily had seen once before. But he was no monster. He was simply Val.

Lisbet swung the sword at him. Val leaped aside so quickly the eye could barely follow, then hit her in the face with a closed fist. She rocked back, lunged for his throat. He swept her arm away and clamped his hands around her neck. She jammed her arms between his and reached for the hollow where his jawbone met his skull. He flung her away from him.

Emily started forward, toward the discarded sword. Andrei caught her arm. "What are you doing? Let go of me!"

His hand was like a steel band. "*Sst!* Don't distract me unless you want to see Val harmed."

Emily didn't want to see Val harmed. Or anyone else. Unless it was Lisbet, and that she longed for fervently.

Val caught Lisbet's arm and snapped it. She slammed him to the ground. He sent her sprawling with a kick to the jaw. She picked up the sword and flew back at him, knocking him off balance. He struggled, but she hacked and slashed until she was straddling him, one hand fisted in his hair to pull back his head, the sword pressed to his flesh. Emily wrenched away from Andrei with strength that surprised both of them, and flung the athame.

It struck Lisbet in the throat. "Jesu!" she cried, and clasped her neck. Val pushed her off him. Emily yanked out the athame, leaving a gaping wound and reached for her almost-forgotten charms. A flash of light, the sizzle and stench of burning flesh. Lisbet spat and cringed.

Emily stared at the crucifix. "Why did it work this time?"

Andrei replied, "Because she believes."

Lisbet was far from defeated. Before anyone could try and stop her, she sketched strange symbols and chanted an incantation in a foreign tongue.

The air filled with mist and smoke. When it cleared a great winged creature stood in the middle of the room. Emily held the pendant in one hand, and the athame in the other. "Samael, angel of death, prince of the fifth heaven, genii of fire, demon who tempted Eve—"

"Stupid girl!" Blood spewed from the wound in Lisbet's throat. "The Darkness is mine."

"Not for long, unless he wishes to be." Emily watched Samael change from a large snake with scales of metallic green and blue, a bald head, and multicolored eyes into a great hulking mound of black-charred muscle and flesh, fingers and toes that ended in deadly sharp talons, and several rows of razor-sharp teeth; and finally a rather pretty goat with cloven hooves and eerie yellow eyes. "That was a most impressive display, Samael, but could we leave off the theatrics, do you think?"

The demon returned to his manlike form, and shook out his wings. "I had so hoped to impress you. And no, I *don't* wish to be."

The pendant was almost too hot to hold. "Then I release you in the name of Yod, Cados, Eloym, Saboath, and Yeshua the Anointed One."

Lisbet shrieked and rushed forward. Samael bowled her over with a lazy flick of one wing. "Thank you. I've been wanting to do that for some time."

"Pray take Lisbet away, and keep her there. Somewhere *other*, so she'll bother us no more. And incidentally, you won't bother us anymore, either. Do you understand?"

"Perfectly." Samael winked. "But I'm at your service if you ever reconsider that seduction bit—"

Emily raised both the pendant and the athame. "Samael, angel of death, prince of air, leader of the angels who married the daughters of men, I command you in the name of Yod, Cados, Eloym, Saboath, and Yeshua the Anointed One to return from whence you came."

Thunder cracked. The floor, the walls around then shifted and shook. When the dust settled, both Lisbet and Samael were gone. Emily thanked goodness her papa had made her memorize her abjuration spells.

Val turned to her. Blood flowed from his cuts down his shoulder, across his chest. "Put down the athame."

Had she misjudged him, as well as Michael and Lisbet? So be it, then. Emily dropped the athame and waited.

Val reached out, and drew her close. Emily hugged him tightly, not minding in the least that he was covered in a great deal of Lisbet's blood. Which she was interested to discover had a somewhat enticing smell. Val said, "I'd wanted you to be aware of the beast that is also a part of my nature, though perhaps not so graphically."

He expected her to run away shrieking from him, as a lesser female might. True, this episode *had* given her food for thought. The most charming vampire in all existence was still a vampire.

"That was certainly interesting!" Ana hovered in mid-air. "If a waste of good graveyard dirt. I found your papa, Emily. He was arguing with Albertus Magnus about an ever-burning lamp, and said he didn't have time for my nonsense but you're a good girl and will figure it all out."

A good girl, was she? Who would figure it all out? The hereafter hadn't changed her papa one whit. And it seemed his opinion of her was higher than Emily had thought.

Andrei shook himself as if emerging from a trance. Or a state of shock. "Ana? What are you doing here? And why the devil are you dressed like that?"

Ana looked at her brother. "Oh, rats."

Chapter Thirty-Three

No herb will cure love.
(Romanian proverb)

Lady Alberta and Cezar sat in the drawing room, a tea tray in front of them. Val recognized the corpse of a plum cake.

Cezar held a teacup. Lady Alberta pressed a towel filled with melting ice to her chin. "Good gracious!" she said, as Val and Emily walked into the room. "Speak of something the cat dragged in. My dear, you really should take better care of your clothes."

True, Emily did look rather the worse for wear. Val looked even ghastlier. He said to Cezar, "You're drinking *tea?*"

"Brandy," replied Cezar. "We finished off the tea some time ago. I assume you'd like a fresh pot?"

"Isidore is bringing it."

Cezar looked sardonic, Isidore having informed him upon his arrival that an ass was an ass, though laden with gold. Emily dropped into a chair.

Lady Alberta reached for the brandy decanter. "We were just discussing the *Historia Rerum Aglicarum*. The author, William of Newburg, refers to 'certain prodigies' who sallied forth from their graves to wander about wreaking terror and destruction." She poured herself a generous libation. "Mr. Korzha, of course, doesn't believe in such things."

"Of course." Val leaned against the back of Emily's chair.

Cezar saluted them with his teacup. "The wren has vanquished the eagle, Miss Dinwiddie. I congratulate you."

Emily didn't feel especially gratified. "Which means what?"

"I've discovered a most interesting recipe for a love philter," offered Lady Alberta, her tone somewhat garbled due to the towel held against her chin. "One powders together the heart of a dove, liver of a sparrow, womb of a swallow, and kidney of a hare. I dislike to be vulgarly inquisitive, dear Emily, but the last time I saw you that dreadful Mr. Ross was dragging you off somewhere. Dear Mr. Korzha rescued Jamie and me from that dreadful mob. As Ravensclaw rescued you, I credit." She eyed Val, and his bloodstained appearance. "Or perhaps you rescued him."

Emily scooped up a cake crumb and popped it into her mouth. "It was a little bit of both."

Val gazed down on Emily's untidy curls and wondered what was going on in her unpredictable little head. "Mr. Ross will bother Emily no more."

"Then you did give him his bastings!" Lady Alberta beamed.

"Rather," murmured Emily, "Andrei baked his bread."

Lady Alberta fanned herself with the damp towel. "Ordinarily, one hesitates to speak ill of the departed, but in this case—"

Emily tucked her feet up beneath her in a most unladylike manner. "Lisbet, too, has gone."

"Was, er, her bread baked also?"

"No. Although I wouldn't be surprised if Samael took some sort of revenge."

"Samael?" Lady Alberta held up her hand. "Forget I asked!"

Emily shifted in her chair, glanced around the room. "Where are Machka and Drogo?"

Lady Alberta looked over her shoulder. "I'm sure I don't know. They were both here earlier."

Cezar rose to leave, bent over Lady Alberta's hand. She blushed like a young girl. Val said, "There's something I neglected to tell you. Ana has returned."

Cezar's poise briefly deserted him. "*Ana?*"

Emily smiled. "She's haunting Val. Ana wants to be made corporeal so she can be tupped."

Lady Alberta echoed faintly, "Tupped?"

"That's what she called it, among other things. The beast with two—"

Lady Alberta fanned herself more briskly. "Never mind!"

Cezar had regained his composure. He murmured, "Secrets, Val?"

Val walked Cezar to the stairway. Secrets were merely one of the tools he'd used to survive. All three of them would endure some sort of malaise as a result of Lisbet's banishment. Andrei would suffer worst. Lisbet's claws had sunk deepest into him.

"And you will suffer least," said Cezar. "I give you my blessing, Val. And suggest you take advantage of it before I change my mind."

"And the consequences?"

"Miss Dinwiddie has met the *provocare*. She is your *ailaltă*. Even the Council cannot naysay you now." Cezar touched Val's arm. "Go, be happy, *camarad*."

Val stood in the doorway as Cezar descended the stair.

When he turned back into the room, he found Emily watching him. Her mind remained closed.

Having quietly polished off the last of the plum cake, Lady Alberta shook crumbs off her skirt. "I think perhaps I shall retire."

Emily wriggled one dirty foot. "Leaving me alone with Ravensclaw? How very un-chaperone-like of you."

Lady Alberta tutted. "It would be remiss of me if this were the first time, but since it isn't, forbidding you would be like locking the barn after the horse." She paused halfway out of her chair. "Or do I mean the cart? At any rate, it hardly matters. The die has been cast."

"Lady Alberta!" Emily sat up straighter. "My business here is done, and I will soon be going home. I wonder if perhaps you'd care to return to England with me. I can offer you a comfortable home, and would be grateful for your company."

Lady Alberta very pointedly didn't meet Val's gaze. "What a lovely invitation, and so kindly extended. Yes, my dear, I believe I would."

"I shall take Jamie, too, of course."

Val folded his arms across his chest. "Of course."

Emily stood up. "I believe that I shall also now retire."

Val was alone in his drawing room. What the devil had just transpired? He felt as though he'd been flattened by a gaggle of stampeding geese. A pity brandy no longer served him, or he would have been tempted to down a gallon of the stuff. In no mood for further conversation—not that anyone appeared eager to converse with him—he withdrew to his own bedchamber.

Tea awaited him there. Val picked up the pot and flung it into the fireplace. His feelings—feelings, for God's sake! Shouldn't he be beyond such stuff?—in no whit improved by this demonstration of temper, he stared at his reflection in the looking-glass. Torn and bloodstained clothing . . . He looked like the walking dead.

Hell, he *was* the walking dead. Scant wonder Emily wanted no more to do with him. She had seen him as he really was, and no amount of glamour or persuasion would erase that from her mind. Not that Val would try to sway her. Even if he could.

He had disillusioned her, exactly as predicted by that blasted Michael Ross.

Val had thought himself perfectly content until Emily forced her way into his life, and proceeded to turn his comfortable existence upside down and inside out; had reminded him of all these unsettling mortal emotions he had long forgot. It wasn't blood that Val needed now to survive.

He *would* survive, of course. If Emily was so disillusioned as to walk away from him, then Val must let her go.

Nor could he blame her. He had allowed her to be frightened and, worse, harmed.

It wasn't as if he hadn't known from the beginning that this moment must come. Val tore off his ruined clothes and approached the copper tub of hot water Isidore had left for him, scrubbed savagely at his skin. This self-scourging didn't lessen his unhappiness, but finally he felt clean. As he was stepping into a pair of breeches, Emily walked into the room.

She closed the door and leaned against it. "Now, where were we?"

You were tossing me back into the sea like an underweight haddock, thought Val, but only to himself, as he pulled up his breeches and fastened them. Since Emily had previously demonstrated some interest in his bare chest, he left off his shirt. "Andrei has gone to Mr. Ross's lodgings to retrieve your list. I know where it is."

Emily still stood by the door. "You read Michael's thoughts."

Difficult not to do so when they had been so close, and a true cesspit those thoughts had been. "I did."

She bit her lower lip. "And Papa?"

"If not an accident exactly, his mishap wasn't planned. Mr. Ross meant to steal, not to do harm. Once he was in possession of the amulet, however—" Val shrugged. "You know the rest. Abercrombie has your stolen books. I'm sure he could be persuaded to return them to you. For a slight fee."

Emily was carrying a small earthen bowl and a candle. She placed them on a table and set the mixture alight, then moved to stand on the hearth. "I also have Marie d'Auvergne's necklace. Unless you want me to give it back."

What the devil was she wearing? It was frilly and frothy and shockingly low-cut. As well as startlingly flimsy in the firelight. "Would you return it if I asked?"

She pursed her lips thoughtfully. Val added, "Never mind. Consider the necklace another treasure to be kept in your Society vaults." And what in Hades was she burning? He smelled acorns, mistletoe, and oak.

Emily remained silhouetted in front of the fire. "Even my ancestress Isobella didn't have *this* much adventure," she remarked. "Lady Alberta chose my negligee. Lady Alberta seems to know more about such things than she should."

"Such things"? Val's curiosity was piqued. Before he could pursue that intriguing topic, however, Emily spoke again. "I keep thinking that perhaps I could have prevented some of this. Perhaps I'm truly *not* fit to be overseer of the Dinwiddie Society."

"Don't be absurd. Of course you are." Val crossed to

her, picked up her hands, and inspected her scraped palms. They were already healing. It wasn't surprising. Emily did have Cezar's blood running through her veins.

And his, for what it mattered. "The failure is mine. I was unable to keep Lisbet from knowing how I felt. You wouldn't have been in danger otherwise." Val released her and started to turn away.

"Bosh!" Emily caught his arm. "I would have been in *worse* danger, because if I'd come in search of the athame alone, Lisbet would have squashed me like a spider." She moved her fingertips over his bare chest, touched the newly forming scars.

Val shuddered and caught her hand. "Emily—"

She pressed her fingers to his lips. "Shush! I have decided I must be blunt. That fight with Lisbet—"

Val couldn't bear to hear the words. "I understand."

"No, you don't. It was . . . Well. It was the most erotic thing I've ever seen."

Val was bemused. "You've seen a lot of erotic sights?"

Emily stood on tiptoes to kiss the hollow at the base of his throat, then slid her lips over his chest. "I hadn't seen any until I met you."

Val tangled his hands in her hair, and tried hard to concentrate. "What are you saying, Emily?"

She looked up at him. "It was the strangest thing, feeling Cezar in my head. I didn't like it very well."

Val was pleased to hear this, jealousy being one of the all-too-mortal feelings he'd been experiencing of late. He was less pleased when she drew away. And positively horrified when she said, "How *do* you feel about me, Val?"

He reached out. *Touch me, Emily.*

Like this? Emily stroked her hand gently across his chest. Val groaned.

He couldn't help himself. Val had to touch her in turn. Emily shivered as his fingers trailed down the length of her neck. "You would be wise to leave now, elfling. Vampires don't have hearts."

She stood on tiptoe and pressed her lips to his. *Piffle. You have mine.*

He grew very still and Emily drew back to study him. "I won't die of love, you know."

"I know." Thanks to that abominably provocative bit of nothing that she wore, however, he might well die of lust. "What do you want from me, Emily?"

"I want you to make love to me. Flesh to flesh. Heart to heart." She colored fiercely. "To teach me the Buzzing Kiss and the Reverse Lips. And most of all—"

"Most of all—?"

She smoothed his long hair with her hands, tugged and brought him closer. "Most of all," she murmured against his mouth, "I want to experience the Fixing of a Nail."

Chapter Thirty-Four

All meat to be eaten, and all maids to be wed.
(Romanian proverb)

He lowered his lips to her throat. Pleasure hummed through her veins. His teeth found her pulse, nipped and licked. A melting sensation, a growing warmth . . .

Her hand clutched his shoulders as he traced her mouth with his tongue, nibbled at her lower lip, teased her with feather touches until she opened for him. His tongue twined with hers in a mating dance.

His lips slid across her silken skin to the soft flesh of one breast. Her hands fisted in his hair. He laughed and licked her breast, her belly, and the inside of her knees; covered every inch of her body with slow, merciless kisses; loved her with long slow strokes of his tongue. His fangs scraped the inside of her thigh.

Her body burned. She whispered, "Val."

He looked up at her. The devil danced in his eyes. And then . . .

"Hah!" said a familiar voice. Emily opened one eye to find Ana perched on the foot of the bed. The ghost appeared irritated. Emily said, "Too late."

"Too—you didn't!" Ana bounced indignantly.

"I did." Emily savored the recollection. "Several times. And what a revelation it was. So you see it does you no good to try and stop us now. I already know what happens next."

Ana shook her head. "Things have certainly changed. I'd have been shocked right out of my garters to find another woman in my husband's bed. And he *is* my husband. You can't get around that."

"Stuff and nonsense!" Emily sat up. "He *was* your husband and you aren't wearing garters, anyway. For that matter—" She paused as strong warm fingers moved under the mound of covers to wrap around one bare leg. "Neither am I. Ana, I need to speak privately with Val. Will you leave if I promise to find some more nice graveyard dirt?"

"I don't know that I shall ever leave. I'm feeling cross." Ana put her foot on the lump beneath the covers, and gave it a shove. "Burning acorns and mistletoe and oak to keep me away. That should be against the rules."

Emily thought of Lady Alberta. "I'm not sure there *are* rules for things such as this. And if there are, I don't want to know them, because I suspect it's far better to make them up as one goes along. Now shoo."

Ana crossed her arms beneath her bosom and thrust out her lower lip. "I won't."

"You will, unless you want to make *me* cross." Emily attempted to look stern, not an easy undertaking considering what those strong, warm fingers were doing to her leg. "Because if I can banish demons, and I can, I can surely get rid of one pesky ghost."

Ana pouted all the harder. Emily raised her hand and began to chant. "Air, Fire, Water, Earth . . ."

"Oh, very well!" snapped Ana, and disappeared.

The lump beneath the covers stirred. "Did you really get rid of her?"

Emily patted him. "Temporarily."

Val sat up, caught her hand, and raised it to his lips. "Miss Dinwiddie, you are remarkable."

"No, I rather think you are, after last night. I had no idea—well, perhaps I had a little, because Lady Alberta explained certain things. How Lady Alberta knows what she does, *I* don't want to know, but she was almost prescient in predicting the effect of the negligee." She glanced at that item, whose remnants lay in a frothy puddle on the floor. "Are you blushing?"

"No." But she was. Val pulled Emily back down beside him on the bed.

Her tangled hair tumbled over her shoulders. *You won't send me away?*

Why would I do that?

Some idiotic nobility of character?

Vampires aren't noble. Didn't your literature tell you that?

"I wonder who wrote those silly books." Emily rubbed her nose against his. Val had been so concerned that she'd turn away from him after seeing what he really was. Silly man. Emily might have been cross with him for so misjudging her, were she not in such a splendid mood.

"It wasn't so much a matter of misjudging you," said Val. In so intimate a position as this, he was privy to all her thoughts. "As the inescapable fact that I am *vampir*."

"So?" Emily nuzzled his neck. "I'm freckled. It's much the same."

Val caught her hair in his hands and tugged until she was looking at him. "What did you just say?"

He was going to be difficult, she could sense it. Emily exhaled. "You are *vampir*, I have freckles. It's what makes us different. I, for one, don't think being different is necessarily a bad thing."

Her logic astonished him. It was also beside the point. Val rolled her over on top of him. "I won't do it, Emily."

Emily propped her elbows on his chest and rested her hands on her chin. Males were so dratted stubborn. "You said I had charmed you."

Val felt the cogs of her mind turning. "You have. But I won't make you like I am. It's too dangerous." A pause, then he said casually, "I believe you planned to leave soon?"

Emily dropped her head on his shoulder. "Vampire you may be, but you're *my* vampire, and I'm not going anywhere without you."

Val smoothed his hand over her hair and wondered whether the events of the past few days had turned his brain, because he was certain he had heard with his own very excellent ears Emily invite Lady Alberta to return with her to England. As well as demand to take Jamie. "Surely you don't mean to abandon the Dinwiddie Society."

"I've no intention of abandoning anything or anyone." Emily twined her fingers in the soft hair on Val's chest. "I suspect there may be some other items of interest to you in our vaults."

Val pulled her upright so he might see her face. "Not another amulet."

"Well, no. I think." Emily screwed up her courage. "I haven't asked before because I was afraid you would refuse me, but—Come back to England with us, Val. Help me with the business of the Society."

Val swept his hands down her back and lingered on her hips. "Help you how?"

At least he hadn't said no outright. "In any way you wish. We could spend part of the year in England, and the rest anywhere you like. I haven't forgotten that you promised to show me your dungeons. And you still don't know what will be the outcome of giving me your and Cezar's blood." She paused. He remained silent. She leaned closer and kissed his chin. "I need you, Val."

She was so determined. Val couldn't help but feel a little sad. "No, you don't. Not really."

"Impossible creature!" Emily pinched him. "Maybe I don't need you to manage the Society, but I *do* need you. And though it's probably prodigiously unladylike of me to say so, I think you might need me, too. How dare you smirk at me like that when I have just offered you *carte blanche*?"

Val wasn't smirking, not really, just looking very fond. Since Emily was feeling fond also, some little time elapsed before the conversation resumed, at which point Emily was lying half on and half off the bed.

She straightened herself. "I dislike to point this out, but if you don't bring me across, you *will* lose me eventually, because you'll stay all ripe and juicy while I shrivel up like an old prune."

Emily sounded sublimely unconcerned. Val wasn't deceived a bit. "It's most unlikely that you'll shrivel. You have Cezar's healing blood."

"What does that mean?"

"We'll have to wait and see."

Emily was exceedingly tired of being told she must wait. However, Val had said "we."

He had also reminded himself that he had always wished to count Emily's freckles. Val had just gotten to two hundred when they were interrupted by a knock on the door.

Val watched with amusement as Emily grabbed for the sheet. "There's someone I'd like you to meet."

Emily looked down at her naked self. *"Now?"*

He tucked the sheet up under her chin. "Come in!"

Jamie stepped into the room, gaped, slapped his hands over his eyes. "Crivvens! I shouldna be seein' this!"

Emily squirmed about until she sat upright with the sheet clutched tightly to her bosom. "It's all right, Jamie. Ravensclaw adores me. And he's coming back to England with us, so you might as well get used to such shocking sights."

Beside her, Val stiffened. Emily poked him with her elbow. *Aren't you?*

He looked down into her hopeful little face and gave up the struggle. *It would seem I am.*

"There!" Emily beamed at Jamie. "I adore him, too. And I shall box your ears if you say another word."

The devil with their audience. Val cupped Emily's face in his hand. *You can't possibly adore me as much as I adore you, elfling.*

Yes I can.

No you can't.

Can.

Can't. I love you, Emily.

He loved her. Emily flung her arms around Val's neck and kissed him on the chin. Jamie slipped away to the kitchen, there to inform the rest of the household—gathered to enjoy Mrs. MacCamish's oatmeal bannocks—that Ravensclaw and Miss Emily were as comfortable together as an auld pair of slippers, and furthermore it was his considered opinion that Miss Emily was no longer unkenand.

The sound of a clearing throat came from the doorway, reminding Emily—in the nick of time—that she and Val were not alone. She snatched up her sheet, which during the exchange of adorations had become considerably disarranged. *Now you've gone and compromised me, you wretch. My reputation is in shreds. You'll have to marry me.*

Flippant she might appear, but she waited anxiously for his answer. Val felt her suspense.

The die was cast. His fate was sealed. And had been since the moment Emily Dinwiddie walked through his castle door.

You are beyond compromised, elfling. I suppose there's nothing for it now but to marry. Supreme sacrifice that it will be.

Emily poked him with her elbow. *Supreme sacrifice, indeed!* One last question remained to be answered. *Can you procreate?*

Under the right circumstances.

Would I enjoy them?

Flower petals are involved.

Emily's toes curled. She was very curious to learn what those circumstances were. But first—

Emily turned her attention to the man and woman who had entered the bedroom, and had waited patiently through this silent exchange. He was compact and muscular, with pale blond hair and strange amber yellow eyes and high cheekbones. She was plump and black-haired with a triangular face and a pouting mouth. Neither seemed the least surprised to find a female in Ravensclaw's bed.

Val roused himself from thoughts of procreating and touched Emily's hand. "May I present my friends, Vasile Dragomir, also known as Drogo, and his wife, Michaela. Drogo and Machka were also victims of Lisbet's malice; and with her departure, freed." Drogo made an elegant bow. Machka yawned.

Forgetful of the sheet, Emily sat bolt upright. "Shapeshifters! Why didn't anyone tell me? I'm so glad to see you're safe. Perhaps you might tell me what it's *like* to be a shapeshifter? There are any number of things I would like to ask!"

Drogo sat down on the edge of the bed. "Ask away, Miss Dinwiddie. We are in your debt."

"Indeed," murmured Machka, as she leaned against his shoulder. "No more fleas."

Already deep in questions, Emily reached for Val's hand. *Ravensclaw?*

Um?
I love you, too.

Contrary to Lady Alberta's dire predictions, Emily chose to be wed in a simple ceremony performed by Cezar, who was among other things a Dacian priest; and enlivened by Ana, who in honor of the occasion performed a dance of veils that was no less astonishing for her semitransparent state.

Jamie served as ring bearer, and filched not a single thing.

Zizi, Bela, and Lilian attended, in great good spirits, for it had long been obvious to them that Miss Emily was the master's *ailaltă*, and now he finally had realized it himself. Drogo and Machka were also present, the latter becoming so moved by the occasion that she rubbed herself all over the former in a manner startlingly reminiscent of a cat in heat. Mrs. MacCamish prepared a special nuptial feast, in honor of which Lady Alberta left off her stays. Andrei stood guard at the door.

It fell to Isidore to propose the wedding toast.

Nimic peste putintă la dragoste se-ntelege.
Love will find its way.

A Brief Dictionary of Romanian Words

Ailată–other

baĭat–boy
Breaslă–guild, brotherhood
bună–hello

camarad–comrade
cătea–bitch
Consiliu–council

Damnatiune!–Damnation!
Dudevite dracului!–Go to the devil!

Fraternitae–fraternity

Iubită–lover, sweetheart

La dracu!–Damn!
Locotenent–lieutenant

neisprăvit–do-nothing, scamp
nelegiuit–evildoer
nefinistat–unfinished

pisică–cat, wild cat
provocare–provocation, challenge
puşti–boy, lad

Rosçat–redhead

Stăpân–master

Strigoii–undead

Trădător–traitor

vampir–vampire
vrajă–charm

zână–fairy
Zau!–really!